I0452564

ALSO BY SHARON GERLACH

Malakh (novella)

The Secret Dreams of Sarah-Jane Quinn

The Wyckham House

Condemned

Blink of an Eye

Where I Belong

Sharon Gerlach

Office Politics

Running Ink Press

A Running Ink Press novel

This is a work of fiction. Names, characters, places, and incidents are products of the author's imagination or are used fictitiously and are not to be construed as real. Any resemblance to actual events, locales, organizations, or persons, living or dead, is entirely coincidental.

All rights are reserved. No part of this book may be reproduced in any manner of whatsoever without written permission, except in the case of brief quotations embodied in critical articles and reviews.

Running Ink Press, LLC
1419 N Lee St
Spokane WA 99202

Copyright 2008 Sharon Gerlach
ISBN: 978-0-9832912-4-4

Edited by N.L. Gervasio
Cover image Copyright 2011 Untitled Images
Cover design by Joshua Gerlach

First Running Ink Press paperback printing: October 2011

Printed in the U.S.A.

In Thanks

I owe thanks to so many people for this book, from the anonymous people who created the modern office slang such as "crop dusting," "prairie dogging," "seagull managing," "Adminisphere," "umfriend," "percussive maintenance," and "blamestorming" to the equally anonymous employees in every office where I've worked who helped define my characters, up to and including the unfortunate gentleman who has been immortalized in Chapter Nine, along with his Post-It Method (which has been renamed). That was an actual conference I attended, and my opinion of it runs along the same lines as Frannie Freeman's.

So many people have been rooting for this book: Nikki, Christel, Tony & Cat, Lori--who even started a group for fans of Frannie Freeman called "Franatics" on a writers site we both belonged to; Gini, Gary, Jerry, and Rachel. I'm glad to finally have officially delivered it into their hands. Their support has meant so much to me.

And always, thanks to my husband and my children, whose sacrifice of time spent with me have made this - and all my other works - possible.

Office Politics

FRESH MEAT

She walks in like a deer approaching a watering hole favored by its top ten natural predators: eyes wide and fearful, face pale, a fine tremor racing through hands clasping a leather notebook to her chest. Her conservative plaid Pendleton skirt swishes around her kneecaps in a frenzy of pleats, and the coordinating jacket over a muted maroon blouse must make the office temperature seem like a suburb of hell.

"Fresh meat," I say in a low voice, tossing a paper clip over the low cubicle wall at my neighbor Stella. She picks it up and bounces it off the head of our coworker Gretchen, who is my best friend. Gretchen looks up and catches Stella's slight nod toward the New Girl passing behind her cubicle. She rolls her eyes. No one wears wool in this office, even Pendleton wool, and no one wears a suit jacket except the administrators. Or perhaps I should say Administrators, for that's how they see themselves, with a capital A—capital A for Assholes, Stella always quips.

"I give it two hours before she finds a way to shed the wool shell," Gretchen wagers.

"One," I say.

"Fifteen minutes. What's the wager?" Stella asks, scrutinizing the New Girl closely. She sees what Gretchen and I miss: the fine sheen of sweat stippling her more-than-likely freshly-waxed upper lip.

"Starbucks Frappuccino," I suggest. I love Frappuccinos and would find a way to exist on a diet made up solely of said beverage if I could. That and Arby's French dip sandwiches.

Gretchen sighs expressively. "Didn't I just buy you a Starbucks card for Christmas?"

"Yeah, for ten bucks, you skinflint. I was out by the end of December."

Stella snorts. "I don't like Starbucks. How about pizza for three from Domino's. They deliver," she adds quickly as Gretchen's brows lower ominously.

Gretchen's husband is a general manager for Pizza Hut and she views consumption of any other brand as a betrayal. Unfortunately, although I like Pizza Hut better than Domino's, we're not located within the delivery range of any of them.

"Make it pizza for four," I say, nodding toward New Girl. "The friendly thing to do is invite Fresh Meat to join us, since the wager is about her."

"Fresh Meat," Stella repeats distastefully. "Geez, Frannie. Why don't you just call her by her name—er, what *is* her name? I've forgotten."

It's Gretchen's turn to snort. "Who cares? Malaria will run her off within two weeks, just like she did all the previous assistants Sam's hired."

Malaria—more commonly known as Malia, pronounced like Maria but with an L instead of an R—is our immediate supervisor. She met her husband Sam, another Administrator, while employed as his assistant. She worked her way up into management—we aren't really sure how since she's as incompetent as a comatose monkey, but we suspect she did most of the work on her back or on her knees—and then ruined Sam's life by accepting his martini-induced marriage proposal. The man hasn't been the same since.

We watch as New Girl, led by none other than Malia herself, stops outside Sam's office door. Malia motions her into Sam's office ahead of her. We begin the count; sixty seconds and New Girl will be ushered out to sit in a chair outside the office while Malia lays down the ground rules to Sam about his attractive new assistant.

"Forty-two seconds," says Gretchen, raising a brow as New Girl is ushered out and the office door is promptly closed. It's a record.

"Okay, who's going to take her in hand?" I ask. A muted argument has already started inside the office, and New Girl's face has taken on an alarming shade of Humiliation Red. "Rock, paper, scissors?"

"Nice try, Frannic." Stella grins. "I took the last one, and Gretchen took the one before her."

I push my chair away from my desk, grousing. "Oh, all right."

It's not that I don't like connecting with new staff; it's just that…well, okay, I *don't* like connecting with new staff. I like to ease my way in to conversations and relationships, unlike Stella, whose very molecules are gregarious. Stella is the outgoing, quirky one; Gretchen the glamorous, aloof beauty; and I am—well, I am the mediocre one in every way except job performance. I can run an office with both hands tied behind my back in a semi-conscious state, but I long to be charismatic like Stella or cosmopolitan like Gretchen. Instead I'm dismally average: my hair is medium-dark, my skin is medium-pale, my dress size is medium-large (okay, perhaps I have consumed too many Frappuccinos and French dip sandwiches).

New Girl watches me approach as though I'm the angel of death. I see she's been relieved of her leather notebook. The rising voices inside Sam's office tell me she will not be reunited with her cowhide shield any time soon.

"Frannie Freeman," I introduce myself. "Don't try to say it when you have several margaritas under your belt."

"I don't drink," she says warily.

"You will."

"Morgan Cassidy." She shakes my hand. I keep hold of it and use it to haul her to her feet. "Wow, it's hot in here." She shrugs out of the jacket. Damn! Stella's won; she'll be impossible to live with now.

"How do you feel about pizza, Morgan?" I ask as I lead her away from Cubicle Row, mentally calculating the balance in my checking account and her deepening green pallor.

"Generally I like pizza," Morgan says. "But Frannie, I think I'm going to be sick."

"Yep, I figured so. That's why we're heading to the bathroom."

Morgan's eyes widen. "That's incredible! Are you psychic?" And she throws up all over me. Stella and Gretchen stifle their laughter behind their hands, but not very well.

I sigh. "Nope. If I was, I'd have called in dead today."

Morgan is mortified. "I'm so sorry! I usually don't throw up on the first date—I mean, day!"

Stella and Gretchen completely lose it. Morgan looks like she wants to pass out, and I would like to join her, because I've just noticed Eric Edwards from Sales watching the festivities with utter disgust stamped all over his too-handsome face. I'm wondering if the disgust comes from seeing me thrown-up on or if he now thinks I'm a lesbian because of Morgan's unfortunate misspeak. Either way, I would not object to a crater opening at my feet and swallowing me whole this very minute.

"Come on, Old Faithful." I guide Morgan around the last corner, our coworkers' laughter chasing us into the bathroom.

Damned if *I'm* paying for pizza!

Before we go any farther, I suppose I should explain just what it is that I do for a living. Harper & Lyttle, Inc., where I work, produces business system software, usually by contract but we boast a modest collection of programs built on speculation as well. Speculation software, in case you're wondering, is software created for no particular client. Someone simply has an idea and runs with it, and we try to sell it later on the general market.

I, Frannie Freeman, hold the coveted (by no one) title of Training Specialist III. In other words, because I have three Associates of Applied Science degrees in computer systems and office management, Harper & Lyttle believes me fully qualified to train myself and others in all our products. What this means to me is I'm at my desk infrequently because I'm training others, and I am quite often called down to the Customer Support Center to answer a consumer's questions. I also find myself tethered to a laptop in my off-hours, trying to catch up on my enormous workload, but since I have no social life to speak of, it's not really a problem.

Tension runs high in our department due to understaffing (and the constant friction between Sam and Malaria), thus we have pizza delivery on speed dial and know the shortest routes to the best espresso stands. The girls and I frequently gather after hours at a dimly-lit bar called Tony's, where the live music is loud and the margaritas strong. This gets us through most of the acid-rain showers from the Adminisphere—oh, you know what I mean: the corrosive decisions that eat away logic and those rare feelings of felicity we may occasionally harbor for the Suits, usually only when someone in their family dies.

So Tony's is where we head at quitting time. Fresh Me—er—Morgan isn't with us, not because we failed to invite her, but because our decision to go to Tony's was made at 4:58 PM and she had Orientation in Human Resources the latter half of the day. I rather doubt she would have felt like downing several of Tony's 'ritas anyway. Half an hour in the bathroom—most of that time spent holding my shirt under the hot-air hand dryer after washing it in the sink—put both my wardrobe and Morgan's upset stomach to rights, but I doubt seriously that I'll ever be able to erase my vomit-splattered image from Eric Edwards' brain.

Stella tosses the drink menu into the center of the table and holds up a finger, signalling to our server. He winds his way with a beaming smile through the clutch of tables between us and the bar and hovers at her elbow, touching her shoulder with a lack of restraint that fairly shrieks evidence of a past sexual liaison. He's a tall, dark drink of water: smooth, blue-black skin, ebony eyes, and fantastic, straight white teeth.

"Stella! Your usual?" His voice is buoyant with a Jamaican accent.

"That would be lovely, Darius. My friends will have a margarita each. Make them good." She winks as he moves away, and Gretchen gives her a disgusted look.

"He's—what? Twenty-two to your thirty-three?"

Stella shrugs. "So what?"

"Ever hear of VD, Stella?" Gretch persists.

Stella smiles wickedly. "Sure. It's what they made penicillin for."

Gretchen's blush is neon-red, and I hastily change the subject. "I heard they cut Concept Development's budget. Jeremy Ingram was in a complete snit after the budget meeting."

"Great," Stella grumps. "That means with fewer products, the rest of the department budgets will be cut as well. I wondered why all the administrators were crab-asses today. Even Sam."

"Sam's a crab-ass because he's married to Satan's daughter," Gretchen replies, flicking a glance at me.

"He's a crab-ass because they downsized half his staff two years ago and still expect the same level of productivity," I say, not appreciating the reminder of his marital status. My crush on Sam Harrison is legendary—at least among Gretchen, Stella, and me. "Remember our workload—the reason we drink?"

"Speaking of drinking," Stella says. "It's too bad Morgan couldn't join us. I wonder why they have Orientation in the afternoon after you've worked the whole morning at your new job."

I have the answer. "It's because they don't want to waste their time on you in Orientation if you're not going to come back from lunch. Remember that little gal we had oh-how-many-assistants ago? She smiled at us all and said 'See you after lunch!' and we never saw her again."

Stella's mouth drops open, and Gretchen clenches her teeth, hissing, "*Frannie!* She was hit by a delivery truck on her way to the deli! I think she's still in a coma."

"Oh," I say blankly. "I forgot about that."

"You're hopeless…and oh, let's add alcohol to your hopelessness," she grumbles as our drinks are delivered. Darius gives Stella a seductive grin and weaves off to the other side of the room.

"Pardon me," Stella murmurs. "I must go find a reason for a dose of antibiotics." She's off after Darius before we can stop her.

Gretchen shakes her head and flicks some of the salt off the rim of her margarita glass. "So when do you think Sam is going to divorce Malaria?"

"Never," I say sharply. She winces and I relent. "If he was going to, he would have by now."

"Fran—"

"I'll be fine," I say brightly. "I'm going to start dating again. Maybe I'll lose some weight, buy some new clothes. Things are going to change, you'll see."

If I'd had any clue of crapstorm about to transpire, I'd've found another job by week's end.

I hear Domino's is hiring.

THE GREAT PAPERCLIP WAR

Bud Mitchell has presided over the office supplies as head of the Inventory Control Office since time out of mind (seven years, actually, but it seems like longer). His iron-fisted techniques have, I'm sure, saved the company oodles of money over the years he's meted out, in his miserly way, the common necessities of running an office.

On one memorable occasion Stella asked him if she could get some file folders. "How many?" asks Bud, and Stella—who was reorganizing her desk and tossing out the ancient, dog-eared folders from 1972 she'd inherited when she was hired—says she doesn't know. Bud makes her go organize everything into little piles, count how many folders she needs, and that's exactly how many he lets her have. Stella nearly implodes, but Bud won't budge, and so on our lunch hour she and I schlep through Office Depot and she purchases her own.

Which brings me to another point of contention. When one buys one's own office supplies, at least when one has Bud Mitchell as the head of Inventory Control, one tapes the receipt to said office supply bag or box so that Bud can see one is not in possession of contraband. This really sticks in Stella's craw, and over the past few weeks I've noticed her hand slowly inching toward her stapler anytime Bud comes near. One wrong move and I'm positive she plans to whack him in the head. Whether or not she'd leave the stapler closed when she does so remains as yet a mystery, but I have fantastic visions of Bud running through the office shrieking with eight or nine staples sticking into the back of his bald scalp.

During the last two years of Bud's reign over the inventory, he's developed an odd compulsion regarding paperclips. Now paperclips are cheap, at least the plain steel ones are (which is all Bud allows us) but you'd think they're made of platinum the way he counts and tracks and protects them. It's not uncommon to see Bud stalking through the cube farm, totting up how many paperclips he estimates you have in your possession.

I buy my own paperclips, because I like those fancy colored ones. These offend Bud for some reason, and on more than one occasion I'm sure I've seen him making the sign to ward off evil spirits when he passes by my colored-paperclip-filled cubicle...like he's doing now.

"Gretchen!" Bud exclaims, shocked.

I look up to see Gretchen about to huck a large Gem clip at me to get my attention. Such trading of office supplies, usually paperclips, goes on all the time, which makes nearly impossible Bud's self-appointed task of making sure the clips are distributed equally amongst all staff.

Gretchen pauses, caught in the act. "Oh, er...Bud. Hi."

"What are you *doing?* Throwing *office supplies* at each other?" He shoots me a scandalous look.

"Hey, I wasn't doing anything!" I protest.

"I was just...ah...giving Frannie a paperclip," says Gretchen lamely. "She...er...looked like she needed one."

Bud eyes the small, broken-handled coffee cup I

brought from home to keep my colored clips in—because, according to Bud, if the supplies are in company-owned receptacles, they belong to the company—and narrows his eyes on me.

"I'm watching you, Frannie," he mutters, and stumps away. Gretchen manages to wait until he's out of earshot to snort with laughter.

"I'm watching you, Frannie!" she mimics. I throw a bright pink paperclip at her.

"How did I get dragged into that? I wasn't even doing anything."

"He's still offended because you bought your own clips, and colored ones, at that. Remember how he nearly had a stroke when you got those brass ones?"

I shudder. "Don't remind me."

Gretchen glances at the clock and shuts off her monitor. "Come on, it's time to go."

This morning the administrators are making us a big pancake breakfast. The Powers-That-Be think we like this crap instead of getting annual bonuses. Stella and Morgan got roped into helping, and I wonder if we'll be able to see through Stella's cloud of disgruntled profanity hovering in the air in the convention room.

Morgan, marshaled by Malia to keep her from having any fun with Sam, is clearing tables and fetching juice and syrup for hungry coworkers. She looks green-faced; she threw up before Malia came to get her. Stress takes her in the stomach, but fortunately she's refrained from vomiting on me this week. Stella is nowhere to be seen, which means she snuck out the back door to have a cigarette. Gretchen and I queue up in the short line, continuing our conversation about Bud Mitchell.

"Seriously, Frannie, it's gotten quite ridiculous. I think you should talk to Sam about it."

"I already talked to Malia." I reach around her to grab a plate and shoot a glance up the serving table. Sam is cheerfully dishing out hash browns, looking relieved to have Malia out of his hair. I look away quickly, before he feels my eyes on him.

"And she's done nothing!" Gretchen complains, holding out her plate for the scrambled eggs our CEO is serving. "Bud should have retired four or five years ago before the paperclip fetish was allowed to take hold. It's time to go to Sam."

By this time we've reached the hash browns, and Sam hears his name. "What do I need to do?" He's smiling, but he addresses my plate. I notice he has no trouble looking Gretchen in the eye.

"Do something about Bud and his paperclips," Gretchen blurts. I nudge her with my elbow. *"What?"*

Sam's eyes do something they haven't done since the night he drunkenly proposed to Malia: they raise and meet my gaze. I feel my withered infatuation spring to vibrant life under their scrutiny. Damn.

"If it's a problem, Frannie…"

"It's no problem, Sam. Bud just has his quirks."

Gretchen rolls her eyes and moves on. I notice Sam's hand is still hovering a spoon of hash browns over my plate, but he's making no move to deposit them. His eyes are locked on mine, and I can feel the heat of a blush in my face.

"Ah…can I have my hash browns, Sam?"

"What?" he asks blankly. He realizes he's just standing there staring at me. A flush creeps out of the neck of his shirt, staining throat and face alike. "Sorry, Fran."

"S'okay." I move away, my whole body feeling hot and cold and Sam's eyes. Gretchen is waiting for me at the pancakes.

"What the hell was that all about?" she whispers out of the corner of her mouth.

"Dunno."

"Right."

She accepts two sausage links and moves away from

the serving table. Her gaze on me is skeptical. I don't blame her. Before he proposed to Malia, Sam and I played the flirting game. When handing me files, his fingers would brush mine. He would sometimes stand too close to me, his arm brushing against mine. On one memorable occasion, I stepped back from the coffee maker in the break room to find Sam standing directly behind me. I have not forgotten one detail of that full-body, back-to-front contact. I don't think Sam has either; he has not looked me in the eyes since the Christmas party two years ago. I wonder if he regrets suggesting the martini bar that led to his marriage from hell.

I'd thought we were pretty cool about our attraction to each other but obviously not, because Malia has been vicious to me ever since they came back from Vegas. For instance, Gretchen and Stella both have received raises the last two years, but I've received nothing. My requests for raises have stopped at her desk and have not been approved and passed on to Sam. And she treats me like complete crap. That's how I know it wasn't a one-sided infatuation.

Stella joins us at our table with a plate of her own, smelling like Marlboros.

"Aren't you supposed to be helping?" Gretchen asks, raising a brow at the mound of scrambled eggs on Stella's plate.

"Screw 'em," Stella says, shoveling eggs into her mouth at breakneck speed.

"Here comes Malaria," Gretchen warns idly. Stella chokes, grabs her plate, and vanishes.

"You're bad," I say, chuckling. Malia is nowhere near our table.

"Yep. Hurry up; I've got loads of work to do."

I scarf down the last of my pancake and we ditch our plates in the large garbage can near the serving table on our way out the door. I feel Sam's eyes follow me all the way to the elevator. As the doors swish shut, I catch

Gretchen's smirk.

"Shut up."

"An interesting development. All you'd have to do is crook your finger, Frannie."

"Not interested in married men."

"So you say, but I saw the look you gave him."

"Okay, I'll rephrase: I'm not interested in having an affair with a married man, even if that man is Sam."

"Don't we have some stupid team-building hike in May? Maybe we could push Malia off a cliff."

"Not funny," because it's all too easy for me to fantasize about.

The doors open and we're greeted with the acrid smell of plastic burning, which gets stronger as we approach Cubicle Row…and strongest in my cubicle. Wrinkling my nose, I hunt around until I find it: the first major move in the Great Paperclip War. My broken coffee cup, full of my neon-colored plastic-coated paperclips, is sitting on my coffee warmer. The plastic has melted, and all I have is scorched metal and plastic goo.

I hear a snicker and look up in time to see Bud Mitchell disappearing around the corner. I dump my purse into my chair and race after him. He's surprisingly spry for sixty-four, and he rounds another corner and disappears from view.

Not to be outdone, I pick up the pace, my low-heeled pumps sliding on the tiled floor. I hit a wet patch by the water fountain as I round the corner and my feet slide out from under me. I have enough momentum going now that I slide like a puck on a shuffleboard and take out the man scrambling to get out of my way. Down he comes with the grace of a rhino, and I find myself in a tangle of arms and legs with none other than Sam.

"Fran," he says in surprise, and then realizes his left hand has fallen squarely on my right breast. He snatches it away and groans as he sits up, rubbing his bruised ribs.

He climbs laboriously to his feet and holds a hand out to help me up. "Is it time to talk about Bud Mitchell yet?"

My face is going to burst into flames at any second. I slink away, my humiliation complete as Sam's soft laughter follows me around the corner.

"Bud Mitchell, I'm gunning for you!" I mutter darkly as I slip into my cubicle, soothing all my bruised spots and my humiliated ego as I avoid Gretchen's inquiring look.

Later I'll wonder why Sam was heading toward the department when he should have been slinging hash browns. For now, I can't erase the embarrassment of falling—and in a skirt—in front of him…or the feel of his fingers splayed on my breast.

Cheap thrill, baby, but it's all I've got.

THE MAD STAPLER

"What the hell?" Stella waves her staple remover in the air in frustration. It's one of those new-fangled jobbies with the long handle and a metal piece at the end that you slide under the staple. They work pretty well most of the time, but when they don't you end up wrangling the damn staple 'til the cows come home to get that sucker out.

"Try the old staple remover. Sometimes it works better." Gretchen doesn't even glance up from the report she's proofreading. Her trendy tortoiseshell glasses are perched on her perfect nose, so I know she must have a headache; she normally only wears her glasses when she has one.

Stella blows out a breath. "It's. Not. The. Staple. Remover."

Gretchen looks up over the rim of her glasses and I peer over the cubicle wall between Stella and me. The problem isn't that the new-fangled staple-remover won't remove the staples. It's just that she managed to extract the heavy-duty staple from the 180-page report only to find that every two pages are attached to each other.

Gretchen and I burst out laughing.

"That's pretty funny," Gretchen says. Stella sends her a fuming look; neither of us needs a translator to know she doesn't find it funny at all. "Maybe they're trying to get your attention."

"Whose report is it?" I ask, trying to see the name at the top. Production has taken to formatting the headers so tiny that only a scientist with a microscope can hope to identity the perpetrator of—er, the employee who generated the report.

"Eric Edwards," says Stella with a slow smile. As with the fuming look, we don't need a translator for this one. Gretchen shoots me a glance.

It's no secret that after Sam married Malaria, I turned my attention to greener pastures. No sense in longing for what will never be mine, right? And Eric Edwards…why not? Handsome, urbane, charming—and gainfully employed. What more could a girl want? The problem: why should he even notice little Frannie Freeman, whose average looks and average figure (hey, I've laid off the Frappuccinos and the French dips) are about as interesting as a drab female sparrow? And if Stella is interested in him, I might as well write him off my list of possibilities. I can't hope to compete with that particular opponent.

Stella was born LaTisha Monique Espinoza. Espinoza, I kid you not. African-American to the smallest molecule of her DNA. Apparently the name came from an adoption in the family a couple generations back.

She divorced her husband four years ago, and a more bitter, acrimonious divorce I've yet to see (except in my fantasies where Sam leaves Malaria and professes his undying love for me, that is). We call the man Satan for what he put Stella through. When the divorce was granted, the judge asked her what she wanted her name changed to. She'd been watching that movie *How Stella*

Got Her Groove Back and French romances incessantly since Satan threw her over and left her with a raging case of the Clap—oh, did I say that out loud?

Anyway, Stella threw out a name: Stellamaria Binoche. Don't ask. Gretchen and I won't let her watch any more subtitled French movies, but the damage is done. Stellamaria Binoche she is. Gorgeous and hip and outrageous, too. I won't stand a chance.

"Who's in charge down there anyway?" Stella raged, referring to the Sales office. "And why isn't Bud watching the flagrant misuse of staples as closely as he watches the damn paperclips?"

That gets my blood pumping. I haven't forgotten the melted, plastic mess of paperclips Bud left on my coffee warmer. And I won't even begin to tell you about the scathing butt-chewing Malaria subjected me to—with her door open so not only the whole office but Sam, too, could hear.

Gretchen looks alarmed at my expression, and she changes the subject rapidly. "So call Eric and ask what's up."

"Maybe it wasn't Eric," I chime in. "Maybe someone in Production did it. You know, there's that really handsome guy down there who looks like Denzel Washington."

"Yeah?" Stella snaps. "*You* go out with him, then."

Ouch. Touchy subject, apparently. I look at Gretchen, who is frowning at me.

"Frannie!" she hisses in consternation. Belatedly I realize Stella has already dated this fellow, and it went rather poorly. I recall something about buttercream frosting and a third party named Conchita…

"Oh, sorry. I forgot."

"Call Eric and find out who the Mad Stapler is," Gretchen advises. Losing interest, she goes back to proofing her report. I notice she's using one of those magnifying rulers. I make a mental note to consider microscopes for Christmas presents this year.

Meanwhile Stella is ripping out staples like she's going for an Olympic gold medal, her mouth muttering silent curses. I can almost see the little thought-bubbles hovering over her head, full of profanity. Gretchen snickers.

Morgan comes around the corner—she has training with Malaria this afternoon, so no doubt she was throwing up in the bathroom—and as she passes my cubicle on her way to her desk, she whispers out of the corner of her mouth, "Pssst! Frannie! Malaria alert and a Bud sighting." She sails on to her desk, where she sits rubbing her stomach and swigging Pepto-Bismol.

Malaria proves not to be a problem, but after a couple of minutes I feel eyes on the back on my head. I spin around to find Bud Mitchell in the empty cubicle to my right, hunched down with just the top of his head and his eyes peering over the divider that stands eighteen inches off the desks. He's trying to see how many paperclips I have.

"BUD!" I warn loudly. I grab my paperclip receptacle and stuff it into my sweater pocket.

"How many, Frannie?" Bud demands, his eyes wild with the excitement of catching me with more paperclips than I'm allotted. "You have at least a whole box of clips! ALL TO YOURSELF!!"

Doesn't Human Resources screen these people? "Get away from my desk, Bud!"

Stella is on the phone, trying to get past the battalion of secretaries in Sales so she can speak directly to Eric Edwards. She holds her stapler out to me. It's tempting...

"What's going on?" Malaria's sharp voice cuts across the chaos.

Bud flings his arm out, pointing at me like he's going for a Golden Globe. "Frannie has A WHOLE BOX OF PAPERCLIPS!"

The commotion has drawn Sam out of his office; his

eyes swing between Bud, me, and Malia like a pendulum. "Bud, Frannie. My office now, please." Malia looks viciously gratified.

Ah, shit. Chewed out by Malaria one day, and Sam the next. With any luck, God will take pity on me and strike me dead before I reach Sam's office.

"She has the evidence in her pocket, Sam!" Bud bursts out before the door is even closed. Silently I hold out my paperclip holder to Sam. There are only a dozen or so clips clinging to the magnetic lip.

Sam sighs. "Bud," he says gently. "Paperclips are cheap. What isn't cheap is the amount of time our employees are spending arguing over them. Ease up a little, all right?"

"But—"

"Frannie is a reasonable lady. I'm sure she'll agree to not hoard the paperclips."

I lift a brow at Sam, but say readily, "Sure. I won't take more than half a box."

"And no more colored ones," Bud adds ominously.

I open my mouth to tell him it's none of his damn business if I bring in my own colored clips, but Sam inclines his head a fraction, and I know that isn't what he wants me to say.

"All right, Bud," I agree resignedly. "If it will make your inventory job easier, I won't bring in my own clips." Is there nothing I won't do for Sam? He owes me big-time... for this and the accidental grope the other day.

"Thank you, Frannie," Bud says, surprisingly docile now. His eyes glint in the fluorescent light. Oh sweet Jesus, the man is going to cry because I relented! Isn't this what Thorazine is for?

"All right, that's settled," Sam says, rubbing his hands together with satisfaction as though he'd just closed a huge deal. "If you'll excuse us, I'd like to have a word with Frannie."

Oh, shit again. Bud leaves, closing the door behind

him. Sam leans his elbows on his desk, frowning at his desk blotter, which is covered with little Sam-scratchings. I feel my face start to burn; he may owe me for copping a feel, even if it wasn't on purpose, but I certainly don't want to talk about it.

Finally he reaches for a couple of stapled papers and hands them to me: my requests for raises from the last two years.

"Why didn't you say something about this, Frannie?"

I can't look at him. "I didn't want to cause trouble."

"Did you think I wouldn't notice when I approve the payroll that you aren't making as much as Stella or Gretchen?"

I look at him now in surprise. "Well, no. Why should you? It's Malar—Malia's decision to deny a raise. I'm sure she had her reasons."

"I'm sure, too," he mutters. He rubs a hand over his face. "I really wish I'd never gone to that party."

Did I hear that? Did I *really* just hear that? Sam seems to realize he spoke out loud. His face flushes and he avoids my gaze.

"I'm approving these, retroactive to the date of the first request," he says gruffly. "No arguments. I'll deal with Malar—" He closes his eyes and takes a deep breath. "I'll deal with Malia."

"Er—thank you," I say softly.

He almost smiles. His gaze sweeps across my breasts and finally meets mine. "My pleasure, Frannie."

I scramble hastily out of my chair and bolt for the door—*femme fatale* I am not.

"Holy crap!" I exclaim to myself as I slide into my chair. Stella glances up; she's still on hold with Sales. Gretchen quirks a brow at me. "Nothing."

I check the area for a lurking Bud Mitchell, then empty my pocket of the paperclips I'd dumped out of the receptacle before handing it to Sam, and lock them in my desk drawer. A dirty trick, but hey, this is war. My victory feels complete; I've vanquished the paperclip maniac, and Sam is sorry he married Malaria. Life is sweet. I even feel ready to take on the Mad Stapler.

Stella, finally connected with her party, stops speaking and hands her phone to me over our divider. She looks stunned.

"What is it, Stel?"

"Eric. He wants to talk to you." Eric? Eric who? "He stapled the report together because he thought you would receive it." She tosses a note over the wall, one corner of it bearing the puncture marks of a staple. I pick it up and read the bold, confident writing:

FRANNIE—WANT TO GO TO DINNER AND A MOVIE WITH ME FRIDAY NIGHT? SANS VOMIT? ERIC

DATING AND OTHER SOCIAL MALADIES

I look ahead to my date with Eric Edwards with a mixture of dread and excitement. I must say, the dread far outweighs the pleasure, which is really a sad state of affairs considering the empty horizon of possibilities before me. What if I really like him—and he me—now that Sam has finally acknowledged the chemistry between us, now that Sam is finally looking me in the eye again?

And why should I care about that, dammit? Sam's the one who got drunk and martini-proposed to Malaria, the lousy jerk. Now that I think about it, I should have kneed him in the groin while we were lying in a tangle of limbs in the corridor the other day.

I staple my report and bang the Swingline down on the desk perhaps a little too forcefully. Gretchen gives me a sympathetic look; she knows I'm torn. She glances at Stella, who has been abnormally quiet today, as well as decidedly cool toward me. I want to feel badly for her, but it's hard—she knew long ago that I liked Eric, and it's not as though Stella can't find another fifteen prospects on her lunch hour. But most men don't look at mediocrity, especially if it carries fifteen or twenty extra pounds and exudes I'm-not-looking-for-a-casual-affair from its very pores, so I'm elated Eric chose me and not her.

Mediocrity…it's why Sam chose Malaria and not me. Even with ten or twelve vodka martinis under his belt, he still recognized drop-dead gorgeous and went after it. Shallow bastard.

Bud Mitchell rounds the corner, and I automatically stiffen in my chair, glancing at my paperclip receptacle, which holds eleven Gem clips. Yep, I counted 'em out after everyone went home last night. The rest are still locked in my drawer.

He looks around the room to be sure he isn't being watched, and slips into my cubicle, hunkering down. The man's obviously on a covert mission. I never realized working inventory control was so exciting; perhaps I should have transferred long ago.

"Here, Frannie. I have some overstock. Shhhh!" he whispers, and slips me a box of gold-toned Gem clips. Beaming as though he's just given me a solid gold ingot, he duck-waddles out of my cube and tiptoes out of our section. Gretchen snorts with laughter; Stella just snorts, still disgruntled.

"Watch it, Fran," Gretchen says. "He'll be proposing by Easter."

Sweet Christ! I drop the box of paperclips as though burned, and this time even Stella laughs.

The comment attracts Sam's attention as he breezes by behind Gretchen. His step falters and he shoots a look at me, then speeds into his office. His door closes a tad more forcefully than usual.

Stick that in your juice-box and suck it, I think with bitter satisfaction.

Morgan comes out of Malaria's office, looking ill. Well, she always looks ill while she's at work, so it's no different really, but this time she makes a motion at me like she's breaking something between her hands. I get the hint; she wants to take a break with me. That she wants to talk about it while at work means Malaria's been especially debilitating today.

I follow her to the break room, where she swigs on her ever-present Pepto-Bismol and announces, "I'm quitting."

"Oh, Morgan! You can't quit now—you're doing really well."

"Seriously, Frannie, the woman is the devil. She's rude, she's manipulative, she is pure evil. I'm living on Pepto," and she holds her rapidly-emptying bottle aloft. "Damn good thing I'm not prone to drinking, or I'd already be an alcoholic just after this nightmare week. I've never had a job so horrible."

"Have you talked to Sam?"

Morgan rolls her eyes. I notice her greenish complexion clashes badly with her honey-blonde hair. "Honestly, Fran, Sam can't solve everything! You think more of him than he deserves."

I close my eyes and count to ten...and then to twenty, because ten wasn't enough. "I meant because while he's not Malia's direct supervisor, he's in an administrative position higher than she is."

"He's also her husband, which you keep conveniently forgetting," Morgan snaps.

My breath catches in my throat and I step back from her as though she just slapped me. Belatedly I remember she's been lunching with Stella...Stella, whose gossiping tongue doesn't care who it lashes. It's one of the things I don't care for about her, but I just live with it, knowing that's how she is.

"This isn't about me," I said evenly. "This is about you wanting to quit because of a bad boss. You can either suck it up, tuck your tail and run, or do something about it. But taking potshots at me isn't going to make Malia tolerable."

She huffs out a breath. "I don't know why I thought I could talk to you. Stella was right about—"

That's it. I've had enough. "Well, then, perhaps you

should have thrown up on Stella instead of me." I whirl around and stomp out. Sam is coming down the corridor, and I pretend like I haven't seen him even though he looks like he's going to speak, and I duck into the bathroom.

After using the facilities, I wait five minutes before coming out, giving Sam enough time to give up and move on—which really is what I should be doing, metaphorically speaking, but that's another matter. I peek out the door, and seeing no one in the immediate area, hurry out and start back toward my section in what's seeming more like Purgatory every day.

"Fran!" Son-of-a-bitch! There he is, hurrying along behind me. Damned if he hadn't waited around the corner.

"I'm really busy, Sam."

"But—"

I walk faster, out-pacing him, and just before I reach the end of the hall to our section he calls out, "But your skirt is tucked into your pantyhose!"

Can I just freaking die RIGHT NOW??? as I remember I wore a thong today, which I usually don't do at work because of the potential for situations just like this.

His voice has carried into the section and everyone looks up, snickering. Red-faced, I yank my skirt out of my pantyhose and tug it over my bottom, and regret like hell that I didn't call in sick today.

* * * * *

Eric picks me up at seven, bringing a bouquet of wildflowers. I stuff them in a vase before we leave, smiling triumphantly. Yes! A romantic man! Surprisingly, the small-talk as we drive to the restaurant and wait for our meal is comfortable and relaxed. We don't even talk about work except for a teasing comment he makes about the pantyhose incident. He's handsome and smooth all through dinner and a couple bottles of wine.

"You're a great lady, Fran," he says at one point, giving me a half-salute with his wine glass.

My mental eyes roll; this particular line is the kiss of death to any romantic notions a girl might have toward a man.

"No, really," Eric says as though sensing my eye-roll. "You don't have to roll your eyes. I really mean it."

Oh shit—my eye-roll wasn't done mentally. Seriously, who allowed me to drink anyway? I can't be trusted with the stuff.

"There, you did it again." Eric grins. "You're a fantastic woman. You're smart, you're funny, you're formidably competent. I believe you could do anything you put your mind to. You're the go-to girl, Fran."

And I'm comin' to ya, I finish silently, because it seems like the obvious conclusion to that statement.

"And I'm comin' to ya," he says. "I'd like to do this again. Many times."

"Despite the vomit?" I ask, because God knows with Morgan, I'm sure to be spewed on again.

He chuckles. "Vomit and all. I was worried that day, not because Morgan puked on you but because of what she said. I thought perhaps you were a lesbian."

My face flames because he's watching me carefully, but I answer gamely, "Nope. I don't bat for the home team." *Jesus, Fran, zip it!!* Could I sound any more moronic?

"What say we blow this Popsicle stand? I should get you home." It's only nine-thirty, so I'm guessing "getting me home" has the underlying connotation of "getting me between the sheets." I'm not particularly alarmed; I can always say no if I decide not to go that route.

The drive home is filled with the not-quite-comfortable silences that fall between a man and a woman who are debating a session of mattress-thumping together. I'm waffling; one second I want to, the next I think of all the pit-falls of office flings.

Before I know it, we're standing in front of my apartment door. I live in a unique little L-shaped complex. The units are all one level and made to look like individual cottages even though they're all connected. The courtyard in the middle is wonderfully landscaped, with cottage gardens tucked here and there, benches strategically placed in private alcoves. Several water features are scattered throughout, one such attraction on the other side of the sidewalk leading to my door. The rush of water over imported river rock into a pool populated with koi…how much more romantic can you get?

Eric leans toward me. I press back against my front door. His hands cup my shoulders; I let them stay as he bends to kiss me. It's nice. It's pleasant. I'm waiting for the other shoe to drop. Surely there's a reason this gorgeous specimen of manliness is outside my front door, kissing me for all the world like I'm the sexiest thing alive.

"Frannie," his whispers. "I've been fantasizing about this for weeks. I've been Frantisizing." He kisses me again, and I try to stifle my giggles. *Frantisizing?* Are you *kidding* me?

One of his hands has left my shoulder; I expect to feel it on my breast any second. I wonder how different it will feel from Sam's hand, and I impatiently push the thought away. But the contact doesn't come, and I open my eyes.

"What are you doing?" I ask, more than a little irritated, because Eric has his cell phone out. While kissing me, he's been dialing a number, one eye open on the phone.

"I'm calling Conchita," he says, breathing heavily. "You have no idea how much you turn me on, Frannie. The whole lesbian idea…ever since Morgan said that…"

I push him away. "Are you freaking SERIOUS?"

He holds up a finger and speaks into the phone. "Conchita? Eric Edwards—hey, *Frannie*!"

For I've grabbed the phone and I'm talking to Conchita myself. "Eric has to go now. I hope you enjoyed your last threesome with him, because I doubt there will be another. I'm going to yank his balls out by their roots and stuff them up his nostrils. 'Bye!"

"Give me my phone, Frannie!" Eric yells. The ardor flushing his face has fled in favor of the pallor of panic.

"Frantisize *this*, asshole!" I yell back as I hurl his phone into the koi pond. "Would you like some buttercream frosting with *that*?" I slip inside the house and slam the door in his face when he would follow after me, making sure I throw the deadbolt and slip on the chain.

I'm pacing and fuming when my eyes fall on the vase of flowers. I snatch it up and hurl it into the sink, where the vase breaks into several pieces on which I will no doubt cut myself later when I clean it up. My cat yowls; sensing my mood, he headed for the top of the entertainment armoire when I slammed the door in Eric's face. He knows I mean business; he lost his own balls early on in our relationship.

I've had it with pretty boys and office man-whores. The dating world has more perils than befall Penelope Pitstop, and I am sick of the Dudley Do-Rights with their perfect teeth and their studly, puffed-out chests and their Conchitas and their *Frantisizing*.

Get outta my way, Malaria—I'm coming to get my man!

FRANNIE FREEMAN, GO-TO GIRL

I spend the rest of the weekend fuming alternately about Eric Edwards' perverted idea of a liaison and the deep cuts I sustained across three of my right-hand fingers while cleaning the broken vase out of my sink (I told you it would happen). I'd arranged to take Monday off, giving myself a three-day weekend, and I took advantage of it. Staring at myself in the bathroom mirror on Monday morning, I decide I need an overhaul. No more plain-Jane; the Frannie Freeman who returns to work on Tuesday will be chic and glamorous…well, as chic and glamorous as Frannie Freeman can be, at least.

And I'm not half-disappointed as I stare at myself in the mirror before work. My hair, now cut to frame my face in wisps and highlighted flatteringly, brushes along my chin. Features I'd thought average now seem attractive. Funny what a trip to the hair stylist and the Clinique counter at Macy's will do. I feel armed and ready to deal with the Eric Edwards of the world.

"New outfit?" Gretchen asks as I stow my purse in a desk drawer and shrug out of my coat.

"Yeah, went shopping yesterday."

"Nice hair," she remarks. "Let's go get coffee."

I arch a brow; that particular phrase actually means "I have something to tell you privately." Once Malaria had slept her way into a supervisory position (one of her many positions, I hear), telling your cubicle mates you had something to tell them privately was expressly forbidden under the seemingly harmless guise of promoting a hostility-free work environment. The simple fact that most of our hostility was caused by Malaria herself never seemed to occur to her.

We're almost to the coffee room when we're approached by none other than Malaria.

"Frannie, I need your help ASAP."

"I just wanted to get a cup of coffee really quick." I send a resentful look at my watch; I'm technically not on the clock for another seven minutes.

"I'm off to a meeting in five minutes, and I'm having trouble with my PowerPoint presentation. Can you look at it?"

"Sure." I allow myself to be dragged off, shoving my empty coffee mug into Gretchen's hands. She shrugs helplessly.

Malaria's problem turns out to be that she even tried to do a PowerPoint presentation in the first place. It takes me ten minutes to fix it, the last five of which she's *ahem*ing to the point I ask her if she's coming down with a cold. Her presentation fixed and saved onto a flash drive, she hmmphs her way off to her meeting.

Gretchen's been called off to fix the copy machine by the time I get back, and when she's done, I've been called to Malaria's meeting because she can't remember what she named the presentation and needs my help to find the right one. Seriously, how does the woman find her way to work every day?

Sam's eyes widen in surprise when I come in. Since I've laid off the Frappuccinos and the Arby's French Dips, I've shed ten of the extra twenty pounds I carry, and the new business outfit I'm wearing—tailored slacks and an amber-hued silk blouse topped with a long ottoman jacket—is a size smaller than I'd have purchased a month ago.

After his initial appreciative look, his face goes quite impassive and he avoids my gaze. Disappointed, I remind myself that Malaria is present, as well as a number of other Suits. I'll have a chance later to make my second move in my gambit to win Sam, the first being my appearance overhaul.

As I close the boardroom door behind me, I hear whispering in the hallway. When I look up to see who's talking, I meet the eyes of the gossiping couple. Hastily they look away and take their whispered conversation elsewhere. This is the first indication the grapevine's been thriving, but I've been unaware of it.

Funny thing about the grapevine; it grows and thrives all the time. If you're aware of what's humming along it, all the better, for that means the gossip isn't about you. But if you're thinking it's quiet, better watch your back, because that's when you're the target.

I don't catch up to Gretchen until lunch, and by then I've encountered enough whispered conversations that stop when I come into the room I know the vine's been humming about me. *Eric Edwards*, I fume inwardly, a *Swingline upside the head is too good for the likes of you.*

"The thing is, Fran, no one seems to care what the truth is. Eric told his boss that you threw his cell phone into the water fountain when he spent more time with Conchita than you did."

I'm so horrified that the only thing I can think to say is, "Who the hell *is* Conchita, anyway?"

Gretchen rubs a finger across her upper lip. Stella snorts into her soup. She's been very cool to me until now, and I realize she's been angry because she thought I had gone the extra mile, so to speak, in order to ensure Eric would stay interested in me and not her.

Stella says now, "Conchita used to work in Inventory Control. In fact, it's how we ended up with Bud Mitchell."

"She hired Bud Mitchell?"

"Good God, no," Gretchen answers, making a face. "Bud would have found her repulsive. He transferred into Inventory Control after Conchita was fired. Let's just say she was…ah… indiscriminate with her use of the Inventory Room."

"And with how many at a time she used it," Stella adds.

"And everyone believes what he's said about me?"

"Well, Fran, you had Monday off. He was able to come in and tell his story first. It's not fair, but it's the nature of the grapevine."

"Screw that, Stella. I'm going to rip his face off!"

Gretchen bursts out laughing. I push away my microwave lunch, not interested in food anymore. Between my self-imposed avoidance of Starbucks and Arby's and the stress of being gossip fodder, I'm going to be back in a size—ahem—before you know it.

"Forget about it, Frannie," Stella says. "The gossip will die down, and in a couple weeks no one will even remember it. In the meantime, enjoy the notoriety; it's your fifteen minutes of fame."

"I don't want notoriety for being the office whore who bats for both teams," I argue vehemently.

A polite cough in the doorway brings all our heads around. Sam is standing there, face flaming, his eyes fixed determinedly on my right cheekbone. Son-of-a-bitch—is there no end to my humiliation?

Gretchen is mortified and Stella—who finds humor even when the humiliation is hers—covers her mouth to hide her grin and ducks her chin toward her chest.

I cover my eyes with my hand. If I had ruby slippers, I'd be tapping those goddamn heels together 'til the shoes virtually exploded off my feet, chanting *There's no place like home there's no place like home there's no place like motherfu*—

"Frannie, I need some help."

"If this is sexually-related, I'm afraid I'm all used up."

Word vomit. *Jesus Christ,* I think, and it's a plea for an immediate recall; I'm obviously a defective unit. Gretchen's mouth pops open in a perfect O. Stella barks out a laugh and claps her hand over her mouth. Sam's blush goes from fire-engine red to beet purple.

"Aaaahhh…no," he says carefully, staring at my left eyebrow now. "It's about excelling—" He closes his own eyes, breathes in deep, and tries again. "It's about Excel. Microsoft Excel."

"I still have fifteen minutes of lunch, Sam, and to tell you the truth, I really need it. If Morgan is out there—"

"She's in the restroom." Throwing up, undoubtedly. "You're MOUS certified. I hear you're the go-to girl."

Wrong words, and said quite deliberately in a flat, emotionless tone that tells me he's heard the rumors—and believes. Gretchen looks like she wants to sink into the floor. Stella looks like Christmas came early.

I open my eyes and get to my feet, clenching my teeth. Sam backs out the door, apparently alarmed by the look on my face. Perhaps he heard about my penchant for ripping balls out by the roots, for he doesn't seem to want me within a five yard radius of his.

I'm so angry with him about the "go-to girl" comment that he's lucky his stapler is out of my reach. It's in an awkward place for how much he uses it—Sam is fond of stapling things—so I wonder if it's simple prudence that prompted him to move it out of my reach before he came to get me.

It doesn't take me long to take care his Excel problem. "All fixed," I say abruptly, straightening from his desk and moving my hand off the mouse. I start for the door without another word.

"I got a bill from the Sales manager today for a new phone for Eric Edwards." I stop, my whole body rigid, waiting for the umpteenth embarrassing moment of the month to come. "Did you really throw his phone into a water fountain?"

"Yes."

The silence behind me worries me more than him yelling. Everyone is equipped with an expensive company cell phone when they're inducted into the corporate ranks; I sometimes wonder if they have tracking devices on them so they can see where we really are on those days we call in sick but are actually at the beach.

"I told him it was an accident but that I'd authorize payment from our budget to replace it. But—"

I hold up a hand to stop him. I don't need dating advice from a man who can't hold his martinis and makes inebriated marriage proposals.

"Frannie," he says, his tone conciliatory.

"Save it, Sam." I'm out the door without a backward glance and he doesn't follow me; either he's wise or he quite simply just values his balls. He's probably not even in possession of them anyway; no doubt Malia carries them in her purse.

* * * * *

I work late today because I spent an extraordinary amount of time fending off sudden dinner invitations from men in the Production and Sales departments. I make a mental note to find the nearest voodoo queen and somehow obtain a snip of Eric Edwards' hair...

The department is quiet; I'm the only one here now. Sam's light went out about twenty minutes ago but I didn't hear him leave. He must have been very quiet about it, not wanting to attract my attention. It's been very tense today, all the more so because we had to work on a project together for the better part of the afternoon.

I'm about to log off my computer when one last e-mail comes in. *This had better not be about having dinner with some nutter looking for a threesome*, I vow as I open the message. My mouth falls open in shock. It's from my neighbor Betsy, who has never e-mailed me at work in the seven years I've lived next door to her.

"Frannie, I figured it might be awkward for you at work, so I thought I would send you the proof that your date is a scum-sucking asshole. You see, I had a feeling it wasn't going well when I looked out the window and saw him on his cell while he was kissing you, so I videoed it on my phone. The file is attached. Fran—hope you pick better next time. Betsy."

My humiliation is totally complete; my neighbor witnessed my latest dating disaster and took video. I'm sure someday someone is going to send a clandestine video of me to one of those TV shows, and the whole world will know what a loser Frannie Freeman really is.

I click the attachment; it's not that I want to relive the fiasco, but I'm curious what it looked like through someone else's eyes.

What really shocks me is Eric Edwards is worse than I'd thought. Perhaps I'd been trying to rationalize his behavior, not wanting to believe someone could value me so little. Now I see him for what he is: smarmy, sleazy, devious.

"What did I expect?" I murmur. "He's a fucking salesman."

"He's a fucking *dead* man," says Sam from behind me. My chair skids away as I jump up and whirl around, my heart in my throat.

"You scared the shit out of me!"

"As did you when I heard the gory details of your date with Eric, which I see now were highly exaggerated."

"You shouldn't have believed it to begin with." I edge back against my desk as he takes a step into my cubicle. My backside presses against my keyboard and it beeps insistently. I look away to move it, and when I look back up Sam has closed the distance between us.

"Not a good idea," I say.

"My last couple years have been full of not so good ideas." He's standing so close I catch the scent of soap on his skin. He bends toward me and…whispers in my ear: "I much prefer you in a skirt, Frannie…and a thong."

I swallow hard. "You shouldn't prefer me at all. You're married." Funny that should make a difference when I'm trying to entice him away from his Medusa of a wife, but it does.

"Now there's an interesting subject," he says matter-of-factly, and steps back from me. "I'm not so sure that I am."

With a decidedly wicked grin, he gives me a two-fingered salute and walks away, pausing only long enough to give me a look of such searing sensuality that I wonder if there's such a thing as psychic sex.

Holy *shit!*

THE PROOF IS IN THE POWERPOINT

I'm wearing a skirt today—okay, don't even say it. It has nothing to do with Sam. I have a dress plan for the week that I work up on Sunday, and this just happened to be in the repertoire. Or something like that. No thong, though—no way I'm chancing a repeat performance. And I check at least twice before leaving my bathroom stall to make sure the back of my skirt isn't stuffed into the waistband of my pantyhose. Yessiree.

The damn copier is broken again. I'm on my hands and knees—not easy in a skirt—trying to fix it when Eric Edwards saunters in.

"Frannie, can we talk?"

"About what, loser?" My acidic tone is somewhat wasted inside the innards of the mammoth machine.

"See, that's just the attitude that makes logic impossible to achieve." He leans against the copier, and the movement shakes the machine just as I'm taking out the toner cartridge. Black toner sifts onto my hands, and I repress the urge to wipe them on his pristine white shirt. The urge is exceeded only by the one to strangle him with his power tie.

"If you're looking for logic, Eric," I say as I awkwardly get up from the floor, "you'd best not look for it in a pissed-off, hell-bent-on-revenge woman."

"Woman scorned and all that jazz?" He crosses his

arms casually over his chest and beams his best smarmy salesman smile at me.

"No. Woman completely dedicated to seeing to it that you never reproduce." I take a menacing step toward him, crossing my own arms over my chest in imitation of him…remembering too late that my hands are coated with toner. He leaves the copy room laughing and I wonder how I'm going to leave at all; I now have two black handprints over my breasts.

Malia chooses that moment to imperiously stride in, and she stops abruptly, staring in shock and dismay. "Frannie! You have a training meeting in ten minutes!"

I groan. I'd forgotten all about the stupid meeting. I rush to the restroom, where I manage to get the toner off my hands, but there's no helping my blouse.

"Shit, shit, *shit!*" I mutter, looking down at my blouse as I come out of the bathroom. I hear a stifled laugh and glance up in time to see Sam disappearing around a corner, shaking his head.

Sam has not explained his "I'm not so sure I'm married" comment yet; I don't know if that means he's seen a divorce lawyer or if he's seeking an annulment. Either way, in my book he's still married, so I've avoided situations in which we'll be alone together. Not easy, since Sam seems determined to create opportunities to make me completely aware of him to the very molecules of my DNA, the bastard.

"Frannie!" Gretchen exclaims in dismay when I come into Cubicle Row. Sometimes I really wish this corporation had opted for the six-foot tall dividers rather than the four-foot tall ones; you can't even pull your underwear out of the crack of your butt in privacy, and let's face it: no matter what they started out as in the morning, all women's underwear end up thongs by lunch.

"I know. Damn copier. I have a meeting in—" I check the clock. "—seven minutes. Do you have a sweater?"

Gretchen opens a drawer and pulls out a sweater; we all usually keep one handy, because one never knows what the weather is going to be like in the office. One day they roast you, the next the refrigerate you. I often wonder how much government funding the corporation gets for allowing experiments in the effects of office temperature on corporate employees. I haven't had a sweater here in over a year, not since Stella bought me a small space heater. I keep it under my desk where I sit so I get the maximum benefit and the Suits can't see it.

She doesn't hand me the sweater, but motions me to the restroom. "Take off your shirt," she says, quickly unbuttoning her own blouse.

"Gretch?" I back a step away from her.

"C'mon, Frannie, we don't have all day. You have to give that training today, which means using the pointer. And that training room is really warm. You're going to die in a sweater. We'll trade shirts."

"But Gretchen—" She reaches for the buttons on my blouse, and I step back again. "All right, all right."

I shed my shirt in record time—I don't think I even undressed this fast for my last sexual liaison more than three years ago…oh hell, did I say that out loud? Anyway, we're just buttoning up when Morgan walks in, her complexion the usual green. She cocks a brow at us and holds up a hand to halt my hurried explanation.

"I don't want to know." She darts into a stall; Gretchen and I finish buttoning and tucking at top speed before the retching starts. She shrugs into the sweater as we leave the restroom, covering the black toner handprints.

"Gretch—"

"Don't," she says, looking green herself. "It sounds too much like 'retch'. Seriously, Frannie, how does that girl stay alive?"

"I don't know. Maybe she's pregnant."

"But she's *always* sick, not just in the morning."

I roll my eyes as we reach my cubicle, and I grab my Meeting Bag. Meeting Bags are strongly encouraged here. In fact, our employee manual even gives us a list of what to keep in them: one legal notepad, two mechanical pencils, extra lead, a Pink Pearl eraser, highlighters, Post-It flags, paperclips (that one sent Bud into therapy), binder clips, business cards, PDA, etc., etc., etc. Today my Meeting Bag is stuffed to the gills with training handouts. I pat the outside pocket to assure myself I remembered my flash drive.

"Gretchen, my mother was sick morning, noon, and night when she was pregnant with me. Maybe Morgan is like that."

"You don't even know she's pregnant, Fran. Isn't she single?"

I shoulder my bag and stagger a little under its weight. "What, are you living in the Dark Ages?"

"What are you teaching, anyway? Physics?" Gretchen laughs as I adjust my posture to bear the weight.

"Might as well be, for all the attention they're going to pay me. Production is getting a new system, and I get to teach them how to use it."

Stella looks up with a wicked grin. "Lucky you. Give my regards to Mario."

Gretchen snickers. "Oh, is *he* the one...?"

"If either of you even *thinks* the name Conchita, I'm going to thump you. See you later." I hear them laughing behind me, but I don't have time to stop. As it is, I'm running too late to be able to make sure the training room is set up correctly, which it never is.

I definitely don't have time to deal with the extras that have shown up at the meeting: Sam and two or three other Suits. Thankfully, I've brought extra copies just in case. Sometimes I'm frighteningly efficient, as long as it pertains to business and not affairs of the heart.

"I hope you don't mind, Fran," Sam apologizes once

he runs me to ground. I've done my level best to avoid him since I came in. "It's been four or five months since we had training on the new system, so we thought we'd gate-crash. Do you need me to make extra copies of the training material?"

The thought of Sam trying to operate the copier cracks me up. If ever there was a man technology hates, it's Sam. "It's all right. I brought extra."

He smiles. "Of course you did."

I accidentally bump the chair holding my Meeting Bag, and the bag topples slowly toward the floor. Sam catches it, and as he sets it securely on its perch I see him slip a note inside. He gives me a look from the corner of his eye and retreats; the registered attendees for the training have started to arrive.

The training is a fiasco, even with the Production managers and Sam present. The employees in the Production Department don't seem to care about learning the new software. They're talking amongst themselves and not even bothering to lower their voices. Two-thirds of the way through, Sam gets a text on his cell and quietly excuses himself. The Production managers follow shortly after, as though they've just been waiting for Sam to vacate so they can leave.

Once all the management is gone, the staff's whole demeanor changes. Crude jokes are exchanged in undertones and the few I can hear seem to revolve around my date with Eric Edwards. Finally I stop the PowerPoint and grip the edges of the podium until my knuckles are white.

"Are we all done, Frannie?" Mario asks with an innocent smile. He's been the worst, and I suddenly wonder if he and Eric hang out together at sleazy bars, trying to pick up loose women who have no qualms about inviting Conchita.

I'm livid. To tell you the truth, I don't even think twice about what I do next. I don't stop to consider any consequences. I truthfully don't even care about being fired.

"No, I have one more short training clip to show you." I click my way to the flash drive, select the file named *proof.mpv* and double-click. "This is a short demonstration of the power of modern technology. Gentlemen—enjoy."

As the clip plays, they gradually realize this has nothing to do with the new Production software. They find themselves smack in the middle of the conclusion of my date with Eric Edwards. At first their hoots of encouragement for Eric's seeming progress fill the room. By the time Eric's phone hits the pond and the last echoes of my *"Frantisize* this, *asshole!"* fade away, they all seem to have been struck mute.

"So the next time you want to disrespect me, just remember you never know who's taking video. You have your training manuals; teach your own goddamn selves to use the software. I'm done with the lot of you."

I power down the laptop and yank out my flash drive. The men scramble out of their chairs, desperate to leave the room before me just in case I turn violent. I'm halfway to the door before I realize Malaria's standing against the back wall, arms crossed over her chest and feet crossed at the ankles in a seemingly casual stance.

"Well, Frannie," she says, and draws a deep breath. "You've outdone yourself this time."

"I'm sorry, Malia. But they were—"

"I understand that. But you had a choice to ignore it and file a sexual harassment complaint later, which would have been the appropriate response. Instead…"

I hang my head, my cheeks burning, because I know she's right. I lost my temper, and with it went my judgment.

"This will mean a write-up. I'm sorry, Fran." And the crazy thing is, she actually sounds like she really is sorry. But she's gone by the time I find the courage to raise my eyes, and instead I find Sam standing there. His expression is sober, and I duck my chin again, certain I'm reading disappointment in his eyes.

"PowerPoint," he says finally. "Not just for business anymore." He starts laughing. After a minute he's laughing so hard he has to sit down.

"Sam?"

"Jesus, Frannie. That was the funniest thing anyone's ever done in a meeting. I was about to come in and restore order, but you managed just fine."

"You should have stopped me!" I exclaim indignantly.

He gets up, wiping his eyes and trying to stifle his laughter. "Calm down. Malia writes you up, I pretend to lecture you and sign the form. I put a little check mark in the "destroy after one year" box, and in twelve months it's gone from your personnel record."

"You don't have to do that. I did something wrong, Sam."

"So did they. Your manner of dealing with it limits our choices, but I can't say I blame you. Being written up isn't a big deal, Frannie—in fact, in this instance, I'd say it's worth it. And I'll let you in on a little administrators' secret: no one ever looks in the personnel files, not even when deciding to promote someone. It's all just bullshit power games."

He stops at the door and levels a serious look at me. "You really need to go over your notes; things are about to drastically change." He nods once and steps out into the hallway. I can hear the dulcet tones of Malaria starting in on a long-winded, grumpy exegesis regarding my behavior. Sam's responses are voiced too low for me to hear, and then they're gone.

You really need to go over your notes, he'd said, and for a moment I'm offended. Did he think my presentation was poorly prepared? And then I remember the note he'd slipped into my Meeting Bag. I sit down and dive in, sorting through the haphazardly stowed contents until I find the folded sheet of paper. My hands shake as I fumble it open and smooth it flat across my thigh.

8:00 PM HUNTER'S LANDING TAVERN. CASUAL ATTIRE. SKIRT AND THONG OPTIONAL.

PANTYHOSE AND OTHER FIRE HAZARDS

Pantyhose…what can I say about 'em? A quality pair of tights infused with Lycra to squeeze that extra baggage into a trim, attractive figure is not to be underrated. These flimsy, see through, wispy pieces of crap I'm wearing now—all for the sake of fashion—are not worth being rated at all.

For the hundredth time, I stop and take a deep breath, wondering just what the hell I'm doing. There's at least a 50% chance that I'll end up in bed with Sam tonight. Sam…a married man.

Willpower, Frannie. Dredge up some willpower. I don't have to sleep with him. It is completely within my power to say no. *Just say no, Fran. Just say…*

And if I intend to say no, why am I dressing the skankiest I've ever dressed…not that Frannie-skanky is skanky by any definition: scoop-neck shirt dipped just below the collarbones and a snug slim-line skirt two inches above the knee. I suppose the most suggestive thing about my outfit is my spike-heeled shiny black shoes that fairly scream HO!

I stop by the full-length mirror by my bedroom door, and have to admit I look good. *Too* good… Quickly I swap for a pair of snug jeans, clogs and a silk shirt I leave unbuttoned enough to show more of my cleavage than anyone but me and my cat has seen for years.

Not as sexy, but definitely safer. Before I can change my mind, I throw on a jean jacket and head out the door.

Hunter's Landing Tavern is a little off the beaten track, a good forty minute drive out of town. True to its name, it's populated by hunters, fishermen, and a smattering of loggers. It seems a strange place for an urban man like Sam, but he fits in rather well. He's wearing jeans and a button-up plaid shirt that even dozens of washing and a couple years of wearing can't disguise: L.L. Bean. A fireplace occupies one corner, and he's taken a table near it. I'm not fooled; it's not only for the ambience, but for the lack of visibility from outside; there are no windows in that corner.

I slide into the chair opposite, and Sam looks up from the gas fire in surprise. "Hi."

"Fran, I didn't see you come in." He smiles. "Would you like something to drink?"

"I ordered it on my way by the bar. It should be here in a minute." I set my purse aside and toy with the candle in the center of the table. An awkward silence claims us, and I can't help but compare it to the comfortable chatter Eric and I shared on our way to dinner Friday night.

But perhaps it's supposed to be this way. Filling the silence with easy conversation was Eric's way of lowering my guard. Sam lets the awkwardness lie between us, filled with all the things we both wish for and long to do. They don't need to be said, ignored, or disguised; they just *are*.

My drink is delivered, and he looks surprised again as I hoist the Samuel Adams Boston Lager. I bet he expected me to order some fru-fru drink or something tiresomely urbane like a Cosmopolitan.

"So what's up, Sam?"

"I didn't know who else to ask, who else I could trust. You're amazingly efficient and I never see you screwing anyone over."

Obviously he has no clue about my plans to steal him away from Malia. I start peeling the label off my bottle of beer and stop just as suddenly, remembering how Stella always says that when you do that, it means you're horny.

Sam doesn't even notice; he's staring into his scotch and soda. The firelight plays across his face and I notice the dark stubble of five o'clock shadow. I'm doomed. I have no idea how I'm going to stay out of his bed; I'm a sucker for a man edging toward unkemptness.

At last he looks up. "I don't know how I ended up in this situation."

I return his gaze steadily. "You drank enough vodka martinis to fell a draft horse and went to the Garden of Love wedding chapel in Vegas," I reply sharply.

"Did I now?" he says quietly. "Fran, I remember nothing about that part of the night. I'm not sure how many martinis I actually had, but the last memory I have is ordering a club soda. That was after I had an Absolut, a Douglas, and a Muscovy—those are martinis," he adds helpfully.

"I know what they are." I yank the label off my bottle a little more forcefully than necessary, ripping it in half. "At least you didn't say the liquor made you do it."

He gives me a helpless look. "Frannie, I know you think I led you on. But I swear to you, I had no interest in Malia before we went to Vegas for that damned party, and I've had no interest in her since we came back."

"Ah. A marriage of convenience, then."

"I can do without the sarcasm. I'm trying to tell you I think I was roofied."

"Roofied…as in given Rohypnol?" Likely story. And to think I almost wore the skank outfit for him. I take a healthy swig of my beer and start to get up.

"I wanted to ask you out when I got back," he rushes on. His hand raises as though to grab my mine and keep me from leaving, and then falls to the table again to curl around his rocks glass as he thinks better of it. "I was planning on it. That night I even talked to Gus in HR about the fraternization policy. I was going to transfer to another department."

I'm stunned. I don't know if he's sincere or if he's shining me on, but I want to believe really, really bad. "So you could date me."

"Yes."

"But you married Malia instead."

"Did I? That's just the thing. I don't remember *a single thing* after Malia stuck the lime from her drink in my club soda."

"Roofied," I say again, this time considering the possibility.

"I tried to be an honorable man; I tried to make it work. But I swear, Fran, that woman is the devil in human skin. After a while, I started to get a little uneasy about some things."

I quirk a brow, intrigued in spite of myself. "Such as…?"

"Life insurance, bank accounts—she didn't want to combine or change anything. Our 'missing' marriage certificate. So I started investigating."

Intrigue takes a back seat to incredulity. "It took you *two years* to start investigating?"

He seems to sense the rekindling of my anger, and he flushes. "I told you—I tried to make it work. What else would you have me do, Fran? Would I be the man you thought I am—the man I hope you still think I am—if I'd just come back and filed for an annulment?"

"The man I think you are is Malia's," I snap. "Had you come back and filed for an annulment, you'd be—" I stop, horrified at what I almost say.

"Yours?" he finishes softly.

"Free," I reply instead.

"I liked my answer better."

"Don't, Sam. You made your choices, and we have to live within those parameters. This was a bad idea. I knew it was a bad idea, but stupid me—I came anyway."

He reaches out and grabs my wrist before I can reach for my purse. "Frannie, I'm saying that I don't think I'm married at all. I think it's all been a lie." He fumbles a paper out of his shirt pocket with his free hand, shakes it flat and hands it to me.

I have to read it twice before it sinks in. The state of Nevada has no record of a marriage between Sam Harrison and Malia Moreno. It's too good to be true. With technology today, this could be a convincing lie. Sam could have created this so-called proof of his freedom...

But this is Sam we're talking about...Sam, whom technology detests. Sometimes I'm amazed he can even open a spreadsheet. His dark eyes are fixed on me intently.

"I need you to verify this," he says. "Supposedly you can search online but I can't find the link. Marriage certificates are public record; you'll be able to find it. I have to know this letter isn't fake."

"Why me?" I don't understand why he's dragging me into this. He could simply ask one of his friends to help him—they all despise her, from what I've heard. And then when he knows for sure that he's been duped, he can try to convince me of his lack of culpability in his entanglement with Malia. *Try* to...

Would I believe him if he came to me later and claimed he had never really been married to Malia, but had been tricked into believing he had been? Probably not. But if I were involved in the research and discovery... Well then, that's a whole different story.

He sees I've put two-and-two together, so he doesn't bother to explain. He lets go of my wrist and finishes his drink in one swallow. I watch him in this unguarded moment: the way his dark hair falls carelessly into his eyes; the tanned, muscled column of his throat working the drink down; the orthodontist-perfected teeth that sink into his lower lip as the scotch bites its way down his throat. Shit.

Sam is free. I finally allow myself to believe it. "Okay. I'll help you."

He plunks the glass down; his hand stays clenched around it. "Thank you, Frannie." He opens his eyes and stares frankly into mine. What I see scares the shit out of me. I think I wasted time changing clothes; I don't think it matters one iota to Sam what I'm wearing.

In true Frannie form, I panic. "I have to go." I grab my purse and head for the door at top speed.

Now, the thing about pantyhose, even pantyhose worn under jeans, is that the more friction they're subjected to, the warmer they get. By the time I reach the parking lot, I'm pretty sure they've caught fire. My thighs are flaming and it has nothing to do with Sam. I have to stop just around the corner of the building to let the heat die down, and that's where Sam catches up with me. I don't know how I'm going to make it to my car; no way am I walking spraddle-legged across the parking lot in front of him.

"Fran, wait!"

"Not a problem. I think my thighs caught fire."

His brows shoot up. "Sorry?"

"Pantyhose…friction…shit, it's really burning, Sam!"

He's laughing hard now. "All right, all right!" he says, fending off my annoyed slaps. "What do you need me to do? Carry you to your car?"

"No. I have to get them off *right now.*"

He's a bit shocked. "Right here in the parking lot?"

"Yes. Stand guard and hold your jacket in front of me."

"It's fricking cold out!"

"Yeah? Want me to set fire to *your* thighs?"

Now there are any number of possible remarks to

this statement, but Sam refrains. He takes off his jacket, holds it behind his back, and turns around to give me privacy. I kick off my clogs, shuck off my jeans, and slide off the offending hose. The problem appears to be two gaping holes in the inside thigh area on both legs, which has served to plump my flesh into two little balloons that rubbed raw on the denim. Freaking pieces of crap...the pantyhose, that is, not my thighs.

That's my last coherent thought for a while; in a flurry of motion, Sam turns and wraps his coat—and his arms—around my waist. I find my back pressed hard against the rough stucco wall of the tavern and my front pressed hard against Sam.

"At last," he breathes against my mouth.

"Sam..." My lips brush against his. His hands slide under the coat and over my bare buttocks; yes, I wore the thong.

His mouth tastes of scotch and is warm, dark, sinfully inviting. I don't know how long we stand there, intent on making up for every kiss we could have shared over the last two years, so I really can't say how long the spinning blue lights bathed us in their glow before a policeman taps Sam on the shoulder.

"Sir, please turn around and keep your hands where I can see them."

"It's not a very good idea," Sam says over his shoulder. His mouth is twitching like he wants to smile but is afraid the cop might shoot him if he does.

"I won't ask you again."

"All right, then. Sorry, Fran," he whispers with a wicked grin. I'm completely mortified; the only thing holding up the jacket, shielding my near-nakedness from the waist down, is Sam. He takes a step back and turns, holding his hands up in the air.

The cop's flashlight turns on me and bounces in surprise. "Sweet Jesus!"

My bare feet are freezing, as is my bare ass, and my

thighs are still flaming, but I flash him my most charming smile.

The cop barks out a laugh and shakes his head. "I think I'm going to need some ID, folks."

I wonder if *this* is going to hit the evening news.

WHAT HAPPENS IN VEGAS

I'm wearing slacks sans pantyhose today, my rubbed-raw thighs slathered with ointment and bandaged. They still burn. I'm considering suing the manufacturer, but they'll probably win on the grounds that I tried to stuff my chub into casings that were too small. I might stand a chance if I can prove their sizing chart on the package is bullshit. I console myself over the pantyhose disaster by wearing my new shelf bra under a demure white blouse; no one else can see the lacy half-cups that cover and support the underside of my breasts and end just under the nipple, but I know they're there. That secret sexiness gives a much-needed boost to my confidence.

A new software package is waiting on my desk when I come in, a Post-It note attached to the box. *NEW SPEC PRODUCT, ESTIMATED MARKETING DATE IN THREE MONTHS. LOAD IT, LEARN IT, AND WE'LL MEET AFTER LUNCH TO GO OVER IMPRESSIONS. SAM.*

I know it seems funny that a man as technologically impaired as Sam holds a management position in the training department of a software company. Actually, it's a hoot, but let me explain: Sam is quite a talented manager. His people-skills are highly polished and he has a knack for managing the huge workload in our busy office, not to mention his flair for arbitration. I try as hard as I can to bring his technology skills into the twenty-first century, but although Sam gets it—he really does—technology has it in for him, and their skirmishes rarely end well.

Those highly polished people-skills are what keeps a little ember of suspicion burning inside me. I'm still not totally sure he isn't shining me on about Malia. I don't mean about him detesting her; that's common knowledge. They barely speak, at least at work; he barely even seems to notice her. I mean about the roofied lime she supposedly slipped into his soda and the bogus marriage.

"So, Fran," Gretchen says without looking up from the training document she's keying. "What'd you do last night?"

I had told her about Sam's note, and she had promptly cautioned me not to go. In retrospect… Nah, even had I known what would happen, I'd still have gone. More good than bad happened, and almost being arrested for indecent exposure was quite an experience.

"Had a drink," I reply warily, sending a look from the corner of my eye at Stella.

Gretchen spares me a glance. "Thought we talked about your…er…drinking."

"Yeah. I only had one. But I did nearly get arrested for indecent exposure."

Her fingers pause. "Let's get coffee."

Stella rolls her eyes; we're not fooling anyone. I join Gretchen in the hallway, and she doesn't even wait until we're in the break room to start.

"Frannie, *what happened?*"

I cast a look behind me; neither Morgan nor Stella appears to be listening, but I'm not taking any chances. I hold a finger to my lips to shush Gretchen and yank her down the hallway to the break room, which is thankfully unoccupied.

"I went to Hunter's Landing."

"Jesus, Fran!" She shoves me into a chair and takes one herself.

"Everything's fine, Gretch," I'm quick to assure her. "We had an interesting talk."

"Is that what they're calling it these days?"

"He asked me to conduct an online search for his marriage license on the Las Vegas website. He thinks there is a possibility that Malia tricked him about being married."

Gretchen's looking at me with an oddly sympathetic look. "Fran…that's really reaching."

"I tried to look up the certificate, but then their website went down for maintenance, so I haven't gotten that far yet. He says he had three drinks and then a club soda, and doesn't remember a thing after that. She could have been able to—"

She holds up a hand, closing her eyes for a moment. When she opens them again, I don't like the expression in them. I'm going to get "a few home truths" pointed out to me; Gretchen is fond of trotting out "a few home truths" when she thinks you're screwing up your life.

"Frannie, he's married, plain and simple. Some wild goose chase across the internet is not going to change that. So he made a letter to cast doubt on it so you'd sleep with him. You aren't the first one to fall for a ploy like that."

Numb, I stare at her in shock. To tell you the truth, I had pushed all doubt aside and believed Sam wholeheartedly. "I didn't sleep with him," is the only thing I can manage to say.

"Thank God for small favors!" she exclaims, throwing her hands up in the air. "But it wasn't entirely a platonic evening, was it? Not if you nearly got arrested for indecent exposure."

"A long story, but no, it wasn't entirely platonic. Gretchen, don't you start thinking the worst of him. That isn't fair."

"What isn't fair," she replies quietly, "is how he's still stringing you along." I don't answer, and after a moment she adds softly, "You didn't tell him you're in love with him, God forbid?"

"No."

"I won't drag you over the coals, then, because it will only piss you off and I have the feeling you're going to need me."

She doesn't say anything else as we go back to our desks, and over the course of the morning I'm aware of her eyes on me, concerned, and of the black looks she keeps sending toward Sam's office.

Sometimes our company comes out with a great product, and sales skyrocket. The Suits have a big party to celebrate, drink too much (it's one such skyrocketing sale that led to the Sam-Malia union), and generally pat themselves on the back. The rest of us working joes meet at a bar, hoist a beer or two (all we can afford), and go home and look through the want ads for higher paying jobs.

I don't think we're going to see such a scenario for this current software—well, the working joes will still look for higher paying jobs, but the Suits aren't going to be celebrating any time soon. This program isn't going to hit the market in three months, either, for half an hour before lunch I find a glitch. A major one.

"What the hell..." I remark. Stella snickers, but Gretchen doesn't even look up, she's so intent on whatever she's doing. It must be much more interesting than the training manual she was writing, because she's riveted. She clicks her mouse button and her printer hums.

"What's the matter, Fran?" Morgan pipes up. She's not green today, because Malia called in sick.

"The new software…I'm stuck in a loop. I get a pop-up box with an error. I click OK. The pop-up goes away, I try to click out of the function, and the pop-up comes back. It's like some kind of cosmic joke."

"Just click the close button in the top right corner," Stella says.

"No can do. The pop-up box prevents it. Seriously, which idiots write this crap?" Resignedly, I hold down CTRL and ALT while I press DEL to bring up my Task Manager and shut down the program.

Apparently this is the secret code to test the fire sprinkler system, for without warning the fire alarm sounds and the sprinklers come to whirring, wet life.

"SHIT!" Gretchen yells, and yanks the documents off her printer, stuffing them into her shirt.

Suits are popping out of offices, scowling, looking for the perpetrator. Good luck with that; since its construction, this building's been plagued with more glitches than that damn software I just tested. One memorable day a few years ago, the key-card lock system went haywire and locked all the doors on us. It took three hours for the installation company to respond to our call for help, and another two for them to free us. I bet the Suits really tied one on *that* night.

I grab my purse and stuff my Meeting Bag into the drawer in its place, and we join the mass exodus to the door.

Southern California isn't exactly Maine in the winter, but neither is it Hawaii. Add to it wet clothing, and you have a group of shivering employees, huddling together for warmth like penguins. All the women have their arms crossed over their chests to hide certain physical reactions to the wet and cold, a fact Eric Edwards and crew seem to find hilarious. Gradually, I notice a lot of the men staring at my chest and looking away really quickly when I catch them.

I nudge Gretchen. "Hey," I whisper, "can you see

through my shirt?"

She's still distracted; she glances down at me and away, then looks quickly back. "Jesus, Frannie! I can see the details of the lace on your bra! And...and..." She glances around, then makes quick circles in the air at the tips of her own breasts.

I sigh. "I thought so." My own arms go up over my chest just as a dark blue windbreaker is thrust between us. "Thanks, Sam."

"No problem."

As I shrug into the jacket, he moves back into the crowd. Gretchen glares after him. *"Stop it!"* I hiss.

"I'm sorry. It's just..." She pulls me out of the crowd and fishes the papers out of her shirt. For a second, she smoothes them against her chest as best she can, as though reluctant to show them to me. But in the end she hands them over, and watches me carefully as I read.

I look up blankly. "But..."

"I found the online document search. It took a little bit of hunting and following some poorly named links. It's no wonder Sam sent a form through the mail; it's a nightmare to find the online query. He probably called them to get the request form in the first place." Gretchen knows Sam's battle with technology well; she's worked for him three years longer than I have.

"He did." I swallow with difficulty, willing the words on the paper to not blur. I will *not* cry in front of all of Harper & Lyttle over a man who doesn't deserve it. I wish I'd never told her; if I'd kept it to myself, my humiliation would at least have been totally private. Technology, after all, is how I make my living.

"Fran...I'm sorry."

It takes a minute to find a steady voice. "Yeah. Me too."

Not only the marriage license, but the marriage certificate as well, is in the Clark County online database. Roofied, my ass—he had to have been lucid enough to have signed the application for the marriage license or it would not have been granted. Had I searched for the information before ever letting Sam lay a hand on me, last night never would have happened, as it never should have.

Gretchen tries to take the papers back, but I hold them out of her reach as I shrug out of Sam's jacket. He's standing with a group of Suits away from the huddle of employees, manfully withstanding the chill in his wet clothes. He sees me coming and excuses himself, meeting me halfway between his group and mine.

"Fran?"

I slap the coat and the papers into his chest and walk away. My car's not far, and I have my purse. Seems like a good day to go home early.

My apartment complex sits at the edge of a lake. Sandy beach extends to the right, and a long boardwalk extends to the left, shielded from view by tall marsh grasses and cattails. The boardwalk is dotted with clusters of Adirondack chairs, and I claim one, sitting in the chilly air until the sun sinks into the lake.

At last, as the fiery sky fades to twilight blue, I allow myself to consider all possible ways of castrating my paramour.

POST-ITS AND PMS

Some things just don't go together. Post-Its and PMS are two of them. Malaria has decided we need a little brain-storming motivation. I don't know why we need to brain-storm; we aren't the ones coming up with ideas for the software, and we certainly don't need it for writing technical manuals or training people, and we certainly don't need a conference about it during the last hour of our workday.

On second thought, I could use some ideas on training people after the last training fiasco last month. I did indeed get written up; I did indeed get called into Sam's office. And he did indeed check the box to have the document destroyed after a year. I told him again he didn't have to, but he did it anyway.

Things have been very awkward since the sprinkler incident. For two days following, Sam tried very hard to talk to me alone, but I avoided all contact. If he called me to ask for help on the computer, I sent Gretchen or Stella, and it didn't take him long to get the hint and stop asking. The day I went home early, I expected to go back to my apartment to a dozen or so messages, but there were only three on the machine: one from Gretchen and two from Sam. The first was a plea for me to pick up the phone and talk to him. The second was a simple "I'm sorry, Frannie."

He's sorry, all right. One thing I can say in his favor is he doesn't appear to have a stalker gene. He avoids me, I avoid him, and on the surface everything is cool. But I'm not the only one who's noticed Sam's easy demeanor has slipped off-kilter; everyone but Gretchen, Stella, and Morgan blame Malaria. And the funny thing is, the sudden change in Sam's behavior is what's making Gretchen see him in a more sympathetic light. Me, I still want to castrate him, and I don't dare let myself believe he ever honestly thought Malaria staged their marriage.

You see, I lied to Gretchen. I think she knows it, but she hasn't called me on it. That night at Hunter's Landing, after the cops left (thankfully without writing me a citation; my ruined pantyhose save me in the end), Sam says he'll follow me to make sure I make it home all right. I'm not surprised when he shuts off his truck and walks me to the door. I'm equally unsurprised when he kisses me goodnight. What *does* surprise me is that I ask him in for coffee—and he accepts.

We walk silently from our cars to my front door. I fidget with my keys, damn near dropping them into the fountain near my door—the same fountain into which I threw Eric Edwards phone after our disastrous date—and then stop because I remember Stella says that means you're horny. I'm starting to think that everything in Stella's world relates to sex.

I stop at the door and leans against it, slotting the key in the lock. "Well... Thanks for seeing me home, Sam."

We both know that it was completely unnecessary for him to "make sure I get home all right"—although, truth be told, I can't handle alcohol very well. And this awkwardness between us now...should it be there, I wonder, after we spent God knows how much time kissing in the parking lot of Hunter's Landing Tavern?

"No problem. Sorry you almost got arrested for indecent exposure."

I blush, which makes him smile. "Yeah, me too. My own fault for stripping in public, I guess."

And then the awkward silence descends again, but this time fully charged with sexual awareness. He closes the gap, leaning in to kiss me. His lips are soft and warm, and the air around me is scented with that aftershave that I so like. He draws away a couple of inches.

"Would you like to come in for coffee?" I ask, and my blush deepens to a painful hue.

"Yeah. Yeah, I'd like that."

I turn the key and step through the door, waiting for Sam to follow me in. He takes two steps past me, and I turn to close the door, nudging Penguin away from the tantalizing outside air. When I turn back around, he's closed the distance again. His eyes are wide, catching the light from the lamp I left on in the living room, like large drops of coffee fringed with black lashes, incredible eyes. I think they're what hooked me from the moment I first met him. That and his smile.

The heat of his body radiates through the air between us. He tangles one hand into my hair; his eyes half-close and his breath catches in his throat. Me, I don't think I'm even breathing.

He draws me up on tiptoes to his kiss, and it's an easy thing from there to slide his arms around me and pull me against him. Passion explodes between us, raging like the fires of hell, and God knows we're probably both going to burn for this. But I don't care. I can't get close enough, even though he's pressed so tightly to me you couldn't put a sheet of paper between us.

Somehow we're moving down the hallway to my bedroom. The sofa is closer, but I don't want our first time together to be on a sofa. He doesn't protest. He's managed to get my shirt unbuttoned, and my skin against the amber silk glows in the dim lamplight from my bedroom. He's mesmerized, his fingers tracing along the edge of my lacy bra cups. At long last his hand cups one, testing its weight, his thumb sliding across my nipple and sending a *zing!* through my entire body. I wrench away from his lips, gasping in a breath as his mouth moves against my neck. He presses me against him, and my gasp becomes a quavering sigh.

My hand threads through his hair and pulls him to me, my mouth crushing against his. He'd sparked desire in me before—and had been given a sample of it in the tavern parking lot—but I'd never before experienced this unbearable need to consume, to *be* consumed, to both conquer and surrender.

He breaks the kiss and pulls away just enough to ask, "Frannie, are you sure you want to do this?"

I laugh, a husky chuckle that sends shivers through him. "Oh, I'm sure."

And he asks at least half a dozen more times as he lays me back on my bed, before the last barriers of clothing and caution are stripped away and we're skin to skin, his mouth blazing a trail of exquisite sensation over my flesh, dragging me into a feverish dream of desperate animalistic need. I swallow his groan of pleasure, our rocking rhythm adding a delicious friction. His control breaks, and I have no words to describe the places he takes me, except to say I think we might have danced through heaven.

He leaves at 3:00 a.m. I don't ask how he's going to explain himself at home; I don't want to know. I've become The Other Woman, and it makes me angry, deep inside, because I know I should be The Only Woman. Maybe you think I'm deluding myself, but I know the difference between a man just taking sex and a man who is emotionally involved in the act. Mind you, it doesn't change the fact that he's still caught between a shrew and a dream-girl (me being the dream-girl, in case there's any confusion).

My extra pillow still smells like Sam, but it's fading now. Perhaps I'll wash it tonight and put paid to the whole sorry mess.

Speaking of sorry messes... The building had to undergo major repairs after the fire sprinkler incident. We were moved to a nearby location the corporation leased, and we've only just moved back in. It turns out my performing the CTRL-ALT-DEL sequence had nothing to do with the malfunction. I'm quite relieved.

Our new cubicles afford a little bit more privacy, with five-foot walls with little windows in them so we can see each other if we want to. No glass, but we do have mini-blinds in case we *don't* want to see each other. My space heater was completely ruined, but a new one miraculously appeared the day we moved back in. I suspect Sam was behind that, but I haven't said anything about it and neither has he. I now have a set of overhead cabinets with metal doors, and I've slapped up a couple boxes of that magnetic poetry. The last few mornings I've been coming in to some weird-ass phrases, some of them crude—no doubt Eric Edwards and crew—but this morning there's a gem left for me amongst the magnetic graffiti: *she walks in beauty like the night*. Lord Byron, in case you're wondering. Rather sweet, but I'm done with office romances. They rarely end well.

"Fran, you coming?" Gretchen calls out. I grab my notepad and pencil and stand up.

"Yeah."

"What's this stupid meeting for again?" Morgan asks.

"Brain-storming," I answer, rolling my eyes.

"What I really need is one on brain-*finding*," says Stella with a sigh. She's been acting rather odd lately, and just yesterday I found a major error in her work. Stel's a perfectionist, and I can't remember the last time I found a mistake. She agonizes over spell-check and proofreads character by character. I'd have just corrected the error and gone on my way, but Stella is the only one who has access to that particular software, so I had to tell her. She's been fretting about it ever since.

"You aren't the only one," I mutter, and Gretchen sends me a sharp look. "I need to refill my coffee on the way."

Morgan hesitates. "Is this a real refill, or a euphemism for a private chat?"

"A real refill, Morgan," I assure her kindly, and she smiles in relief.

Morgan's come a long way in the last month, mostly because Malia has been out frequently with illness and

Morgan gets to do her real job, which is handle the enormous amount of paperwork Sam seems to churn out despite his technological failings. A rumor's going around that Malia's battling pneumonia, but personally I think she's hitting the sauce and can't make it in due to hangovers or continued inebriation. I think this because she's called me several times during such absences, and she can barely string a coherent sentence together, not that her requests make much sense anyway. I just placate her and go my merry way as usual. Everything gets done and on time. I'm the Go-To Girl, after all.

The key-note speaker of this little conference is dressed like David Copperfield. This doesn't bode well. Stella stifles her laughter and Gretchen gives me a warning look. I'm PMSing badly and I have cramps bad enough to fell an elephant. The filter between my tongue and my brain is often rendered useless by the sudden flood of hormones during these times, and anything—*anything*—is likely to come out my mouth before the brain can stop it.

"I wonder why all the Suits are here," Stella grumbles, giving the huddled group of administrators the stink-eye.

"They only know how to *blame*-storm, so they're here to learn how to *brain*-storm," I quip. See, no filter. Too late, I see Sam passing nearby with the CEO, who thankfully is about 180 years old and, I suspect, two-thirds deaf if his response to our complaints is any indication. I see Sam's mouth twitch as he sends a look in my general direction.

"Filter, Fran!" Gretchen hisses.

I wave a placating hand at her and vow to clamp a lid on it.

The speaker isn't all bad. He performs in a flourishing manner that makes me wonder if he doesn't double as an illusionist, and he speaks with the forced enthusiasm of an infomercial, but some of his ideas are good.

The Post-It Method is not one of them.

According to this gentleman, brain-storming isn't enough. You need a brain-blizzard; traditional, structured brain-storming, where one person writes out shouted ideas on the whiteboard, tragically fails to capture all beneficial thoughts. At this point, the only blizzard I want is from Dairy Queen, and as he walks around the room handing out pads of brightly colored Post-It notes, I have to physically repress the urge to tell him where he can put them.

The point of a brain-blizzard, he says, is to write your ideas—Thoughts, with a capital T—on the Post-Its and slap them up on the whiteboard as fast as you can. When the session is over, someone will compile them all into a coherent list (if they can read your writing, that is), and thus *all* ideas are captured. I see a major problem with this method: Not all ideas *should* be captured, and traditional brain-storming allows those present to immediately nix the more idiotic suggestions so no more time than necessary is spent on them. But hey, I'm game. I'll try anything once, just so I know what I'm talking about when I say it's stupid.

"BEGIN!" the illusionist cries, and the crowd of suits and skirts rushes toward the whiteboards with their Post-It pads in hand and their pens at the ready. He's assigned topics to each section of the whiteboard, and we're supposed to go from topic to topic and slap up our Thoughts. I feel like a moron doing this, so I only slap up a couple notes before I fall back. I notice Sam is hanging back also, viewing the festivities with an expression that clearly says *So this is what we've come to*. I toss my pad on a nearby table and start to take a seat.

"Come! Come!" the illusionist cries, motioning for me to rejoin the group. He sounds like a carnie hawking his scam to a mark.

"No, thanks," I say.

"I'm sure you're *brimming* with ideas!" he insists. I am, but it's better he not know the ones that involve evisceration.

"I'm fresh out," I reply.

The illusionist looks to Sam for help; he only shrugs and vanishes into the crowd. Stella comes to my aid, which is never a good thing.

"She's PMSing," she announces loudly.

You know how there are those moments in a crowded, noisy room when a sudden lull in conversation coincides with an unfortunate remark, as though by silent, tacit agreement the occupants fall mute to witness your humiliation? Well, one of those happens now, and the whole room hears. There's a beat of surprised silence and then everyone is roaring with laughter. I close my eyes and count to ten. Then twenty. Then thirty. Still not enough. I grab the pen and scrawl out a Thought and cross the room with purposeful strides to the board with the subject heading WHAT WOULD MAKE THE OFFICE A FRIENDLIER PLACE? The crowd parts for me like the Red Sea for Moses, and I slap up my note: *PEOPLE MINDING THEIR OWN GODDAMN BUSINESS*. Sam blinks, stares, and closes his eyes for a second, but the note is still there when he opens them again. Another write-up in the making for sure, I think as I make my escape.

A second little snippet of poetry waits for me on my cubicle cabinet, some of the words robbed from the graffiti and put to better use: *you are a balm to my restless spirit*. That one I have to look up on the internet, and find it's a modernly worded quote of Helen Keller. For the first time I let myself wonder if my magnetic poet is Sam.

"You all right, Frannie?" Gretchen asks. Startled, I look up to find her and Stella standing nearby with their coats on. I hadn't even seen them come in.

"I'm fine." I smile, but I don't fool either of them.

"I'm just going to get a couple of things done."

Gretchen shoots a look at Sam's office, but his light is off. So she nods, because it's safe to leave me here if he's gone home.

"I'm sorry, Frannie," Stella says meekly.

"It's all right, Stel. It was just poor timing, like those things always are."

She nods now, and she and Gretchen leave. I sit for a long time in the darkened office, just my cubicle lights on, and it's not until I hear Sam's voice behind me that I realize I'm crying.

"Frannie—are you okay?"

I swipe at my cheeks hastily. "Yeah, I'm fine," I lie, even though it's obvious I'm not.

"Do you want to talk about it?"

The words act as the catalyst that springs me from my chair. "No. Definitely not." I push past Sam and head for the bathroom, foolishly thinking I can dodge him in there; it's the ladies room and he can't come in. But those designations are only social barriers, not physical ones. It's after hours and we're the only two in the building; he doesn't hesitate to barge in after me.

"Frannie, we have to talk about this."

"Oh, no we don't."

I come out of the stall with a wad of tissue and try to staunch my flow of tears but it's hopeless; Sam's too near, too concerned. He reaches out to touch my cheek; I turn away and he catches my hair instead. The tears explode from me and I sob so hard I don't even notice his arms go around me. It's not until I take a step back that I realize he's there, and we go down in a tangle of limbs. Sam takes the brunt of the fall, but he doesn't complain. He holds on to me when I'd otherwise move away. It's a long time before I regain control of myself, before I realize he's propped himself against the wall and I'm curled up between his splayed legs—which are no doubt going numb by now—with my cheek pressed against his chest.

"Frannie, I'm sorry. I never meant for things to turn out this way."

"Not your fault. I knew what I was doing."

"I honestly believed she set the whole thing up, that it was all fake. I wanted it to be true."

He wanted it to be true…but he's done nothing to extricate himself from her in the month since Gretchen found the online proof of his marriage. He wants me…but not enough to serve her papers and end their sham of a marriage.

"What are you going to do, Sam?"

"I'm working on it, Fran." He lifts my chin and forces me to look him in the eye. "I'm working on it as fast as I can."

But it's no guarantee for me, I realize. Perhaps he'll take one gulp of freedom and become intoxicated by it, and never want to be tied down again. While I won't be his mistress, I won't be his sex buddy either.

Something in my expression must have betrayed my train of thought, because Sam's fingers tighten on my chin. "No, it's not like that, it's not ever going to be like that." He crushes me against his chest and for a terrifying moment I can't breathe. Then he cups my face and kisses me hard, once, twice, three times, and he says it, damn him, he says the forbidden words.

"I love you, Frannie."

I reflect that I should have just stayed at the conference and done the stupid Post-It project, and dealt with my PMS in my usual sarcastic manner. But seriously, how much more fucking moronic can it get?

"Sam?"

"Mmmm?"

"I don't want to do any more brain-blizzards."

He laughs softly. "Me either."

We sit in silence for a while longer.

"Frannie?"

"Mmmm?"

"My ass has gone numb."

KNACKERED AND KNOCKED UP

I have more work than I can do, as does the whole Training Department, and the Powers-That-Be have put a freeze on hiring after Morgan came on board. In spite of the mounds of work piling up for lack of sufficient time to do it, for some reason the Adminisphere thinks we need to have a weekly staff meeting to go over progress.

We come out of these meetings with our limbs twitching and our eyes glazed over, and the Suits strut around pompously decrying the poor state of affairs while secretly thriving on the drama of created crises. The rest of us stump back to Cubicle Row, knowing that some stuffed shirt is going to get a hefty bonus at Christmas while we'll be lucky if we see an additional dollar-eighty-five on our semi-monthly checks.

I don't gripe much about the meetings lately; Malaria's frequent absences mean Sam conducts them more often than not, as it should be. He's actually our boss anyway.

The simplistic beauty of corporate idiocy in the case of Harper & Lyttle lies within its management structure. The chain of command is a convoluted Gordian knot that would send Alexander the Great shrieking into therapy. At the top you have the CEO—you'll remember him: the 180-year-old, two-thirds deaf man with Sam at the Brain-Blizzard conference (side note: Bud Mitchell is now exhibiting signs of Post-It Note paranoia along the lines of the paperclip mania. Must nip this in the bud—no pun intended—post-haste). Garland Harper, CEO, MBA, blah blah blah, is a Texas transplant who originally came to California with the intention of starting a vineyard in Napa Valley. Silicon Valley sucked him in instead; he proved to have more of a knack with code than mash, and while busting a hump writing programs for Intuit (of Quicken fame), he designed his own programs on the side. A group of venture capitalists from his home state provided funding, and Harper Business Systems was born. A merge in the 1990's with Lyttle Software, Inc., gave us the corporation as we now know it and for unknown reasons prompted a move from Silicon Valley to Los Angeles.

Under Garland Harper is a battery of Senior Executives who manage several departments grouped together for reasons known only to the Powers-That-Be, who were obviously drinking heavily at the time and more than likely drew department names out of a hat.

Below the Senior Execs is an army of Section Supervisors—which is Sam's title. These folk are pseudo-Suits; in other words, they have management authority and privileges within certain confines but rarely rub elbows with the Senior Execs. These folk are also responsible for upholding the sometimes-mad policies that come down from the Senior Exec level (also pulled out of a hat) and relaying the staff's discontent to deaf ears.

The bottom feeders of the admin pond are the Office Supervisors. These sad sacks are responsible for maintaining the workflow, processing departmental payroll, and filtering paperwork to the appropriate Section Supervisor. While they can dictate our job responsibilities, they have no real authority and have to refer any disciplinary issues to the Section Supervisor. In other words, they are the equivalent of older siblings who try to tell you what to do and run and tattle to the "parent" when you don't do it. This is Malaria's lot in life.

Generally speaking, the fraternization policy—usually strictly upheld—would have required that either Sam or Malia transfer out of the department, because supervising a spouse or significant other is regarded as a conflict of interest. This policy was not, in fact, enforced in the case of the Harrisons; popular rumor has it that no other Section Supervisor would take her.

I don't think I need to point out that with a management structure like this, we are indeed the unwilling doing the impossible for the ungrateful. Sam buffers us from the corporate idiocy as much as he can, but sometimes he's forced to go by the playbook, and weekly progress meetings are in said publication.

This morning, we ladies file in grousing and grumbling; the coffeemaker is broken and Malaria's morning e-mail informed us that the budget request to replace it has been denied. Stella has one of those profanity-bubbles hanging over her head, and Sam looks quite alarmed at her expression as she stalks in and throws her notepad on the conference table. He glances at me only long enough to ask a silent question; prolonged eye contact with his wife present is not a wise move.

"Coffee machine's still broken," I say by way of explanation as Stella slumps in her seat and crosses her arms over her chest, her face scrunched into a grouchy frown. "Budget request was denied."

"Sorry, ladies. The Budget Committee is crunching down on what they call unnecessary expenses, and I'm afraid your coffee habit has fallen under the axe."

Stella mutters something about "the freaking staple usage" under her breath and Sam pretends not to hear her.

"Are we all here?"

"Morgan's in the restroom," Gretchen says, sidling in the door at the last second.

Malaria harrumphs impatiently. Sam sends her a quelling look. I know you're probably thinking by now that he's hen-pecked and subservient—a spineless twat, in other words—but there's a latent strength in Sam that many underestimate. It's what makes him such a good boss; he eases the blows he can't prevent and fights relentlessly for the things he can. Yeah, I know---rah rah rah, I sound like a cheerleader for Sam. So what? Deal with it. Lately we've been seeing the subtle signs of his all-out mutiny against Malia, and to be honest, it's quite fascinating to watch an easy-going man transform into a wild tiger making a desperate bid for freedom.

She huffs out another sigh, obviously pushing the envelope, and I quirk a brow at Gretchen, wondering if I'm the only one who caught a whiff of whiskey. Judging from the frown on his face, Sam smells it too. I dart a quick look at her water bottle, but the liquid is clear.

Morgan skids into the room, green-faced and sweaty, apologizing profusely as she sinks into a chair, avoiding Malaria's disgusted glare. She pops a stick of chewing gum into her mouth and cocks a sickly brow at me.

"No can do, Morgs. They said no."

Her expression sags comically; Morgan without her coffee is as bad as Stella when she swears off casual sex.

Malia snorts and takes a swig off her bottle of water. "Oh, shtop moaning about it. I'm shhure Sam'll buy you a nnnewww one." She doesn't look at Morgan, though; she beams a glare at me, and I realize now she's as drunk as a hoot owl. (Another side note: where *does* that expression come from, anyway? Do hoot owls get drunk? Has anyone ever witnessed this phenomenon?) Sam's demeanor of utter exhaustion now makes a lot of sense. The last two weeks since the Post-It disaster have seen his mood in a definite downward spiral.

I send a panicked glance at Gretchen, who raises her brows. I've never told her about that night with Sam. I haven't told her that he said he loves me, either.

"Okay," Sam butts in sharply, ignoring Malaria. "About the coffeemaker. I'll see if one can't be found in the basement for the short term while I see what I can do about the purchase of a new one. If we don't have a spare, does anyone have one they can bring in from home?"

"I do," I say quietly, avoiding his gaze.

"Of coursssh you do," Malaria mutters. She thinks she's speaking in an undertone, but she isn't; she's clearly audible to everyone.

Sam grits his teeth and plows on. "Now that we have that out of the way, we need to move on to…"

An hour later, Morgan interrupts a spirited disagreement between Stella and Gretchen over the new font production is using for the technical manuals. She's gone quite green again.

"I think I'm going to be sick," she announces. I skid my chair back by instinct, which makes Stella crack up.

"Ooohhh, for chriisssshake!" Malaria slurs impatiently. She rummages through her meeting bag and with a triumphant smile whips out a long, rectangular box, waving it aloft for a drunken moment. I have one of those moments of crystal clarity that only seem to come when some terribly humiliating event is about to occur, and I see the label plainly: Clearblue Easy.

"I mmeant to give it to *you*," and she points at me with package, "ssooo you can check the cons…consh…shnequences of fucking my husband, but Mmmooorgan needs it more."

Dead silence reigns in the room as Malia slams the box on the table and gives it a shove toward Morgan. The color drains out of Sam's face and finds Morgan's. Stella gives a delighted whoop and Gretchen a shocked, strangled squawk. I feel the odd rushing-backward sensation that precedes a faint, and everything seems to go in slow motion: Sam closing his eyes in weary resignation; Malia falling out of her chair, the motion of pushing the pregnancy test across the table setting her off balance; Sam's hand slamming down on the Clearblue Easy box with unerring accuracy despite the fact that his eyes are shut tight; Morgan's stricken cry and subsequent flight from the room.

"Meeting dismissed," Sam grits out between clenched teeth.

"But Sam—" Stella says, and for the first time in the five years I've worked for him, I see Sam completely lose it.

"NOW, DAMMIT!"

Gretchen jumps. Stella throws up her hands, snatches up her notepad and whisks from the room. Malia is lying on the floor giggling maniacally. Sam snatches up her water bottle, takes a drink and nods, and then throws it toward the trashcan by the door. I feel little sprinkles of vodka-laced Sprite hit my flaming face.

Sam pinches the bridge of his nose between his thumb and forefinger and says heavily, "I'm sorry, Frannie." He seems to say that a lot lately.

I'm afraid to stand, my legs are shaking so badly, but Gretchen is there, her hands lifting me from my chair and guiding me out the door. I don't notice where we're going until she half-closes the door of an empty conference room down the hall. We can hear the shouted argument ensuing between Sam and Malia, muffled by walls and distance to the point we can't make out the words.

"Frannie, are you all right?" Gretchen asks as she pushes me down into a padded arm chair.

"Holy shit, Gretch! What the *fuck*?"

Gretchen is silent as she pulls a chair around to face me. "Fran…" She takes my hands, dangling them between us, and sighs heavily. "Frannie, are you sleeping with Sam?"

Hot color rushes into my cheeks. "No."

She huffs out a little breath and tries again. "Let me rephrase. Have you *ever* slept with Sam?"

I look away. "Yes. Once—that night I went to Hunter's Landing."

"I knew it." She shakes her head. "Are you pregnant?"

"Good God, no! I'm not *entirely* stupid, Gretchen!"

"Are you sure?"

"That I'm not entirely stupid?" I ask flippantly. "Yeah, pretty much."

"I meant are you entirely sure you aren't pregnant."

"Yes, I'm sure. I'm not pregnant."

"I am," says a small voice in the doorway.

Gretchen spins around, and my head comes up. Morgan is standing there like a small child, hangdog, her honey-blonde hair hiding her face.

But when she looks up… Gretchen and I are transfixed by the expression of sheer hatred on her face. "That bitch is going down."

"Morgan," I venture, almost afraid to ask. "I…er…thought you weren't married."

"I'm *not,* Frannie," she snaps. "This was a surprise. But I'm not sorry." She lifts her chin proudly. "Bud isn't, either."

Gretchen's mouth falls open. If she gets one more shock today, I'll be visiting her in the hospital. "Aaahh…Bud?"

Morgan sniffs and tosses her blonde hair defiantly. "Yeah. Bud Mitchell."

I start to laugh. Bud Mitchell and Morgan, having a torrid affair and a baby; Malia having a drunken moment of sabotage and self-destruction; Sam losing his temper and pulverizing a Clearblue Easy meant for me, Frannie Freeman, The Other Woman.

And me, still without a fucking coffeemaker.

MARGARITA MADNESS

Blame has landed on us like radiation fall-out, and is just as deadly. Because Malia was intoxicated at work, Sam has no choice but to report the incident to his supervisor—not that I thought he would shirk that responsibility even if given a choice. He comes out of George Stuckey's office red-faced but with a grimly satisfied smile.

Malaria's tucked into her office to sober up, and when she's more or less coherent, Sam ushers her out to a cab and sends her home. The next day he stuffs her into a rehab clinic. Harper & Lyttle doesn't fire you for intoxication during business hours; "alcoholism is a disease" and all that, you know. Bullshit, is my personal opinion. A disease is something that can't be prevented. You get it no matter how you guard against it. Alcoholism is a choice to pick up a bottle and find your way to the bottom of it, again and again and again.

But that's just Frannie Freeman speaking. The Suits have a differing opinion, which involves rehab and second chances. I'm not saying that's all bad; I'm just saying life would be much more pleasant in Cubicle Row if they'd simply outright fired Malaria and had done with it. Call it giving us a dose of quinine.

We all stayed and toughed it out that day, only

because we felt we'd be letting Sam down if we didn't. No reason he should have to stay and fend off the fall-out all by himself. As it turned out, none of us were called in about the meeting until the next day, and by then I'd already talked to Sam about his meeting with Stuckey, because he called me after work. He said George asked if he was having an affair with me, present tense. Sam told me he had no qualms about saying "no" because we'd only slept together that once when we thought—hoped—his marriage wasn't real, and we weren't still doing it.

His telling me proves fortuitous, because I'm called in to talk to Stuckey the first thing the following morning. I don't even blink as I confide to George that I think it was just the tequila talking.

"Whiskey and vodka," George corrects me absently.

"Just a phrase," I clarify. "But seriously, Mr. Stuckey, it was just the alcohol."

And that's the end of it...sort of. The whole department, including Sam, has been placed on probation, and Sam confides in me during the two whole minutes we were left alone this morning that we narrowly avoided one of us being transferred into another section. Neither of us wants that, even though we know that when he does finally manage to extricate himself from Malia it will *have* to happen.

It's not fair that we're on probation; Malia is the one who got drunk at work and caused a scene. But that's one of the little quirks about office politics. Responsibility gets shared amongst anyone who happens by sheer misfortune to be present...and sometimes those who weren't. In other words, the policy for getting screwed over by the company is an equal opportunity one.

Suffice to say, the week totally sucked and I'm glad it's over. The others apparently agree with me on that score, because fifteen minutes before quitting time Sam closes up his office and heads for the door. Two minutes later I get a text message on my cell: *HAVE A GOOD WEEKEND, FRAN. DON'T WORRY. S.*

Gretchen doesn't ask who it's from; she knows. Stella doesn't seem to care; she gets text messages all day long and seems to think it's standard fare for the rest of us. Morgan, who's looking better since she went to her obstetrician yesterday and got anti-nausea medicine, bangs her phone down and turns off her computer.

"This was worse than my first week."

"Mine too," I pipe up.

"I don't remember my first week," Gretchen remarks. "I had a five-day migraine."

Stella grins. "Larry," she says.

"Sorry?" Morgan gives me a querying look, but I have no idea what Stella's talking about.

"Larry was the first week. Rather enjoyable."

Gretchen rolls her eyes, and Morgan and I crack up.

"I'm heading to Tony's, and I'm having a big-ass margarita," Gretchen says. "Who wants to join me?"

"I'm in." I shut off my computer and grab my purse.

"Me, too." Stella's already shut down and ready to go.

Morgan hesitates. "You won't think less of me if I order a virgin margarita, will you?"

"There's nothing virgin about you," Stella quips as we head for the door.

Tony's is crowded when we get there, but we manage to snag a table just as another group leaves. Stella's a regular, so when she hails the server—a good-looking Latino lad—he veers off his original course and to our table. I can tell by Stella's preening posture and his easy familiarity with her that he's...well, *familiar* with her, if you get my drift. Stella is an equal opportunist as well: young, old, and in-between. I don't think she was shocked in the least by Malaria's accusation about Sam and me because she's never made being single a criteria in selecting a man to take to her bed.

"Margarita for Frannie—lime, Frannie? Gretchen will take one too; Morgan a why-bother strawberry daiquiri, and I'll have a Screaming Orgasm."

The server—Enrique—slides a sly gaze over Stella's made-for-sex body and grins as Gretchen mutters, "I'll bet."

The drinks are quick in arriving, and we're barely two sips in when Stella broaches the subject of Morgan and Bud Mitchell. Morgan swallows her mouthful of why-bother and wipes the corners of her mouth daintily.

"Well, it's a long story…"

Turns out Morgan and Bud live in the same apartment complex, one of those über-friendly complexes that calls itself a "community." She was living with her boyfriend, a waiter-wanna-be-actor who unexpectedly threw her over for a large-breasted, small-brained cocktail waitress he works with and took everything but her clothes. Unfortunately, the day he up and moved on her was the day her home pregnancy test (ironically, a Clearblue Easy) showed positive. It also coincided with the Christmas potluck in the complex's Common Room. Feeling down and out, Morgan went to the potluck, where by chance she met Bud Mitchell, who befriended her. Once he learned her plight, he introduced her around. The complex came together to provide her with some acceptable second-hand furniture and a TV, and Bud put her onto the job at Harper & Lyttle. They've been fast friends ever since.

"We don't—you know," Morgan says, blushing furiously. "But he's like a really nice uncle. Neither of us has any family, and he's really excited about the baby."

"You don't…mmmphm?" Stella says skeptically. Gretchen snorts.

"Bud's not a bad guy," I protest as my cell phone chimes. Another text. Since Gretchen is here with me, it can only be one person. I flip open my phone to find another message from Sam.

WHAT ARE YOU UP TO?

Smiling, I text back: *DRINKING HEAVILY. WHAT ARE *YOU* DOING?*

"Oh for chrissake, Frannie," Stella grumps. "Let's have the real story. How long have you been riding the baloney pony with Sam Harrison?"

I choke on my margarita. "I'm not."

"Come on, Fran," Morgan chips in. "You're in love with him, he's in love with you. All we need is a convenient cliff to push Malaria off of. Hey—aren't we having some recreational…thing in May?"

Gretchen and I exchange a look and crack up.

"Seriously," I say. "I'm not sleeping with Sam."

Stella looks me up and down: at my relaxed posture as I voice my denial; the way my hand still rests on my cell phone, almost caressing it. I'm not fooling her one bit.

"Who said anything about *sleeping*, Fran-Fran? But you *have* had…er…*relations*," she guesses. "At least once."

I gulp my margarita down, and as my head spins I realize that Enrique must *really* like Stella, because this baby has almost enough tequila in it to make my clothes fall off. And lookit that, here comes another one, almost before I can wish it up. Enrique deposits another round of drinks and gives Stella a slow, sultry smile as he winds his way around our table and off across the bar.

"Wow," says Gretchen, blushing. "Would you two like to be alone?"

Stella grins wickedly. "Been there, done that. And might do it again," she adds, watching her young protégé across the room. "But back to Frannie. Let me guess—it was the night you almost got arrested for indecent exposure, wasn't it? What were you guys doing, making out in a parking lot or something?"

While I haven't had quite enough tequila to get

naked, I've had enough to loosen my tongue and my inhibitions. "Something like that." My cell chimes again. I resist the urge to look at the message and coolly sip my margarita.

"Oh, read the goddamn thing," Gretchen bursts out irritably. "The cat's out of the bag anyway."

I snatch up my phone.

I'M PACKING, Sam's message reads.

I blink and text back as fast as I can: *SIRIUSLY?* That doesn't look quite right, but frankly I can't hold my liquor and I'm just drunk enough to not give a shit about impeccable spelling.

"So what's Sam have to say?" Stella asks.

"He's packing."

"Packing what? His office? Did he get fired?" Morgan's eyes are wide.

"No, silly." Stella sucks down the last of her Screaming Orgasm, looking for all the world like she's just had one. "He's packing his things and moving out while Malaria's in rehab."

"Got himself a dose of quinine, did he?" Gretchen remarks, giving me a sidelong look. Stella and Morgan howl with delight.

"Your new nickname, Frannie: Quinine. Think anyone will get it?"

"Sam will."

"If he's lucky," Stella replies suggestively. "Does he even know we call her Malaria?"

"I think so. He almost said it that day he called me and Bud Mitchell into his office about the paperclips."

This cracks us all up. I pick up my margarita glass and drain the last dregs as my cell phone chimes again. How the hell did my glass get empty?

LMAO—SO HOW DRUNK ARE YOU, FRANNIE? I snicker, realize the girls are all looking at me strangely, and snicker again.

DRUNK ENUFF, SAM.

Stella signals for another round and now I seriously wonder how I'm going to get home. My phone chimes again, and Stella says, "Jesus Christ, the man has it bad."

ENUFF FOR WHAT, MS FREEMAN?

"Not drunk enough for *that*, Mr. Harrison," I mutter, blushing brightly, and the girls fall over each other laughing.

STILL MARRIED, MR HARRISON?

Another damn margarita comes. Have I told you I'm addicted to salt? Love the stuff. I literally lick any remaining granules off the rim of the glass when I'm done with my drink. Why the hell am I telling you this?

The phone chimes, and Morgan says, "Maybe we should leave Sam and Frannie alone together."

Stella chortles, taking in my nuclear-grade glow. "Well, if any man can make love to a woman from this distance, it's obviously Sam Harrison."

"Shut up—I can't hear!" I shush them as I'm reading my message. The girls hoot with laughter, and people at other tables look over at us, some with amusement, others with disgust.

MORE OR LESS. WELL, MORE ON THE LESS SIDE. ARE YOU TOO DRUNK TO MAKE SENSE OF THAT? ;-)

"Fuck you!" I say—or shout, rather. The table next to us breaks up laughing. *SCREW YOU, SAM.*

"Frannie!" Gretchen hisses. "How much tequila is in those things, anyway, Stel?"

"Knowing Enrique, enough to bring down an elephant." She smirks at me with amusement. "But hell, after this week, we deserve it."

"No shit," says Morgan. Stella catches her rubbing her tummy, and leans over to rub it too.

"How long, Morgs?"

Morgan smiles serenely. Something in her expression, some inner peace and contentment, holds us all transfixed for a moment. "I'm just over three months along. We're looking at an August baby."

My phone chimes. *BEEN THERE DONE THAT, FRANCESCA.*

I snort with laughter, and Stella says, "For shit's sake, she's as drunk as a hoot owl!" This reminds me of my random thought in Wednesday's meeting when I realized Malia was shitfaced and I crack up. I *did* tell you I can't handle my liquor, didn't I?

WANT TO DO IT AGAIN, SAMUEL?

"So Fran," says Gretchen, who's looking a little glassy-eyed herself, the judgmental wench. "How did Malaria figure out you slept with her husband?"

"For all I know, he told her," I say, and my voice now has a definite Malia-like slur to it. Stella and Morgan stifle their laughter. "I'll ask him." His message comes in first, though, so I have to read it.

IS THAT A PROPOSITION, MS FREEMAN?

"What's this 'Ms. Freeman' crap anyway?" I grumble as I text back.

YOU MAN ENUFF FOR IT? BTW, HOW DID SHE KNOW? I type this in with some difficulty, for the girls are now trying to get my cell phone away from me so they can read the whole thread. "Back off, buzzards!" I smack their hands away and pick up my glass, only to find it empty.

"Who the hell is drinking my 'ritas while I'm busy, anyway?"

"Somebody cut her off," Morgan says, but she's snickering and I know she'd rather see me continue on and provide some comedic relief.

ARE YOU SOBER ENUFF? I THINK NOT.

"Says you," I mutter. I notice—in a vague, bleary sort of way—that he hasn't answered my question, and then another text comes in.

I TOLD HER.

I'm speechless, and I hold out the phone to Gretchen. "That answer your question?"

"He *told* her?" she marvels, and I can almost see her Sam-meter go up several notches. Or maybe that's just because I'm as drunk as a skunk. (Side note: do skunks get drunk like hoot owls? Do I give a shit? What about squirrels? I like squirrels; they're damn funny to watch...) Another message comes in while she has the phone, and I can't stop her before she opens it. She reads it silently and then hands it to me.

"Well, all right then, Frannie," she says quietly and smiles.

LOVE YOU FRANNIE FREEMAN, his message reads.

I smile back at Gretchen and I'm sure it's the tequila that makes me reply now when I wouldn't after the dumb-ass Brain-Blizzard conference: *LOVE YOU SAM HARRISON*.

Enrique comes by, undulating like a snake. Or like he's already making love to Stella. Or perhaps it's only that I just downed one hell of a lot of José Cuervo.

"A Screaming Multiple Orgasm, Enrique," Stella orders. "Frannie, you going to have one?"

"God, I hope so," I reply fervently, and promptly pass out.

BURNING DOWN THE HOUSE

Conventions: the bane of the business world. I can't say they don't have their uses; I just don't see why I have to be involved. I suppose it's because I view conventions as a sales tool and I don't view myself as a salesperson. In fact, I couldn't sell ice to a person dying of heat stroke in the Mojave.

Unfortunately, Malia's duties have been distributed amongst Gretchen, Stella, Morgan and me, and I drew the short straw. Stella has a date, Gretchen did the last convention, and Morgan has a mortal fear of public speaking. It stands to reason, or so says Sam, that I'm the best person for the job due to my experience with training. He assures me that I don't have to sell anything, at the same time advising me (with a definite gleam in his eye) that a bit shorter skirt won't be a detriment at all. Since I hadn't planned on wearing a skirt at all, I'm a bit disgruntled by this suggestion. Sam gives all indication that he's gone deaf and blind, because he doesn't seem to hear my protests or notice my irritation.

Speaking of Sam… We haven't talked about his relocation to a posh apartment other than his mention of it in our text-messaging Friday night. I saw him stuff a change of address form into an interoffice envelope addressed to Human Resources on Monday—he deliberately made sure I saw it—but we haven't discussed it. I haven't been much in the mood to talk anyway; my hangover from Friday's margarita madness is only now starting to fade. That's the bad thing about tequila: great while you're drinking it, damn nasty after-effect.

We also haven't discussed the dark mark on his neck, the edge of which is just barely visible above his collar. I don't want to come across as a jealous lover already, but I'm reasonably sure I've not made out with Sam since he spent the night with me six weeks ago, and I'm wondering if I wasn't a bit premature in telling him I love him… Well, of course I was—for God's sake, he's still legally married.

An IM pops up from Gretchen: *What's the matter?*

I write back: *Was that a* hickey *I saw on Sam's neck?*

Gretchen: *Hmmm…I wonder how* that *got there? hahaha*

Me: *NOT FUNNY, GRETCH!*

Gretchen: *What's the last thing you remember from Friday night?*

Me: *Something about a screaming orgasm. I…er…didn't have one, did I?*

Gretchen snickers. *You'd have to ask Sam.*

Me: *I didn't see Sam Friday night.*

Gretchen: *You're right; you were too drunk to focus. How the hell do you think we got you in your apartment? You don't think WE carried you?*

Me (blushing furiously now): *YOU CALLED SAM?!?!?!*

Gretchen: *Well, no—we texted him. From your phone. He thought it was pretty funny.*

Me: *Why didn't anyone* tell *me about this????*

Gretchen: *From how things were…ah…progressing, we figured you'd know all about it in the morning. You mean he didn't stay?*

Me: *Stay? I didn't even know he'd been there.*

Gretchen giggles again.

"Oh for chrissake!" Stella mutters. I hear her typing furiously, and a second later I get an IM from her, copied to Gretchen: *JEEZUZ, FRANNIE, YOU WERE SUCKING ON HIS NECK LIKE A FRIGGING VAMPIRE. IT WAS REALLY EMBARRASSING, TO BE HONEST—YOU WERE LIKE AN OCTOPUS. I MEAN, HE'S OUR BOSS, RIGHT? REGARDLESS OF HOW GORGEOUS HE IS, I NEVER REALLY WANTED TO SEE MY BOSS WITH A HAR—*

"Fran?" says Sam from behind me. I jump, squeaking in surprise, and quickly close the instant messaging window.

"Will you stop sneaking up on me?"

He chuckles. "I said your name three times. What more do you want?"

"Sorry. I'm still hung over from Friday."

Sam's change of expression is extraordinary, and I dimly recall Stella saying something Friday night about if any man could make love to a woman long-distance, it's Sam. His fingers wander up to touch the hickey just below his collar.

"I can imagine..." he murmurs. He looks up to find Gretchen watching open-mouthed. A red stain floods his cheeks and he looks quickly away. So it *was* me! Sweet Jesus, what else did I do? "Ready to go?"

"Sure." I reach for my laptop case and Meeting Bag, but Sam gets there first. As he straightens, his eyes fall on my cabinet door and the latest from my secret poet: *mine eye stirred up my heart to love.* This snippet I had to look up on the internet as well; hey, I never said I was a poetry expert, so you won't be surprised when I say I've never heard of George Gasgione. His mouth tightens, and that's my first indication he's not my hit-and-run poet.

"Secret admirer, Frannie?"

"Guess so." I arch a brow at him, but he only smiles.

Sam stows my bags in the back of a luxury sedan I've

never seen before (which he tells me later he borrowed from his aunt so I wouldn't have to climb into his truck in a skirt) and opens the passenger door for me. When he gets behind the wheel, he hesitates before starting the engine, and finally turns in his seat to look at me.

"Here are the rules. You will not cross over this line," and he draws an invisible barrier down the center of the front seat. "You will *not* drink tequila, you will *not* shed your clothes as though you just joined a nudist colony, and you will *definitely not* put those lips anywhere near my neck again."

I stare at him, eyes wide, hoping like hell he's kidding—I didn't really strip off in front of him, did I? And why should I care if I did, anyway? He's seen everything I've got—more than seen it, in fact, and I was stone-cold sober when I showed him.

He glowers at me. "Well, at least not until..."

"Did I *really*..." I motion toward his neck, and he faces forward, gripping the steering wheel tightly.

"*Yes.*"

"Ah. Er...did we...?"

He laughs once, surprised. "No, Fran—what d'you take me for? You were completely snockered. You *did* ask me for a screaming orgasm and I doubt very much you meant the drink, but I told you no. I'm trying to behave and do this right."

I'm pretty sure my blush can be seen from outer space. No doubt there are communications passing between the space shuttle and Houston Control this very moment wondering just what that glow is down there in SoCal.

"Well, all right, Sam," I manage. "That's very noble of you."

"You have no idea," he says fervently. He turns the key and guns the engine, and I can't help snickering a little.

The Convention Center, much like the training room

at Harper & Lyttle, is rarely if ever set up correctly, and this time is no exception. While I unpack my gear, Sam goes to find our audio-visual guy. When he comes back with a kid who looks barely old enough to drive, I'm pretty certain he must have just grabbed the first person he came to who looked as though he could fumble his way around a computer.

"Fran, Stewart'll get you all set up. There are some people I need to talk to—be right back."

Be right back in this business is a euphemism for *I'm going to vanish for the next three hours, leaving you to sink or swim.* And it *is* a long time before I see Sam surface from a group of men and women in business suits.

Stewart turns out to be a twenty-year-old tech genius, and I vaguely recall seeing him lurking in the corridors of Harper & Lyttle. He seems to know me, however, for everything he says to me is preceded by or followed with "Ms. Freeman." He makes short work of setting up the equipment properly, and it's only as he ducks under the table to plug things in that he realizes there's a problem.

"Hey, Ms. Freeman, do you have a surge suppressor?"

I look at my laptop case and Meeting Bag, which are flattened and set aside, then at my snug skirt. Do I *look* like I have a surge suppressor?

"No, Stewart. 'Fraid not."

He springs to his feet with a beaming smile. "Not to worry, Ms. Freeman. I'll ask the convention coordinator for one." He dashes off into the crowd, leaving me to fend off milling clients wanting to see demos. I panic for a moment, but when I look around for Sam, he's smiling encouragingly from across the room.

I can do this, I tell myself, *but I could so this much more efficiently if Stewart would get back!*

As though my annoyed thought has summoned him, Stewart reappears, winding his way through the crowd with a battered power strip in one hand and a can of root beer in the other.

"Time is of the essence, Stewart," I remark, a bit acidic, glaring at the root beer.

"Sorry, Ms. Freeman. I was really thirsty." He sets down his pop and ducks under the skirted table with the surge protector. With a whiff of burning rubber, I now have power. Stewart pops back up, and I yank him close enough to hear my suspicious whisper.

"Everything all right down there, Stewart?"

"Sure, Ms. Freeman," he whispers back. "It's just an old suppressor, and it kinda sparked a little when I plugged everything in. It should be fine."

And everything *is* fine…at first. I start the demos and answer questions, and this is what I really enjoy doing: showing people how to use our products. Most of the attendees are Harper & Lyttle clients who have already purchased versions of the products we're demonstrating and are looking for upgrades or technical advice. It's not uncommon for companies seeking a new product to frequent a training convention, and it's a group of such gentlemen that Sam reappears with. He's carrying a can of Pepsi and I give him a black look. I haven't been within sniffing distance of a beverage since we arrived.

And I'm apparently not going to get any closer to one, either. The men begin firing questions at me, and I answer them as fast as I can. It's almost like a game to see which of them can trip me up, but I know our products well. I even know a bit of code, so I can easily answer the question they obviously intend as the sudden death round.

"Well, you were right, Sam," says a shifty-eyed specimen of latent chauvinism. "She knows her stuff."

Sam grins. "Told you. Frannie, this is Richard White from Business Solutions Accounting, Inc. Richard, Frannie Freeman, our top training specialist. So, gentlemen, can Harper & Lyttle expect your call soon?"

"That was the deal, Sam," says Richard. He shakes

Sam's hand and then turns to take mine. "Ms. Freeman, a pleasure."

"Likewise," I murmur, giving Sam a sidelong look.

It's about that time I smell smoke, and the faces of Sam's entourage simultaneously register shock and dismay.

"Ah…is your demo supposed to do that, Ms. Freeman?" says Richard White in alarm.

I whirl around to find smoke billowing from the table. The skirting has caught fire and our whole booth is going up in flames. Stewart panics, his face so white his freckles stand out like polka dots, and he leaps into action, rescuing my laptop and flinging my computer case out into the middle of the floor. My Meeting Bag is already burning, and by the time the convention coordinator employs the extinguisher it's too late to save it.

I look at Sam and shrug, and smile brightly at Richard White as I lean against a neighboring booth, crossing my ankles to show my legs to their best advantage. I wore the shelf bra tonight under my crisp white blouse and hours ago shed my suit jacket. For a daring moment I have no qualms about displaying my wares, and Sam's eyes just about pop right out of his head.

"And that, gentlemen, is just how hot our software really is."

* * * * *

My cat is all over my smoke-scented laptop case as soon as I set it down. He loves it when I bring in something new, even if it's just an odor. Along with his balls, he lost his wandering-outdoors freedom when he hooked up with me.

And Sam is all over me almost before the door is closed. I admit I take advantage of it for a few minutes;

it's been a long time, and damn, this man is seriously sexy. But he *did* say—oh! he should *not* be touching me there...!

"Sam...you said you were trying to be good," I remind him.

"Oh, I intend to be good."

"I meant *behave*, you were trying to *behave*."

"I never was much good at that." My shirt's almost completely off now, and the shelf bra is not proving to be much of a barrier. "Do you realize that you probably just sealed a half-a-million dollar deal for Harper & Lyttle tonight—a deal Sales has been working on for more than a year?"

Holy shit! "Does this mean I get a raise?"

He laughs softly, pressing me tightly against him. Oh, yeah—I get a raise all right. "You were fucking incredible."

"The night's not over yet."

Sam pushes my hair off my face, tangling his fingers into it. "Frannie," he says quietly, "I screwed up badly, and I've lived in hell for two years. No way I'm going back there, no matter what."

I've heard this before in a dozen or more movies, and oh, how cliché can we be? The subordinate having an affair with her handsome, married boss, and the promises of "I'll leave her any day now."

But this is Sam, and in the five years I've known him I don't believe he's lied to me once. Even when he came back from Vegas with an unexpected wife, while he might not have been able to look me in the eyes, he never lied to me about it.

"Fran," he says now, his voice barely a whisper. "I know what you're thinking, and there's nothing I can say that will prove I'm being honest."

I consider this for a moment, not an easy task when Sam is holding me so close and I'm half-naked. And I decide it really boils down to one question: "Why now?

It's been two years since you married her. Then all of a sudden...since the pancake breakfast..."

He gives me a smile of singular, heartbreaking sweetness. "That was the first time you've looked me in the eyes since Vegas, Frannie. You're not very good at hiding what you think or feel. I couldn't believe it...two years and you still..."

"I *always*," I say. "And it was *you* who wouldn't look *me* in the eyes, Sam."

He shakes his head. "No. I tried, Fran, but you were determined not to. But that morning...I don't know what was different. You looked at me, actually saw me, and there was no blame, no accusation, no disappointment, just...everything that had been there before Malia. And I realized in that instant that what I thought was honor was just stupidity."

"Yeah," I agree smartly. "We all already knew *that*. Took *you* long enough."

"Too long." He kisses me once, and again, and again...

Guess I get that screaming orgasm after all.

NO GOOD DEED GOES UNPUNISHED

"What the hell is this crap?" Stella grumbles, peering at the flyer that was delivered to our inboxes sometime early this morning before we came in.

"Dunno. Haven't looked at it yet." I open my drawer to put my purse away and find a surprise. I quickly quell my delighted smile, but Gretchen sees anyway. Nothing gets past that woman. A little frown creases her brow; she's not entirely happy with how much time I spend with Sam, considering the circumstances.

I don't know of any woman in an office setting who doesn't make her way through the day without the aid of chocolate and I consume more than my fair share, but my secret addiction is pistachios. In the bottom of my drawer is a large bag of the shelled nuts. I don't need a note to know who they're from.

"Whatcha got there, Frannie?" Stella asks.

"Pistachios." I don't explain who gave them to me and neither of them asks. Stella has not said a word about Sam since the margarita incident, not even to ask in her usual brazen manner what happened after they left that night. I find this odd, but I'm not complaining. Perhaps she's aware that her penchant for gossip could have disastrous consequences were she to wag her tongue about this particular subject.

She sniffs and says, "Mmmm" with a decided air of disappointment. Stella lives on a diet of chocolate, alcohol, and coffee. If it doesn't fall into one of those food groups, she can do without. "What's the latest from your magnetic poet?"

I glance at my cabinet door. "Huh," I say, for I don't recognize this quote either. Apparently my hit-and-run poet is much more learned in such things. "*Strong in the love that came so late our souls shall keep it always now.* Who wrote that?"

"No clue."

"I'll Google it," Gretchen offers.

The flyer turns out to be about Employee Action Resources (EAR), an employer-provided service to help you handle emotional problems, relational problems within the office, and drug or alcohol addiction. Seriously, I don't know who comes up with these acronyms; some moron paid nine bucks an hour trying to get back at his skin-flint employer, no doubt. EAR is supposed to make it sound like they'll lend you an ear when you have a mouthful to let loose. Thanks, but no way am I spilling my guts to some counselor paid for by my employer. That's the height of professional suicide, if you ask me. I crumple the flyer and toss it in the trash.

"Hey," says Morgan, breezing in five minutes late. Her greenish hue, helped along by both pregnancy and the enormous stress of working with Malaria, has completely faded and we're seeing a bit of rounded tummy now. "Did anyone notice we got a new coffee machine?"

"No lie?" Stella bounces to her feet. "Who bought it?"

"Elizabeth Akers Allen," Gretchen says.

Stella, Morgan, and I exchange a look. "Who the hell is she?" I ask.

"Not the coffee machine," Gretchen replies impatiently. "The poet who wrote Frannie's latest snippet."

"Never heard of her," Stella says. Big shock there. "C'mon, Frannie, let's go see if we can figure out how to make coffee."

"It's not like it's rocket science, Stel," I reply as we head off.

No, not rocket science, but it may take a nuclear physicist to get this baby running. This is one damned fancy machine and I'm not entirely one hundred percent sure I even know where to put the grounds. And while we're on the subject of coffee, who the hell decided two measly scoops of Folgers is going to make your taste buds perk right up, anyway? It's barely-flavored, bitter hot water. Now I've got some pretty good Puerto Rican beans at home, and I grind up two tablespoons per cup of water—

"Mother*fucker*!" Stella swears loudly.

Water gouts, grounds ooze, and the machine makes steamy whooshing sounds like a mortally wounded rhino. Stella tries to staunch the flow of boiling-hot wet coffee grounds with a paper towel, which is a little like trying to stop arterial bleeding with a Kleenex.

I spring into action, grab a fistful of paper towels, and ram them into her hand.

"Well, that's helpful, Frannie, thanks a lot!" Stella shouts grumpily. "I don't think the grounds basket is in right. Here—" and she yanks it out.

This proves disastrous. Water shoots out in all directions like a sprinkler head, dousing us both and leaving little coffee-ground deposits on our clothes and in our hair. I grab the basket, dump its contents into the garbage and shove it back into place, ending the fountain of scalding water. The end result is about four ounces of discolored water with coffee grounds floating in it like drowned ants.

We barely have time to assess the damage when a Suit elbows his way by us and dumps the contents of the pot into his coffee cup. A leather notebook is stuffed under one arm and it's obvious he's on his way to an Adminisphere meeting that will more than likely rain down on us another moronic non-solution to some issue we're aren't having, thus creating a problem that will require an equal amount of time spent blame-storming. Maybe they'll do some brain-blizzarding instead.

"Thanks, ladies," this fine gent says on his way out. Stella and I stare at each other, flabbergasted, as we hear him remark, "Your girls are real nice, Sam, but they can't make coffee for shit."

Sam pokes his head into the break room, eyes wide as he takes in the destruction of women and machine alike. "Fran—what the hell?"

But I'm ready for him. I keep a Post-It pad in a drawer in the break room, which I have to replace nearly every day because someone swipes it. I write out a quick Thought and slap it on his notebook: *INSTRUCTION MANUAL.*

"Real men don't need instructions, Frannie," he quips with a positively lewd smile. He swipes the Post-It pad, grins, and ducks out of the room.

The real reason for the meeting—which I know only because of my direct involvement with both the situation and Sam—is the pending deal with Business Solutions, Inc., who did indeed call on Tuesday.

The nature of the business beast is very territorial, and this time proves no exception. Eric Edwards has actually been in the middle of preparing a lengthy presentation and sales pitch for Business Solutions, and for them to call out of the blue raving about the woman who wouldn't have sex with him and threw his cell phone into a pond does *not* improve relations between our departments. The only issue there appears to be is the fact that *I* swayed Richard White's decision, and of course the rumor spreads like wildfire though the company (sped along by Eric, I'm sure) that there must have been some involvement of sexual favor. Sam spends the better part of the morning placating the section supervisor in Sales and defending my honor, and when he's done he's thoroughly pissed.

I recommend margaritas à la Enrique to help him unwind. *That's* an enjoyable night.

Philosophically speaking, I suppose I should be grateful the guys in Sales think I'm attractive enough to warrant sexual interest. On the other hand, I find insulting the implication that only my body and not my expertise in my job would generate interest in our product.

By Thursday the hullaballoo has died down and Sales is preening their collective feathers about bagging the deal with Business Solutions, Inc. Do I get so much as a nod of acknowledgement? Nope, thus proving that no good deed goes unpunished.

I shoo Stella out—she has a tricky training project to complete—and set myself to cleaning up the break room. After taking the coffee machine halfway apart to clean it, making coffee seems quite simple. I start a pot and go into the bathroom to clean myself up. When I come back out, I run smack into Eric Edwards.

"Well, well, well," he says, turning up the wattage on his smile. "If it isn't Frannie Freeman, Training Specialist aka office wh—"

"For your safety and well-being, Eric, I suggest you don't finish that sentence." I try to step around him, but he blocks my way, stretching out one arm and trapping me in the alcove that shields the women's room door. "Let me out."

Eric leans in closer, and I find myself pressed against the water fountain trying to elude him. It's one of those with the push bar on the front, so you guessed it: I get a nice shower of cold water down my back.

"There's no end to what you can do, is there, Frannie? Amazing how in half an hour you manage to seal a deal we've been working on for a year."

"Well, perhaps smarm and sleaze weren't the way to close it, Eric."

His face suffuses with anger. "Yeah, I guess sex works better, eh? And not just with the clients, either. Everyone knows about you and Sam Harrison. Working your way up the corporate ladder, are you, Fran?"

"Wow, it's a big secret that I work with Sam," I say sarcastically, but inside I'm panicked. Everyone *knows*? But we've been so careful!

"I love all the euphemisms people use these days for sex," Eric replies with an evil, knowing grin. With that he withdraws his arm and saunters away.

I watch him go, waiting until he reaches Cubicle Row before I holler, "Yeah, you're welcome for me doing your job, jerk!"

He flips me off and rounds the corner, and I sigh, heading slowly toward my allotted space to continue my salmon day—you know the kind of day I mean: the one where you struggle to get everything done and only end up screwed in the end. Oh yeah.

And people wonder why I drink.

HEARTS AND FLOWERS AND ALL THAT CRAP

Sam has been an almost constant presence at my apartment and having spent so much off-work time with him, I've finally gotten the full story of the Vegas incident. Pillow-talk can be a wonderful thing sometimes; the only problem with it is I have not gotten to sleep before two in the morning the last four nights, and I'm seriously dragging ass and thanking God it's Friday. We are *soooo* sleeping in tomorrow, and if Mr. Pollyanna-I'm-a-morning-person even cracks an eyelid before nine, I'm going to club him into unconsciousness and there is not a court in this land that will convict me.

Anyway—Vegas. The Powers-That-Be had decided the Suits deserved a Christmas party separate from us losers at the bottom of the dog pile. We're only four hundred or so miles away from Las Vegas, and the corporation is very successful, so they flew anyone with "supervisor" in his or her title to Vegas for a big shin-dig they had catered at the Paris Hotel. Sam, in his infinite wisdom, suggests the martini mar that ultimately leads to his confinement in hell, and the Powers-That-Be are all over *that* suggestion like a cheap suit.

Sam has downed his three martinis (you'll remember: the Absolut, the Douglas, and the Muscovy), has found courage at the bottom of the third, and asks Gus Haldemann from Human Resources what his options are if he wants to date—*seriously* date—a subordinate. Gus is no fool; he's heard the talk about us and has actually been preparing to talk to Sam himself. The only options are for me to transfer out of the department or for Sam to, and Gus promises to look into the ramifications of both scenarios to see which would have less impact on the workflow.

Not long after, along comes Malia with her allegedly roofied lime, bringing with it Sam's amnesia. The next thing he knows, he's waking up in a Paris Hotel room with a wedding ring and a wife, and can't remember acquiring either.

While I'm at Sam's apartment one night, he pulls out a photo album Malia had put together. He has it in a banker box labeled in bold, black letters; *DIVORCE*. I don't want to look in it; when Malia (with a demonic gleam in her eye) passed around the photos from the Garden of Love wedding chapel, I flipped through the pages without looking at the photographs. I was so afraid of seeing a radiant, happy Sam. I think at the time I was still in denial that it had happened, that he was now forever out of my reach. And perhaps that's why I know Sam is right: *I'm* the one who wouldn't look *him* in the eyes. I was afraid of what was there—or of what *wasn't* there anymore.

But I look because Sam asks me to (we *have* established there isn't anything I won't do for him, right?) and what I see is a far cry from what I feared. Sam, blank-faced and obviously stoned; and Malia—oh, I want to grab the bitch by the hair and swing her into a convenient wall. Several times.

First I should explain Malia. I have mentioned, I do believe, that she is drop-dead gorgeous: dark hair and eyes, impeccable complexion, immaculately dressed. And while she may wear her hair in an elegant chignon, she does not and has not *ever* worn it twisted in a messy up-do and secured with a claw clamp like me and Gretchen do. She also never wears anything but business skirt-suits and fashionable, spike-heeled shoes. You'd never catch her in slacks, a trendy blouse and low-heeled pumps.

In the wedding pictures, however, that's exactly how she's dressed and just how her hair is styled. I see what Sam is seeing: an imitation of me, and it seems obvious (at least to us conspiracy theorists) that this is precisely why Sam is suckered into nuptials.

"The brazen ho!" I exclaim, and Sam quickly stows the album in the box and ushers me out to the truck to take me to dinner before I become more agitated.

So it seems she knew of Sam's attraction to me and his desire for a serious relationship with me, and for reasons known only to Malaria herself, she decided to take extreme measures to prevent anything from coming of it. It's going to be very hard not to sock her in the eye when she comes back to work. It's going to be a messy enough divorce without me adding assault to the mix. I suppose I should be glad that alienation of affection has been abolished in California, although to tell the truth, I think it would be hard for her to bring such action even if it weren't. No one harbors any illusions that the Harrisons' marriage is based on love and affection.

"Frannie?" says Sam sharply and I jump, realizing I've been daydreaming. No sense in that when I have the real thing right across the table from me.

"Sorry. Wool-gathering." I smile, and he reaches across the table to take both my hands, winding our fingers together. He has elegant hands; an artist's hands, my mother would say. Long, slim, strong fingers... I suppose what he does to me with them could be considered art. It's got *my* vote.

Sam smiles back, one of those slow, sexy ones he started giving me about three years ago that hooked me through the nose. "Happy?"

"Mmmm," I answer, squeezing his fingers. "Very. The M&M's were a nice touch."

For Valentine's Day, I get not only dinner out at a nice seafood restaurant I adore—which is where we are now—but three pounds of personalized red and white M&M's with my name on one side and his on the other. Okay, saccharine sweet, I know, but I thought it was rather romantic. They were waiting for me at my desk when I came in to work this morning, along with a bouquet of daisies in a vase and a new magnetic poetry arrangement: *Each day through my window I watch her as she passes by say to myself you're such a lucky guy to have a girl like her is truly a dream come true out of all the fellas in the world she belongs to me.* "Fellas" has been handwritten and taped to the top of another word, because my poetry kit didn't come with that particular word.

"What happened to the classical poetry?" Gretchen wonders. "That sounds like a song."

"That's Motown," Stella says, grooving to the Temptations playing in her head.

I smile. "That's Sam." I know because we have Motown on the stereo a lot while we…well, mmmphm.

"That's pretty bold," Stella says, and casts an impressed glance toward Sam's office.

By now it's no secret that Sam has moved back into the apartment he lived in before he married Malia and that he has no intention of going back to her. I have no idea whether it's common knowledge that he's seeing me; I haven't heard anything on the 'vine, which probably means everyone's talking about how many times he's spent the night at my house—remember the nature of the grapevine. That doesn't stop me from choosing a restaurant three counties away. Just because people talk doesn't mean they need to see.

"Ah, Frannie," Sam says, grinning. "The M&M's were corny, but I don't care. I did, however, get chewed out for giving you daisies, even though you're a daisy kind of girl."

"By whom?" I can't imagine anyone being bold enough to approach the subject of Sam's relationship with me.

"Gus Haldemann. He said you deserved about eight dozen long-stemmed roses for waiting so long."

"Hell with that," I say. "I deserve friggin' gems for even speaking to you after you married her."

He smiles again, his fingers brushing over my naked left-hand ring finger. "I'm working on that, too, Fran."

"Sam, I didn't mean—"

"*I* mean it." He kisses my fingers and lets them go as the server comes with our meal. And everything is going well—going great, actually—until a shadow falls over our table.

"Frannie! I didn't know you'd be out on Valentine's Day!"

Oh, *shit*. I close my eyes for a brief second, willing away reality. But when I open them again, there's my mom beaming down at me, obviously pleased that I'm out on Valentine's Day with a man and not my girlfriends. And now she's eyeballing Sam, and she doesn't even wait for an introduction.

"How do you do? I'm Francesca's mother, Sylvia Freeman."

Sam takes her offered hand, sending me a look from the corner of his eye. I'm sure he would have stood up out of respect had we not been in a booth, because that's the sort of man he is. "Sam Harrison."

Mother looks quite blank for a moment, and I know she's recycling every bit of gossip I've ever passed on to her. Eventually she'll unearth the Vegas story, and there's no telling what will come out of her mouth. See, I come by it honestly.

Then she smiles brightly. "So sorry to hear about your divorce, but next time I'm sure you'll choose more wisely. You can't go wrong with Frannie."

I close my eyes again and shake my head. Sam stifles a laugh. "No, you sure can't."

"Umm, Mom, where's Dad?" I ask pointedly, hoping she'll get the hint and go back to her own table, leaving us alone.

Mom looks startled. "Oh, quite right, dear."

And then she begins to rearrange our table, moving my plate over and setting Sam's next to it. She lays her hand on his shoulder and smiles brightly at him.

"I'm sure you won't mind us joining you for dinner? It's not every day our Frannie is out with such a handsome man." And there she is, motioning across the restaurant to where my father sits at a shadowed table.

"Mom!"

"We'd love it if you joined us," Sam says courteously, his mouth twitching. He slides out of his side of the booth and into mine. "Edge over, Fran."

Mom stops a server and has him bring over their plates. I reach for my margarita (Sam has allowed me one), but his fingers close over mine on the stem of the glass. Mom's brows wing up into her hair and Sam gives her a beaming smile. Dad joins the festivities and Mom ushers him into the booth ahead of her.

"I don't want to slide, dear," she says, patting him on the shoulder. She inches her elegant frame onto the edge of the seat. "Sam, this is my husband, Franklin, Frannie's father. I always add that because these days you just never know. People get divorced and remarried at the drop of a hat." She reaches across the table and pats Sam's free hand. His fingers over mine twitch. "Don't you worry about it. I know aaaaallll about it, and you did well to leave that Malia. Malaria, Fran calls hers. Women like that are an illness, Sam, and it's best you just cleanse yourself and move on with your life."

"Mom. Word vomit."

"Really, Fran, using a word like 'vomit' at the dinner table is very crass."

I sigh and turn my attention to my father, who is quite often overlooked when he's with my mom. He's a quiet, self-effacing man with an incredible sense of humor when you get him going. "Hi, pops. How you doin'?"

"Doing well, Frannie, doing well. How 'bout yourself?"

"Good, Dad."

"So Sam," says Dad, and I figure he's going to launch into business talk, which could be good or bad. My dad was a corporate man, but he was one of the rank-and-file with a healthy contempt for the Adminisphere. "What are your intentions with my little girl? I'm sure they're honorable…?"

I choke on the gulp of margarita Sam has finally allowed me. Oh, can someone just *kill me?!* Mom perks up, tapping a bright red, perfectly manicured nail on the table.

"Strictly honorable," Sam assures him with a bland smile, for all the world as though that interlude last night in the laundry room never happened…and as though he hasn't spent every night but one in my bed since he left his wife.

"Well, good. That's good." Dad nods appreciatively, and as Mom takes a breath to begin a new monologue, he steps into the second of silence and takes command. "So tell me, Sam, what's it like these days on the corporate ladder? Still as big a cluster-fuck as always?"

"No, sir. A bigger one." They both laugh, and Sam slides his arm around my shoulders as they launch into what Mom always calls man-talk.

I glance at my mom, and I'm surprised to find her smiling serenely. She reaches over and gives my hand a squeeze, flicking her gaze at Sam. Then she goes on with her meal as though there's been no interruption, and I finally relax. Sam's passed with flying colors, and while I may have to explain the Malaria thing, my parents have been remarkably well-behaved.

We pass a pleasant hour finishing our meals and enjoying after-dinner coffee, and as Sam holds my coat for me, he bends close to my ear and whispers, "Ready to go home, Quinine?"

"Oh, shut up!" I whisper back. He chuckles as he drops the coat onto my shoulders and turns to shake my father's hand and kiss my mother's. She surveys him with a discerning gaze, then reaches up to cup his face in her hands. I'm sure she's going to spout some nonsense about how glad she is her little Frannie's found a worthy man, blah blah blah.

"Sam, we must discuss my grandchildren. Frannie's getting on in years, and I'm no spring chicken. I'd like to see them before I'm dead."

Sweet *Christ!* Sam's face floods with color, but he says gamely, "I'm working on it, Sylvia. I'm working on it."

GRETCHEN SINGS THE BLUES

It's a cosmic truth that when something fantastic happens, the universe must shift proportionately to maintain balance, and some unsuspecting schmuck takes it in the shorts.

After departing from the restaurant—and my parents—we go back to my apartment. Sam puts on some Motown and dances me around the room to the Temptations, predictably ending at my bed. He pulls me close, the heat of his body nearly scorching even through our clothes.

"Your mom's a hoot," he says with a chuckle. "Apple didn't fall too far from the tree, eh?"

"Right," I say, rolling my eyes. "I doubt very much my mother's ever come out of the ladies' room looking anything but impeccable, let alone with her skirt tucked into her pantyhose."

He laughs softly and kisses me. My dress floats softly to the floor as we embark on the best part of our evening. His hands skate over my skin, those artist's fingers leaving fire in their wake, and it's no wonder that I don't at first hear the phone ring. But I wouldn't have answered it anyway; better to let the machine pick up.

But when Gretchen's tearful voice comes over the answering machine, passion flees. I dive for the phone, but she's sobbing so hard I can't understand what she's saying, so I simply holler over her.

"I'm on my way, Gretch. It's okay, I'm on my way." I hang up and send an apologetic look at Sam as I start yanking on a handy pair of jeans and a tee-shirt. He's smiling in a resigned way. "I'm sorry, Sam. She's my best friend—"

"No apology needed. Better to stand between a lion and its dinner than a woman and her best friend." He grabs me around the waist as I sail by to find my sneakers and plants a firm kiss on my lips. "I'll be here, keeping your fat cat company."

With a last, tense smile thrown over my shoulder at him, I race out the door. It's a twenty minute drive to Gretchen's and I'm imagining the worst the whole time: James has been killed in a plane crash; one of the kids has been hit by a car; Gretchen's pregnant again. There's no end to the horrifying scenarios I can think up. In case you haven't already guessed, I'm not the one to rely on in an emergency.

The door is unlocked when I get there, and Gretchen in sitting in the middle of her wrecked living room, tears streaming down her cheeks, hugging a bunny slipper to her chest while the kids run rampant through the house. The two older ones are wailing at the top of their lungs, and the two youngest are squabbling. The three-year-old pushes the eighteen-month-old onto the floor, and her wails rise above the chaos of noise.

I look around the room and notice there are a good many items missing, most of them valuable. "Christ, Gretchen, what happened? Did you guys get robbed?"

She only sobs harder. The preschooler pulls the toddler's hair, causing her screech to reach ear-splitting proportions. Gretchen simply sits in the ruins of her house, wailing into the bunny slipper. While I may panic in a crisis, I'm quite adept at assessing the most immediate need, as long as there's someone to keep me calm. Since no one's bleeding or unconscious, I relax marginally, step through the rubble, and hoist the baby onto my hip. The cacophony has become unbearable, so I stick two fingers in my mouth and whistle.

"Yo!" I yell into the sudden silence. Gretchen's the only one still making noise, but since she's sobbing quietly I address the kids. "You two—" and I point at the oldest ones, "—I need your help, so zip it. I want you to start picking up the living room."

"G-gl-glass," Gretchen sobs. I run an eye over the debris and sigh. "All right, never mind. Here's the deal. You two are going to go wash your faces, brush your teeth, and get into bed. I will be in to tuck you in after I clean up."

"B-but Aunt F-fr-frannie," sobs nine-year-old Luci, "w-what about—"

I close my fingers against my thumb in my shut-up-now motion. "Now. I'll be in as soon as I'm done."

The kids shuffle off to the bathroom, snuffling, their little chests hitching, and my heart squeezes. Meanwhile, the preschooler is tugging on the baby's foot, making her wail again "You! Stop! Go sit on the so...fa," I end lamely. Belatedly I realize the sofa is gone. Gretchen starts to laugh, a hysterical, maniacal giggle that shuts the kids up like nothing else.

Sofia's three-year-old brain can't comprehend her mother's hysteria; her eyes wide, she edges closer to me and clutches my legs.

"Okay." I close my eyes and take a breath, wondering if I should have brought Sam. I hadn't expected the whole family to be in hysterics. "Okay, Sofia, sweetie—Aunt Frannie needs you to be a good girl. Can you go sit on your bed quietly while I change the baby's diaper?"

She nods and scampers down the hall to the room she shares with the baby. Gretchen's laughter has subsided into sobbing again, the only sound in the quiet house. It echoes eerily, and only now I realize that almost everything is gone: the Turkish rug, the elegant sofa set, the teak occasional tables—all gone. Biting my lip, I follow Sofia to the bedroom and make quick work of changing little Beatrice. A thorough wipe-down with a lukewarm washcloth calms her considerably. I pop a pacifier into her mouth as I lay her in the crib and turn to Sofia.

"Come on, sweetie, let's get you ready for bed."

Down the hall to the bathroom. I shoo out the older kids, who are dawdling, give Sofia's face a quick wash and help her brush her teeth. Back to the bedroom, where I stuff her into a footed fleece sleeper and tuck her into bed with a cuddle and a kiss. A deep breath, and down the hall to the older kids' room. Through it all, the counterpoint of Gretchen's sobbing sets my pace.

Luci and Marta are sitting on their beds, still crying quietly. I grab a fistful of Kleenex from the carton on the dresser between their beds, sit down beside Luci and motion Marta to come join us. With an arm around each child, I let them soak my shirt with their tears, not sure what's causing their desolation but having a healthy suspicion.

When at last they calm, they're so sleepy I barely have time to mop up their faces before they conk out. I tuck them both in and cast a last glance at them as I turn off the light. Now I brace myself to handle Gretchen.

Back in the living room, I find Gretchen slowly sweeping the debris into a pile near the wall, her tears a never-ending river flowing toward her chin. I recognize the shattered remains of a mosaic glass vase I gave her for Christmas three years ago as well as a number of other collectibles. I take the broom from her and guide her to the dining room, the only remaining chairs I can find.

"Okay, Gretch, *what happened?*"

"He left us." Gretchen loses the small amount of

composure she's managed to gain. Her head sinks to the table and she sobs so hard I'm afraid she's going to rupture something. My stomach lurches; I remember how hard I cried after the Post-It conference, and I wonder how men can manage to evoke such strong emotions in us women.

I sit adjacent to her, silent, my hand smoothing her mussed hair, until she finally raises her red, swollen eyes to me. "He left us. Me and the girls. What are we going to do, Frannie?"

"He left you on Valentine's Day and took all the furniture?"

Gretchen nods, the movement convulsive. "There was a letter...he left it on the mantle. A carnation and a box of stupid little sweetheart candies for each of the girls, and a goodbye letter for me." Fresh tears spill from her eyes and I marvel that the human body can produce so many at one time.

"What happened?" I ask quietly.

"A—a woman. Some girl he works with."

The parallels are not lost on me; I'm in the same situation, only I'm the Other Woman. *But it's different*, I remind myself firmly, and you can say I'm justifying my actions all you want, but I don't care. It *is* different, because if Malia hadn't interfered, Sam and I might have been married a long time ago.

"Is it...is it just a fling, Gretch? Is he coming back?"

She shakes her head, squinching her eyes closed and dislodging more fat tears. "No. He says he loves her, and that he hasn't loved me for a long time."

And the story tumbles out, word after desperate word, and the subtle signs of anxiety and stress I've been associating with her opinion of my relationship with Sam make perfect sense now. Gretchen has suspected for some time, and has been worried sick about what James is going to do. His choices determine the fate of her little family, and she's now like a desperate tigress needing to protect and care for her cubs.

"I can't make it alone, Frannie. There's no way I can afford this house. And it's going to be a fight to get one red cent out of him, even for child support."

"That's bullshit, Gretchen. He makes good money. Why should he live high on the hog while his wife and kids struggle? Pin his fucking ass to the wall."

"In the meantime, Fran, how do we live? It's going to take court action to get anything from him. He already said he's done with it all, good luck, have a nice life, fuck off. You name it, he said it."

"I've got some savings, Gretchen, I'll help you."

"No, Frannie, I can't ask that of you. I'll call a lawyer Monday morning and we'll see what we can do about getting immediate action for support. I just...can't believe it," she ends on a bewildered note. "Wh-what's wrong w-w-with me?"

And I know exactly what she means. It's the same question I asked when a relationship I'd been in for two years ended abruptly when the fellow met another girl he "had more in common with." Seven months later, once I'd done with my pity party and decided that swearing off men was rather inconvenient for a twenty-four-year-old, I suddenly became very aware of Sam as a man rather than just a boss—coincidentally around the same time he noticed me as a woman. And then he married Malia, and I thought that it must be something about me, something was wrong with me.

But that wasn't true, and it's not true about Gretchen, either. She's beautiful, sexy even after bearing four children for the ungrateful asshole she married, and funny as all hell.

"Nothing is wrong with you, Gretchen. I asked myself that...oh shit, how many times in my life?" I sigh. "People have selfish desires. Some act upon them. It doesn't say a thing about you and me, only about them."

Gretchen nods silently, her eyes crawling across the

room she'd so carefully put together. A perfect wife for a rising executive, she'd created a warm, inviting home in which to host dinners and raise kids and boost her husband.

"What happened, Gretch? Did he break everything he couldn't carry?"

"No. I...I went a little crazy, Frannie. I didn't...I didn't know how to hold it in. I thought I might explode." She looks ashamed, but I understand that, too. I won't even tell you the things I broke when Sam came home from Vegas married to Malia Moreno.

"It's okay, Gretchen. I got that vase at Pier 1. Nineteen-ninety-five." And incredibly, she laughs.

I help her clean up the rest of the house and drag the sofa from the family room into the living room. Finally I push Gretchen toward the shower, and I go do the few dishes in the kitchen. When she comes out, she's obviously hit the wall. Her eyes droop and her step drags, so I haul her into her room and tuck her up in bed, sitting next to her until she's almost asleep.

"Go home, Frannie," she murmurs drowsily. "I'm okay."

"I'll stay if you want, sweetie. Sam will understand."

A fleeting smile comes and goes on her pale lips. "Go home to Sam, Frannie. Go home and make love to him until he can't see straight, and hold on as long as you can. Hold on, Frannie, because even love like yours is vulnerable."

"Oh, Gretchen..." My heart is breaking for her, but my thoughts of breaking James's neck are best left unvoiced. It won't serve to help her right now, and it would be bad for one of the kids to overhear.

"Go home," she murmurs again, and drifts off to sleep.

I linger for a few minutes more to make sure she's really sleeping and not playing possum, and then I slip out the door and head home.

Sam is drowsing but not sleeping when I slide under the covers next to him, dislodging my fat black-and-white cat Penguin. He pulls me close, and his kiss is deep and leisurely.

"Is everything all right?" he asks a long while later.

"No," I reply, "but I'll tell you about it tomorrow."

He rolls toward me, his body pressing against mine, his artist's hands painting me with his passion, and if I died this very moment I'd have no doubt whatsoever that he loves me with every fiber of his being.

"I love you, Frannie," he whispers, his arms tightening almost to the point I can't breathe.

I kiss him softly. "I love you back."

Then words and time become meaningless. There's nothing but Sam and me, and the love between us, and that, my friends, is what heaven really is.

WITH FRIENDS LIKE ME

"It could happen to anyone, Sam." I yank the sheet off the mattress a little too forcefully, ripping it from his hands.

Patiently he picks it back up. "You never know what's between two people in a marriage, Frannie," he says calmly. "Perhaps there were issues Gretchen never told you about because she was embarrassed to talk about them."

"Seriously. Why should she be embarrassed to talk to me, of all people? My life is strung together with one humiliating moment after another."

Sam chuckles. "Yeah," he agrees, and chuckles again.

"Shut up!" I throw a pillowcase at him, laughing. We finish stripping down the bed and he takes the bedding to the laundry room.

One thing I've found about Sam that I hadn't known previously: he's a very tidy man. The only time his clothes litter the floor are when we've undressed in a hurry. Otherwise they're neatly folded or draped over the back of the chair beside my bed. Likewise, his stuff isn't strewn around the house everywhere. He leaves his cell phone and keys on the telephone table just inside the front door, and the only other things he's brought to my apartment are the toiletries he prefers. I don't know if he's just trying to make a good impression or what. I wonder how long it will take him to realize that I'm making a concentrated effort to keep my apartment neat. I'm no slob, but I'm also not a neatnik, either. I'll let the apartment edge toward squalor and then go on a manic cleaning frenzy about twice a month.

"Fran," he says quietly, laying his arm across my shoulders. I jump; I hadn't heard him come back in. He guides me down to the edge of the bed. "You can never really know what's going on between two people. If his unhappiness was making her miserable, perhaps it's best that he's gone. Granted, she *should* pin his ass to the wall; just because he's unhappy doesn't mean he doesn't have obligations."

"There's always counseling. He should have tried to fix things first."

"I agree."

There are many things I haven't asked him regarding both his marriage and pending divorce; perhaps it's because I'm not sure I'll like some of the answers. But I take a chance now.

"Did *you* try?"

A smile brightens his face. "Finally."

"Finally what?"

"Finally you're asking. I've been waiting, but you've been remarkably…"

"Self-controlled?" I offer.

Sam grins. "Yeah, that too. No, Frannie, I didn't try counseling. There was no point. I already told you I tried to make it work, but after the first few weeks it was obvious nothing short of exorcism was going to help. My circumstances aren't like Gretchen's."

I can't help but grin back. "Exorcism, Sam?"

"I told you—she's the devil in human skin." He kisses me on the forehead.

"So did you—ah—"

He takes my chin in his hand and scrutinizes me

carefully. "Aren't you an inquisitive wench," he remarks conversationally.

"Wench!"

"The answer's not the one you want, Frannie," Sam replies seriously, his smile fading. "I told you I tried to make it work. But it's been a very long time, not since the first month we were married." My next question—have there been other women besides me in that time—must show plainly on my face, for his fingers tighten. "No. No one. Anything else you want to know?"

"Yeah," I remark smartly. "You plan on doing anything with those steaks marinating in the refrigerator?"

His smile comes back. "Yeah, but I'm not so sure you're going to benefit from it." He spins me around so I'm lying across his legs, looking up at him. "I'm right where I'm supposed to be, Frannie. Finally."

$$* * * * *$$

Gretchen comes to work on Monday. I'm not sure how she managed to drag herself out of bed, let alone doll herself up like she does every day. But other than the dark, sunken circles under her eyes and tension in her expression, she's more or less on an even keel. I went to see her on Sunday and took her and the kids to lunch. It's obvious that the whole family is holding on by their fingernails. I give her to Wednesday before she hits the wall again and calls in sick, but I'm wrong. She makes it all the way through the week.

Friendship, that ever-fickle animal of joy and crushing sorrow. I think the main problem with it is you get so comfortable together you sometimes don't notice when there's something wrong, and that the problem is you. I've never said I'm the most considerate friend, nor the most attentive. I'll never win any Best Friend of the Year awards, and I'm totally undeserving of the BFF keychain Gretch gave me this Christmas. Growing up with an older brother, a no-nonsense pop, and a mom who was neither touchy nor feely, I sometimes think my feminine gene has a crooked leg that bends me toward a more masculine, blunt, and straight-up personality. But I love her; she's the sister I never had, and maybe I don't express it well, but she knows. At least, I *think* she knows.

By Wednesday I'm a little uneasy. Gretchen is uncommunicative, but she's that way with everyone this week, so in my infinite wisdom I decide it's best just to leave her alone and let her come to me when she's ready to talk. But me—being me—can't leave things unresolved (it's that crippled chromosome, trying to fix everything), so I call her that evening. I don't like to talk on the phone, so I'm really stepping out to make sure she's all right. Yeah yeah yeah, I know—with friends like you, Frannie... Bite me.

Gretchen isn't very talkative, which is understandable, and I'm off the phone in less than five minutes, which usually pleases me. I can't explain the niggling dread in the pit of my stomach; I just know instinctively something is wrong between us. Call it women's intuition if you want—all you male oinkers out there can call it a glimpse of simple logic if it so pleases you—but there's no denying there's been a shift in the dynamic.

I let it ride all day Thursday. Gretchen has been running errands on her lunch hour, so there's no chance to talk to her, but I catch Stella shooting me silencing looks when I periodically ask Gretch if she's okay. I go home feeling like the only schmuck who hasn't been let in on the secret, which then means the secret's about me.

Sam tells me not to worry about it; Gretchen's peaks and valleys will eventually level out into plains or some shit like that. I love the man to the bottom of my heart, but he really shouldn't try to make up analogies.

Friday is even worse, and I resolve to talk to Gretchen at lunch whether she wants to or not. While I may not be stellar best friend material, the cold shoulder is hurtful and undeserved no matter what you think.

So just before the noon hour I scoot out of my seat, round Cube Row to the other side where Gretchen sits. She gives me a half-smile but goes on with her work as I crouch beside her chair, ignoring Stella's warning frown and Morgan's suddenly apprehensive expression.

"Gretch, will you come to lunch with me? I want to talk to you."

"I'm really busy, Frannie," she says without looking at me. "I have—"

She's been "really busy" all week, and I'm not buying it anymore. I ruthlessly interrupt her. "Did I say something to hurt your feelings? Did I forget to call you back or something? Please, Gretch, *talk* to me."

She stops typing abruptly, shoves her keyboard tray under the desk and turns deliberately in her chair. Her face is set and cold. "Fran, I don't want to talk to you about this."

"What do you mean? Why not?"

Her eyes close and she breathes in sharply, gripping the arms of her chair. "I come in every day and I see you all happy and glowing, and it's Sam-this and Sam-that and Sam-and-me. And that's great, Fran, I'm really happy for you, but it's too damn close to my situation right now, and I can't…I can't stand to be so near it."

"Gretchen, it's completely different!"

"Oh?" Her perfect brows arch. "Is he still married, Frannie?"

"Well, yes, but—"

"And is he married to you?"

"No, but—"

"Then tell me how it's different."

I can't believe she's even bringing this up. She *knows* Malaria stole Sam right on the eve of our beginning.

"The whole situation is different! She tricked him; there's never been any love there. Gretchen, you *know* this."

"I only know what he's told you, what you've believed," she responds stubbornly. "Now please excuse me, Fran. I have a lot of errands to run."

She grabs her purse from one of her upper cabinets and steps around me. Stella joins her hastily, shrugging helplessly at me as she goes. I stand up, legs shaking, and Morgan pops out of her cube like a prairie dog.

"Just give her some time, Frannie. It'll be all right."

But will it? I won't give up Sam, and I don't think it would be fair of her to expect me to. She knows how long I've loved him. I go back to my cube and eat lunch alone. And when Gretchen comes back from lunch I pretend nothing has happened, but something is broken between us now. I reflect that Gretchen wasn't the only unsuspecting schmuck who took it in the shorts.

FALLING IN LOVE...AND IN PARKING LOTS

"Hey, Morgs, you ready?"

Morgan blows her bangs out of her eyes "Just about."

She has one foot propped on her knee and is attempting to breathe while she ties her shoe, a task that's becoming more and more difficult of late, she claims. Over the last three weeks her tummy has popped out and now resembles half a watermelon stuffed under her shirt. Morgan needs to keep fit while she's pregnant and I just need to get out of the office, so she and I have taken to walking the fitness track that circles the company grounds at the edge of the parking lot. Harper & Lyttle paid a landscaper to make it all pretty-like, so it's surrounded by a strip of grass wide enough to picnic on and dotted with benches and picnic tables. They even put little shade trees near most of them.

Gretchen has still been very cool toward me, and I've stopped asking her if she's all right. Stella is torn and impatient with both of us; you'll remember her helpless shrug as she followed Gretchen out the door the day Gretch let me know my BFF services were no longer needed—at least not as long as I'm involved with a married man.

She doesn't want to hear the things I know, such as

the quagmire this divorce is; the astronomical bills Sam pays without flinching for a private investigator who is retracing Sam and Malaria's steps in Las Vegas; the times he's so stressed I'm afraid he's going to fly apart after he's been to see Malia at the Betty Ford Center—and before you ask, I'll just say now that he participates in the Family Program the Center offers. He's explained to the Center that they're divorcing, but treatment seems to be more successful with the support of family members, and he's the only one who would go. And before you say he has a "taking care of people" complex, let me just say I already know that.

Sam and I have spent almost every off-work minute together, and I have to confess I'm a little worried as the thirty-day mark—and Malia's release—approaches. I wonder if things will change, if she will make increasing demands on his time, excusing herself under the pretense that she's still recovering and he's the only one who cares. And I wonder if she'll ever realize he only gives a shit in basic humanistic terms, such as he doesn't like to see another human being suffer.

While things are still on a questionable legal and moral footing, I've tried to keep our relationship confined to a very small sphere: him and me—and Penguin, of course, who adores him—but Sam himself proves to be a problem there. For instance, my parents called and invited us out for a barbeque last weekend because my brother is home for a visit. I was going to beg off, but Sam insisted we go. He thinks I'm being superstitious and silly about keeping the different aspects of my life apart from each other. I think I'm being prudent. No sense the family getting attached to him in case this thing falls apart; and no sense them having a tarnished opinion of him if it doesn't. The ever-practical Frannie Freeman at your service. (Side note: We went to the barbeque like he wanted to, and now my family adores Sam almost as much as I do. In fact, I think they would adopt him if they could. He and Dad talked shop and Mom doted on him like a favored son. I swear, even the frigging *dog*—)

Morgan gulps a breath and hoists herself to her feet. "I feel like I weigh roughly the same amount as a baby Beluga whale."

"Just wait," Gretchen says without looking up from the book she's reading. "In another two months, you'll resemble one."

We all laugh, and Morgan and I head out the door. Things are civil between Gretch and me, but they aren't mended, and there's still that distance. We don't get lunch or go shopping together anymore, and I miss that time with her desperately. But she's still put out by my relationship with Sam, and I can't help feeling she expects me to end it just to appease her. I have my own ideas on that subject: Not. Going. To. Happen.

Halfway through our second lap, Morgan clutches my arm. "Slow down, Fran," she says, panting. "I'm not a hundred-and-fifteen pounds anymore and I have a critter pushing my lungs into my esophagus."

"What a wonderful visual. Thank you, Morgan," I remark, and she chuckles. I slow my pace and our walk becomes a stroll.

"So tell me, Frannie," Morgan says out-of-the-blue. "When are you and Gretchen going to start being friends again?"

"We're not *not* friends…are we?" I cock a brow at her, and she shakes her head.

"Not as far as I've heard, Frannie. I'd tell you if she said that." And I believe Morgan would. She thinks the whole thing is silly. "But as long as you two are holding each other at arm's length, nothing is going to mend."

I sigh. "It's not going to mend as long as Sam and I are together without the benefit of his divorce being final."

Morgan is silent for a long time. "Doesn't it bother

you, things being so up in the air? No guarantee of a commitment to you as long as he's married to her?"

And I admit to her what I've not admitted to anyone else, even Sam. "More than you know."

We walk on.

"You know, Frannie," she says after a while, "when Chuck and I moved in together, I thought it constituted a commitment. We signed the lease together, pooled our resources, split the bills. And I thought, when that pregnancy test came back positive, that everything would be all right, because we were more or less married already, right? Only it turned out to be less than more, and I—"

I don't know how it happens or why, but sometimes it's like the planet pauses for a moment but my momentum goes unchecked and I tumble to earth. There's no rational explanation for it—there's nothing to trip me or cause me to stumble within a five-mile radius—but down I go, bouncing hard off my right knee. Morgan walks on, oblivious, still chattering about her former boyfriend, until she finally realizes I'm no longer beside her. She stops abruptly.

"Where'd you go?"

I start to laugh. Morgan turns to find me huddled on the smooth walking track, tears of pain rolling down my cheeks and blood soaking the shredded knee of my jeans, whooping like a loon.

"Jesus! Frannie, are you all right?" She hurries back and kneels beside me.

"Nothing hurt but my pride," I assure her as though pain isn't screaming from my knee to all points beyond. She helps me up and with one arm around me guides me off the track and through the grass to the parking lot.

"What happened? One second you were there, the next—poof! You were gone."

My laughter is turning nearly hysterical at this point, and Morgan is snickering herself. "It—it just *happens*—

Morgan!" I wheeze, and soon she's laughing as hard as me. We weave our way across the parking lot like a couple of drunken sailors, hooting and cackling, and when we get to the side door that's the quickest route to our department, I pause, wiping the tears from my cheeks.

"M-Mor-Morgan," I gasped, and start giggling again. "When you start—start thinking about Ch-Chuck and what an as-asshole thing he did to you, just sing the *Na-Name Game Song*."

"What?" Her brow creases, and she runs through the song in her mind. Her eyes widen when she gets to the part I mean, and we sing it together: *"Fee-fi-fo-fuuuck…Chuck!"*

We're howling with laughter by now and can barely make it through the door. Somehow we manage to comport ourselves with a miniscule amount of decorum as we pass through the lobby to the elevator, but once the doors shut behind us we're shouting with laughter again.

As circumstances would have it—because Fate seems determined that I not have one single humiliating moment that isn't witnessed by him—Sam is passing the elevator as the doors open, his legal pad tucked under his arm as he heads to another interminable meeting. He glances up as a matter of form and does a quick double-take.

"Frannie!" He looks stunned. "What the *hell?*" Morgan and I burst into laughter again, and he shakes his head. "No. I don't have time," he mutters to himself, and beams a glare at me. "Can't I leave you alone for a minute?"

"Apparently not," I reply, trying hard to gather some self-control. I catch Morgan's eye and we're off again, our gales of laughter chasing Sam down the hallway as he beats a hasty retreat.

Into the restroom we go. Morgan helps me clean up,

and the process of gently scrubbing out the fine threads of denim embedded in my skinned knee sobers us considerably. She ducks out of the restroom for a moment and comes back with some first-aid supplies from the kit in the break room. My knee is already bruising and I know from long, sad experience that by nightfall it will be all the colors of a stormy sky.

She bandages the wound and helps me up again. "Come on, Frannie. Let's see if you can make it to Cubicle Row without causing any more trouble."

This gets us both snickering again. Gretchen and Stella gape in astonishment as she deposits me in my chair. As she settles into her own cube, I'm sure I hear her sing under her breath *"Fuuuck Chuck!"* as she giggles uncontrollably.

That evening, while I sit with a huge ice-pack on my knee, Sam laughs until he cries. I'm a bit put out, to tell you the truth, because by now my whole body is feeling the effects of my sudden impact with Earth. But he makes up for it by carrying me to bed and fetching me some aspirin. He cuddles close, his body a giant heating pad, and eventually the pain subsides and I relax, feeling pampered and protected: a golden memory that carries me through the darkness ahead.

HOUSE OF CARDS

"Do you want a baby, Frannie?" Sam asks one night out of the blue. His hand slides from its comfortable resting spot on my hip and splays across my stomach.

"What, right now?"

"No. I mean in the future."

I smile in the darkness and snuggle against him more securely. I'm sandwiched between him and Penguin, and while I'm cozy and happy now, in about an hour I'm going to feel like I'm roasting in the pit of hell.

"Sure. Three or four, even."

Sam hooks his hand under my hip and turns me over to face him. "With me?"

His uncertainty is cute. "No, with one of those other guys lined up outside my door," I quip. "Of course with you, silly."

"And what about right now? Do you think about it?"

I shift uncomfortably. "Well, yeah. But I don't think now's the time. How about we get you divorced first, and then we worry about the particulars of getting me pregnant?"

He smiles and sinks down under the covers until we're eye-to-eye. "Well, just let me know when you're ready," he murmurs. "Until then, can we just practice?"

I chuckle and melt into his embrace. Yes, practice

makes perfect, and we must make sure we do this right. But I feel flattered and loved and excited at the prospect, and it's almost enough to make me forget that Malia gets out of rehab tomorrow.

Sam takes the morning off to retrieve her and drop her at her house to be watched by the housekeeper, much like a child. He comes back later than expected and completely out of sorts, and at first opportunity— close to quitting time—he corners me in a secluded alcove and kisses me breathless.

"That woman would try the patience of God," he growls as he straightens his tie and wipes my lipstick off his mouth. "That stuff tastes like shit, Frannie."

"Oh yeah? And how much of *that* have you eaten in your life, smart one?"

He gives me a quick hug and kisses my neck. "I have an unexpected meeting with Garland Harper in about fifteen minutes, which means I'd better be there in five. Don't know how long it will take, so I might be late for dinner."

"Sam, if you have things to take care of with Malia—"

"Frannie, I'm not her babysitter. I'll be *home* a little late." And he kisses me fiercely and darts away up the stairs. That's the last sane moment I recall.

I go back to my cube, and I have one of those instances of niggling dread like the one that preceded my and Gretchen's problem, and try as I might, I can't shake it. Angry as she is with me, she's still attuned to my moods, and she keeps sending me concerned looks.

Sam isn't done with his meeting by the time I go home. I cast a worried glance at his office, everything still as he left it. But he's a big boy, and if Garland Harper has decided to chew him a new asshole—and it's not unheard of—Sam can handle it. It's embarrassing and demeaning, but it's another one of those equal opportunity occurrences: It happens to everyone. So I go home and while away the time watching meaningless sitcoms and scarfing a Marie Callender's potpie.

But Sam doesn't come home, and neither does he call. When it's time for bed, I go alone, and I can't lie to you—I'm thinking the worst: he's with Malia. The thought keeps me wakeful toward dawn, driving a tidal wave of anxiety and dread before it that makes me speed fifteen miles over the limit to get to the office as fast as possible the next morning.

He's not there, either, but the department is buzzing about the destruction of his office. As I stand in the doorway and stare in awe, my mind flashes back to Valentine's Day and the debris from Gretchen's emotional collapse. I know the physical signs of a mind in turmoil, and I wonder what caused Sam's utter loss of control. I back out, utterly terrified for him now— terrified for myself, too, because my heart already knows something is dreadfully wrong.

Stella comes up behind me. "What the hell, Frannie? You think Malaria did this?"

"I don't know, Stel. Something bad happened for sure."

"Didn't he tell you what happened when he came home?"

I swallow over the lump of fear in my throat and answer quietly, "He didn't come home."

"Oh, Fran...I'm sorry. I'm sure there's a reasonable..."

She trails off, staring at the papers flung all over his office—the remains of a five-hundred page report; the pens and pencils and paperclips scattered on the floor from the toppled receptacles; the mini-blinds yanked from the office window and laying in a mangled heap on the floor. The telephone handset hangs over the edge of the desk like a lynch-mob victim. I gaze at it, and I don't know what draws me toward it, but I step over the wreckage and press the disconnect button. Then I press the outside line button twice and watch the display. My phone number flashes. So he *had* called me…and then for unknown reasons hung up before it rang.

I hurry out of his office and go back to my cube, where I sit motionless, my heart pounding, my mind frozen with clawing panic. *No! Don't let it happen, don't let it be over!*

The day drags and I admit I accomplish zero. Zilch. Nada. The blinds are closed between my cube and Stella's and Gretchen's, and I sit alone in my isolation, desperately trying not to panic. And when quitting time comes, I don't wait for the others but run as fast as I can to my car and speed home. To my intense relief, I find Sam's truck parked in a visitor's slot in the parking lot.

"Where have you *been*? Did Malia wreck your office? Jesus, Sam, I've been worried sick!" I dump my purse by the front door and rush into the living room where he sits in the wing-back chair, elbows braced on his knees. My step falters and I stop, belatedly realizing that things are not okay.

Sam doesn't look at me as he says quietly, "Sit down, Frannie. We have to talk."

Since the dawn of mankind, no good has ever come from a conversation preceded by these particular words. I know what's coming like a meteor of doom; I don't want to talk because that makes it real, but I sit on the edge of the sofa, because as we all know by now—let's say it together—there's nothing I wouldn't do for Sam Harrison.

"Sam—"

He looks up and I can't help but recoil. His face is granite, his eyes ice, and there's something uncompromising, unyielding, in his expression.

"Sam, don't say it."

"I'm going back to Malia."

The breath leaves me, and I don't think it's ever coming back. "You…can't mean that."

"I do mean it. It's been an incredible time, Frannie, but this is the end of the ride. I...have commitments elsewhere."

I stand up, my legs numb, my heart exploding. "Are you out of your fucking mind?" My voice is a stranger's: controlled, hard, inflexible. "You told me you'd never go back to her. You said you loved me!"

"It worked, didn't it?" A cool smile curves his mouth but doesn't reach his eyes.

"Oh, bullshit, Sam!" I yell, trying not to show that he just struck a mortal blow. I'll bleed later. I'll lie down and die respectably. But here and now it's war, because I know this can't be happening, this isn't the Sam I know, and I refuse to believe that I love a lie.

"No bullshit, Fran."

"You can't fake what was between us! You don't honestly expect me to believe that this was all just a fling while she was in rehab and now she's out and crooks her finger, you go running. You forget I've known you for five years. I know who you are—" I take a step toward him and he holds up a hand.

"Don't touch me."

I stop, my hand falling to my side. "I know who you are inside," I finish quietly. "You can't fake that."

"But I did." He stands up, his hand going into his pocket for his keys. There's no stopping the inevitable; he's leaving, it's over, and in a moment that will come all too soon my heart will shatter and I will lose my mind.

I take a deep breath, trying to get enough air. I feel as though an elephant flopped on my chest. "I don't know what happened. I saw your office—that didn't look like the work of the calm, cold man you're trying to be. But go on—leave if that's what you think you have to do. But I'm not the one who's lived a lie; that's *you*."

Sam gazes at me impassively for a long moment, then he gives a half-smile. "Whatever gets you through the night, Fran." He pauses at the door. "See you around."

I don't remember the moment the door closed, because every molecule of my being is attuned to the sound of his truck engine starting. That's when I can crumble; when I can admit my house of cards, built on a man of sand, has tumbled down; when I can fall into desolation and wail my misery to the sky. But not a moment before, because he doesn't deserve to witness my heart breaking.

The truck rumbles to life, he revs the engine, and I hear him speeding down the street. The tires squeal as he takes the corner too fast. But still the tears don't come. I find myself on the floor, holding the phone in one hand and clutching Penguin to my chest with the other, but I can't think of anyone to call. Gretchen is angry with me, and I can't face her I told you so's; Morgan had dinner plans with Bud; and Stella…well, Stella's solution would be to drink enormous quantities of tequila and take home a version of Enrique.

Finally I press a button for a preprogrammed number. When in peril, one calls for a hero, and now I call for mine.

"He left me." My voice breaks. "I need you, Daddy."

At last I shatter, into so many pieces they can never all be found.

THE ENEMY OF MY ENEMY

The week following my break-up with Sam shows we aren't going to be able to work together without the benefit of a little time and space. I take a month's leave of absence, shooting my vacation balance in the ass. There's a cabin that my dad rents all the time by a lake up in the hills, so I retreat there to give myself some distance. I have enough savings—thanks to my retroactive raises—that half a month's lost salary won't be a hardship, but Mom and Dad pay my rent and my bills for me anyway.

Following my and Sam's split, I spent a weekend crying on my daddy's shoulder. My parents may have their faults, but condemnation isn't one of them. They listen and evaluate and advise, but they don't blame, and to tell you the truth, it's a more soothing balm than any of my girlfriends could have given me in those first hours. I feel like I've lived through a bombing; Dad tells me that's shell-shock. I was hit hard and fast and without warning, and he'd expect nothing less than devastation. He takes me fishing, and while we're sitting on the lake surrounded by the quiet calm of nature, our hands and jeans mucked with bait, he tells me he'd seen this sort of thing time and again during his own career.

"Many a naïve soul misses the signs that people like

me, on the outside looking in, can see plain as day. I saw none of those signs with Sam, Frannie-pie. So either he's an actor worthy of an Oscar, or there's some serious shit going on in his life that you know nothing about."

Either way, Sam is gone. Seems to me it doesn't matter so much why he left as it does that he left at all.

Sam's easy-going personality has completely slipped sideways and the week before I took my LOA was pure hell. He yelled at Stella one too many times, and she stuck her bony finger in his face and snapped back: "Don't you bark at *me*, Rover!" *That* shut him up.

As for me, I might as well have been invisible because he said virtually nothing to me all week, although when I came in that Monday morning I found my magnetic poetry arranged all in a large, tight rectangle, with one coherent phrase in the very center: *it has to be this way*. Yeah, whatever. The day I left on my LOA I put up my own message: *love was a lie or goodbye was either way you don't deserve me*. I hid the rest of the magnets, and the girls haven't mentioned any more messages left for me.

Malia returned to work right away after her release, and I think the only thing she learned in the Betty Ford Center was how to be the perfect seagull manager. Oh, you know the kind: they fly in squawking, crap all over everything, and fly out again, leaving you to clean up the mess. She's been especially nasty to me, but I suppose in retrospect I can't blame her. I did, after all, sleep with her husband for the entire month she was in rehab. Not precisely the way to win friends and influence people.

I went to talk to Gus Haldemann against my better judgment three days into Hell Week. I say against my better judgment because I don't know if I ever mentioned it before, but Gus is Sam's best friend. He doesn't ask the particulars of why I want to transfer, but he is very kind about it all. I'm sure there's some insidiously evil plan behind his kindness—men always seem to have one—but frankly I'm too tired to worry about it. The bottom line is the Board of Directors has put an indefinite freeze on transfers. Sam and I are both stuck where we are, together in the same sinking ship.

But I refuse to be one of those rank-and-file drama queens always in the restroom weeping when an affair with the boss heads south, so I refrain from talking about it at work so I won't cry. Gretchen came to my house to see me, and we made up over ice cream. Ben & Jerry are the only men allowed in my life right now other than blood relatives and my feline boyfriend, and I think they're fantastic as long as they keep making Chunky Monkey and stay the hell out of sight.

The solitude has been good for me. The girls come up every weekend and we drink margaritas and watch the sun set into the lake and rip on the male of the species. The gaping wounds in my heart have scabbed over, but to tell you the truth, I don't think I'll ever heal a hundred percent.

But there are lots of squirrels out here, and I like watching them—so does Penguin, although he doesn't attack them. I think he's afraid they might be able to take him. A squirrel enjoys a simple life: a brain the size of a gnat (much like men) and every action driven by nature's design. I've named them, the ones that frequent the clearing outside my front door, and I can tell them one from another. Sweet Jesus, I've lost my mind!

* * * * *

When I go back to work, a semblance of our former working environment has settled into place. It's only a mirage, but I'll take it over the armed camp any day. Sam's foul mood has passed, and Malia is still seagull managing (and drinking, too, I suspect, but I'm minding my own business), but the respite feels like the calm before the storm. Something is building; I can feel it as sure as I could feel it back in January, and I can only hope I don't get sucked up into the eye this time.

No magnetic tidbits wait for me—not even the one I left. I don't put any of them back up.

"Say, Fran," says Stella around my cubicle wall. "You want to take my three o'clock training today? I'll take your two-thirty tomorrow."

"Who's your three o'clock?"

I lean back in my chair, sucking key lime yogurt off a plastic spoon. I'm down below size ahem—stress, that wonderful weight loss program; NutriSystem's got nothin' on it—so I'm not eating any of that fat-free crap, and I'm enjoying every bite. A party in my mouth, you could say. In case you haven't guessed, I'm fond of limes. Oranges are good, lemons are better, but limes are incredible. I always put a slice of lime in my water; it adds a better flavor than lemon. I tried crushing a few raspberries into my glass once, but that was just plain weird. The berries got all soggy, and—

"Sales," Stella says. I choke on my yogurt.

"Not freaking likely."

"Who do you have tomorrow?"

"Production."

"E-gads, that won't work! Hey, Gretch!"

"On the phone!" Gretchen sing-songs. She's been on the phone interminably since I came back. I toe-tap the cube wall we have in common, shaking it.

"Who are you talking to all the damn time?"

"Knock it off, Fran!"

Morgan pipes up. "She's talking to Gus again."

"As in *Haldemann*," Stella emphasizes slyly.

Gretchen kicks the cube wall from her side, and we all break into laughter. But it hits a sore spot with me. Sam's best friend and my best friend. How's *that* going to work for social gatherings?

She hangs up and gets up on the little step stool she keeps under her desk so she can see over the cube walls.

"You guys are rotten!" And she flounces out of the department.

"Guess she's not getting back with James," Morgan remarks.

"Gus is better-looking," Stella says.

"Hell with looks. He's not a schmuck like James," I chime in. "I'm getting coffee."

I make my escape to the break room just in time to see Gretchen disappearing down the stairs to the lobby, walking with Gus Haldemann. Crap. And in the break room I find the coffee pot empty. Double-crap. I rinse the pot and as I'm dumping the grounds, someone comes in.

"Coffee pot was empty. I'm just making som—" The words die on my tongue. Sam is holding out a filter.

"I'll wait."

My hands shake as I take the paper filter. We work in perfect synchronicity, just as we did every morning during our affair: he hands me the coffee can, I take off the lid and he holds it while I scoop grounds into the basket, I hand him the can and he puts the lid back on and stows it in the cupboard as I jab the brew button. We just stand there silently, side-by-side, watching the coffee brew, close enough to hear each other breathing, and I feel the scar tissue over my broken heart peel away, layer by layer, leaving the wound gaping and raw.

When the coffee is done, he hands me my mug. I fill it and then his, but he makes no move to pick up his. Instead, he braces both hands against the counter and closes his eyes. I can see his pulse hammering in his throat, as I'm sure he could see mine if he opened his eyes. I can't run because he fills the only avenue of escape. I put my mug down; I can't carry it without spilling it because I'm shaking so badly.

"Frannie—"

I interrupt. "Please let me out, Sam."

He draws in a deep breath and steps aside. I see

Morgan stop in the doorway, surprised to see us alone in the same room. She doesn't say anything but gives me a sharp, concerned look as I pass her. I'm unaware of Sam coming after me until I hear him call out.

"Frannie, your coffee!"

I don't stop until I reach Cube Row, and then I go into Morgan's to wait for her. I don't know if he'd come after me all the way to my desk, but I don't want to talk to him. A moment later I hear them coming closer.

"I'll just put it on her desk," Sam says. I hear my mug clatter down into my coffee warmer.

"Are you feeling all right, Sam?" Morgan asks. "You don't look well."

"I don't feel well," he admits.

And Morgan, bless her little heart, remarks with no small amount of acidity, "Well, I hear malaria can be debilitating. You should get yourself some quinine."

His office door shuts a little forcefully, and I bolt for the restroom where I join the ranks of all the previous drama queens before me.

I don't realize someone's in the restroom with me until she clears her throat, and I come out of the stall to find a vaguely familiar woman leaning against the wall, arms crossed, waiting for me.

"Frannie Freeman, you and I need to talk."

I hold up my hand. "Oh, please. The last time those particular words were said to me, they were followed by a royal screwing."

"Sorry—should have known."

I run the tissue under my eyes carefully so I don't smear my mascara. "Do I know you?"

She laughs sarcastically. "You've only seen me every day for the last three years when you come in the building. I'm Christine Requa, the building receptionist."

Now I recognized her. "I'm sorry. I didn't—"

"Recognize me? No one pays me any mind," she says with a grin. "And that is why you and I have to talk."

"If this is about Sam Harrison, I really don't ever want to discuss that man again in my lifetime."

Christine Requa runs a critical eye over my state of disrepair. "If that were true, Frannie, you wouldn't be in here crying. I can help."

"Help with what? You have a miracle cure to get me over him?"

She smiles like the Cheshire Cat. "No. But I might have information that makes a difference."

"Difference in what?"

"In whether you write him off or win him back."

I drop the tissue in the garbage, study her face for a moment, and then turn to brace myself against the sink counter. Do I head into the future, leaving Sam behind, and hope that I can somehow heal enough to love someone else so I don't spend my life alone? Or do I get a drink with Christine and hear what she has to say, and formulate my plan of attack against whatever forces wrested that man out of my arms?

Christine watches me with a knowing expression, as though she knows my dilemma. "It's your choice, Fran. I can walk out of here and we'll never speak of this again. Or you can give me a listen."

"And just what am I going to be listening to?"

"I have information I think would interest you," she says, "and I don't want a thing in return for it. If you're interested, meet me tonight at seven, Marty's Café. It's on—"

"I know where it is. I'll think about it."

"I saw you both in the break room a little while ago. I think you'll be there." She studies my face for a moment, and then grins. "I certainly hope you will."

She pushes out the door, leaving me to debate whether I want Sam bad enough to wage war to get him. Can I forgive him for what he did, no matter why he did it? And I know—I *know*—he left me for reasons completely different than the ones he gave me. You can say I'm delusional all you want, but I *know*.

I walk back to my cube in a daze.

"Hey, Fran, want to go to Tony's after work?" Stella calls out.

It can't hurt to at least *listen* to what Christine Requa has to say. I don't have to take any action.

"No," I say slowly. "I have plans."

THE EQUALIZER

Marty's Café boasts a bar in the back, and when I don't find Christine Requa in the dining area, I push through the mirrored doors to the lounge and wind my way through mostly empty cocktail tables to where she sits in the corner. She smiles broadly when I slide into the chair adjacent to her.

"I took the liberty of ordering for you," Christine says. "I hear you're fond of tequila."

"Tequila unfortunately isn't fond of me," I remark, eyeing the shot of tequila, salt, and lime before me.

She laughs. "I heard that, too. Go on, drink up, Fran. You're going to need it."

"I'm a lightweight; I'll save it 'til I really need it. What have you got for me?"

Christine leans back in her chair, staring into her snifter of brandy for a long moment. "That's what I like about you. No nonsense, no beating around the bush." She sips her drink, smiles with pleasure, and fixes me with a calculating gaze. "I was you four years ago, Frannie."

"What do you mean?"

"I was in love with a colleague, who was married to the coldest bitch on the face of the planet. He and I had an affair. You can probably guess it ended badly, much like you and Sam Harrison."

I tip her an ironic look. "Thanks for reminding me."

"Take that drink now, Frannie." Lifting a brow at her, I go through the ritual: lick between the thumb and forefinger and sprinkle on the salt; lick off the salt and slam the tequila; bite down on the wedge of lime. The liquor makes my insides glow, and the burst of citric acid in my mouth burns in a toothbrush skid from this morning.

"Want to know who his wife was?"

The question doesn't strike me as odd. In the business world there are those of fame whose names are renowned no matter what exact position they hold. Idly, I sort through all the possibilities of the corporate elite.

"It's not a hard question to answer, Fran. He was married to Malia Harrison."

"Fuck *me*!" I exclaim, louder than I should—I'm drinking tequila, remember—and she grins as she shushes me.

"So you see, we have a lot in common."

I motion to the server and point at my empty shot glass. I'm going to need it. "Did you call me here to start the Ditched by Malia Harrison's Husbands Club?"

"You're not understanding." She shakes her head. "Maybe I'm just explaining it badly. Sam didn't *want* to leave you. He was…*encouraged* to give her another chance. *Strongly* encouraged."

The server drops off my shot with fresh salt and lime, and I prepare it. "Doesn't matter. He's gone regardless."

"Let me explain what I know, and then you can decide how to handle what I tell you. It's all the same to me." I grant her a curt nod to prod her on. "Malia is Garland Harper's only child."

"Say what? I'm sorry, but I thought you said—"

"You heard correctly."

"If that were true, it would have been spread all over

the grapevine. How is it that I've worked there five years and haven't heard this?"

"It's not something they want broadcast far and wide. She's illegitimate, you see, from an affair he had early on in his marriage to Evelyn. They've kept it very much on the down-low."

I toy with my *cruda*, but I'm determined to pace myself. "What does this have to do with Sam and me?"

She swirls the brandy around in her snifter, passing it under her nose to inhale the potent fumes. "Unlike Sam, Bradley married her because he wanted to. I mean, look at her—you'd think she'd be suitably passionate to go along with those fuck-me looks, right? Not so. Bradley said sex was scarce and not very satisfying when it came, you should pardon the pun."

"I'm not sure I can pardon *that*," I say with a chuckle. "Sam said the same thing about the sex. And that it's been more than two years since they had it. I thought he was just placating me. I mean, don't all married men tell their mistresses the same thing?"

"In this case, you can believe it. She doesn't seem repulsed by it, he said, but just…uninterested."

"Is she a lesbian?"

"No clue, but she doesn't give off that vibe. Sexually abused, maybe?"

I shrug. "God only knows. Maybe she's just a cold fish, or a man-hater at heart. If she's Harper's illegitimate child, you can probably bet he had little to do with raising her. If her mother was bitter, she'd be likely to pass that on to her child. Can you imagine growing up in a bitter home, poisoned all your life? Could turn you into…well, someone like Malia."

"You sound sympathetic," Christine says suspiciously.

I snort. "Hell, no. The situation she's put me in makes me too angry to be sympathetic. Doesn't mean I don't understand how someone can go from A to Bitch."

She chuckles and passes her glass under her nose again, inhales, and this time takes a sip. "Well, it's not Armagnac, but it will do just fine," she murmurs. The brandy brings a flush to her cheeks as its warmth works through her system.

"What happened with Bradley, Christine? Are you two still together?"

"Things got ugly," she says after a long pause. She stares into her snifter, her expression distant. "Malia found out, showed up at the office—drunk—and caused a scene. We both got fired. She had a nervous breakdown. I—" Her smile twists, self-deprecating. "I wasn't very sympathetic. I said some harsh things. Bradley and I argued over it, he said a lot of things I didn't want to hear, and broke it off. He disappeared from my life. I heard he divorced Malia, but I have no idea where he went."

"Wow," I say.

"I changed my name, looked around, found this position at Harper & Lyttle even though it's beneath my skill level, and damned if I didn't land myself right in Malia's world."

"Completely by accident," I remark skeptically.

"Completely by accident," she assures me. "I'll be honest and tell you that I wasn't sorry to find she worked here. I hold her responsible for my losing Bradley and a little come-uppance for the bitch is never very far from my mind. Things went downhill fast after her breakdown. A little retribution would be nice. And tell me you don't want to just slam her face into the pavement for stealing your man."

"He's not my man. He never was, or he never would have married her." I take a steadying breath, my mind reeling. I'm having trouble putting everything together. "Why am I here, Christine?"

She signals for another drink. "I told you—I have information for you. I could just sit on it—I mean, what's it to me if you and Sam part ways forever? I don't even know you. But letting that happen means letting that utter bitch get her way, and I really don't want to do that."

"Because you hate her."

"Hate is too mild a word for what I feel for Malia Harrison. And it's too mild a word for what you should feel for her too."

"So where did you get this information that you want to give me? I mean, I'm sure neither Sam nor Malia confided their marital troubles."

"No, they don't. Not intentionally, anyway. Let me tell you about my life at Harper & Lyttle..."

No one notices a building receptionist. At the bottom of the dog pile, she's the one who chases you across the lobby and ends up with her arm crunched in the elevator door as she's trying to deliver an urgent message—and she has to chase you because she can't get you to make eye contact as you breeze by her station.

Building receptionists are mostly invisible, and apparently people assume they're deaf as well. Sensitive information is bandied about like small-talk, and Christine can't believe some of the things she's heard. She knows of damn near every "secret" affair in the company—including mine and Sam's—as well as who's up for promotions, who's trying to screw someone out of said promotions, who said what to whom and why, whose head is on the chopping block, and who's being hoisted onto a pedestal.

"What this makes me, Frannie, is the least paid, most powerful person in the company. I have as much—or more—information as the CEO himself." She grins delightedly.

"That would be the information you want to give me," I clarify, only half tongue-in-cheek, "but which seems to never come."

Christine chuckles. "Yeah, I'm all over the place. Let

me explain from the beginning—the *very* beginning—of your and Sam's troubles."

Nearly three and a half years ago, I'd noticed a pattern in the office. When I had an idea about how to streamline a process or of some kind of training we might need or might give to others, the credit would end up being Malia's if I went to her with my thoughts. Now I'm not a glory seeker, but in the corporate world where your value is measured by means of your brain and creativity, someone stealing credit for your ideas is the slow murder of your career.

I'd gone to Sam with my complaint, who then took it up the chain of command. It eventually ended up on Gus Haldemann's desk—that was the year before he became the head of HR. She deflected blame by making it sound like others had given her credit, which she tried to defer on to me, but she wasn't responsible for how others perceived a situation. Of course it caused tension between us; I often refer to that summer as my descent into hell. She made things so uncomfortable in the five months before she married Sam that I'd honestly considered finding a different job. Only my desire to be near Sam kept me from following through. In retrospect, I should have just left.

And then, just two weeks before the fateful martini bar, Sam is walking through the lobby with Gus Haldemann, talking about me. It's not breaking news to Christine that he's in love with me, she says, because anyone with eyes and half a brain can see it. And walking behind them, unnoticed, is Malia Moreno, hanging on every word. Next thing you know, they're in Vegas, and you know the rest of *that* story.

"So I lost him because I complained about her stealing my ideas?"

"No. Well, the first time you did—I think it's pretty obvious she chose him as her next victim just to stick it to you. But he left you last month because she's an alcoholic."

I run my finger along the rim of the shot glass, staring into the amber liquid. Not the first time I've looked for sense in a glass of tequila. And not the first time I've failed to find any.

"That doesn't make sense. She was an alcoholic before he became involved with me. Why does it make any difference now?"

"It makes a difference because Harper appealed to Sam to stay with her, at least until she's dried out."

"The rest of his freaking life, in other words." God knows Malia will probably never stop drinking, especially if she thinks it will keep Sam and me apart forever.

"Who knows? What I *do* know is there was a battle of wills between Sam and Garland Harper—I heard Sam telling Gus Haldemann about it. Malia wanted you fired for your affair—"

"The bitch."

Christine's eyes gleam. "Here's where shit fell apart for you. Sam said if you were fired, he would quit *and* he would leave Malia drowning in her whiskey. Harper said if he did that, you would still be fired *and* he would accuse you of deliberately corrupting that new software we're having so much trouble with."

"Sam and I could find other jobs," I say angrily. "He shouldn't have agreed to this."

"I'm not so sure you guys *could* find other jobs once Harper was through with you. He moves in high circles, Fran. He knows almost everyone who's anyone. All he has to do is put it about that you two are nothing but trouble—you sabotaging software to get back at his daughter for marrying Sam out from under you; Sam dipping his quill in his subordinate's ink."

This surprises a laugh out of me. "God, Christine."

She grins. "I'm not known for being tasteful," she admits. "But in the long run, Sam opted to cave—but not because of Harper's threat. He feels sorry for Malia, feels like he'd be abandoning her at her worst moment. Granted, he's not happy, but he gave his word. He'll see it through."

"Maybe not. Maybe he'll get tired of playing nursemaid to a drunken sot and...."

Christine's grin fades to a pitying smile. It tells me what I already know deep inside: he won't go back on his word to Harper. Despite his infidelity with me, Sam is an honorable man. No, these aren't rose-colored glasses I'm wearing, and yeah, maybe I'm indulging in a little justification here regarding our affair. But this situation isn't your normal "stepping out on a spouse" scenario.

"I heard him talking to Gus, remember," she says quietly. "They were over in the elevator alcove, but when there's no one in the lobby, voices carry pretty clearly. Sam said 'What the hell am I supposed to do? Abandon her while she's lying at rock bottom?' And Gus said, 'Yeah. That's exactly what you do. But I know you won't. Your damn helping-people complex.' Sam got a little irritated, said something about the kettle always calling the pot black, and walked off."

I lick the salt, slam the tequila, bite my lime—and gasp as the tequila burns its way to my belly. Tomorrow I will have many tequila-induced regrets, but today the liquor extinguishes a measure of the pain. I wonder, for the first time, if this is the very reason Malia drinks, and on the heels of that I wonder what could have given her such pain that it must be alleviated by enormous quantities of alcohol. Then I push the thought away—and stomp on it a few times—because I don't want to entertain excuses for her behavior that might make me feel anything toward her but deepest loathing.

"Great. So now he and his best friend are fighting about this."

"Nah. They're fine. You know guys—they don't hold grudges in the same way women do."

"I don't see how any of this is going to help me win

him back. Maybe it will help me understand *why* this happened—and it definitely salvages some of my self-esteem—but winning him back? No. He won't break his word."

Christine shrugs, unconcerned. "All I can do is give you what I know. All you can do is use it however you deem best. There are no guarantees in love, Frannie Freeman."

"No fucking lie."

"But this is a house of cards, Frannie," and I'm startled at the echo of the analogy I used for my relationship with Sam. "Harper's hold on Sam by playing on his honor is precarious at best. A man like Sam is bound to get restless in a loveless, drink-sodden marriage—and being the man he is, he'll eventually seek out the woman he loves rather than some meaningless affair."

"So what do I do? Just wait around? Screw that."

"Call his bluff. If you put him on the spot, I doubt he'll lie to you. And if he knows you know why he left you, it will be much easier for him to return to you than it would be if he thought you hated him."

"Sounds good in theory. In reality, however, things rarely work out how you plan them."

"What do you have to lose, Frannie? The only thing between you and your man is an act of courage. I don't doubt you love Sam Harrison. I also don't doubt you hate Malia Moreno almost as much as I do. You win him back; I get the satisfaction of her abject humiliation. That's all I'm after—that little bit of retribution."

I look down and find another tequila *cruda* in front of me. I don't remember it—or the fresh snifter of brandy in front of Christine—arriving. I wonder idly if Enrique happens to moonlight here. My gaze raises to hers. "It really wasn't just a fling?"

She shakes her head. "That man has it bad, Fran, and he was happy as hell about it. Whatever reason he gave you for leaving was bullshit. He doesn't love her, and he never will. He loves you."

"Yeah, but that was more than a month ago, Christine."

Her smile slowly widens to a grin. "No, that was just this afternoon, straight from the horse's mouth. You forget, they think I'm deaf."

I want to believe that, but then I remember Sam's granite expression and ice-chip eyes as he decimated my world, and it seems unlikely. Instead of pursuing more information, I ask, "What about you and Bradley? Why didn't you fight to keep him?"

Her lashes lower, hiding her eyes. She swirls the brandy around the snifter but doesn't take a drink. "He didn't want me anymore," she says softly. "Said my attitude toward Malia and her problems showed my true colors, and he didn't want to be with someone like that."

"I'm sorry."

"No more so than I." She raises her gaze. "Will you try, Fran?"

I must carefully consider what she's said; it's a lot to take in, and I can't make any rash decisions. He had been cruel in his leaving, cold in the aftermath of our affair, and he hurt me terribly. I do have my pride, you know. So I'll think it over tonight and let her know my decision tomorrow, because things like this have to be weighed and measured—

"All right. You can relax now. I'll try to topple the bitch so you have your retribution." And, to be honest, I want a little of my own. Christine has given me the information I need to equalize Malia and me so that we're evenly matched in ammunition.

"Excellent!" She throws back her head and laughs. Heads turn, and why not? She's a brilliant, vibrant woman. I wonder what gene of idiocy Bradley Moreno possessed that made him unable to see beyond her jealous words.

"Here's to us, Frannie!" She hoists her brandy high.

I raise my tequila shot and correct her: "Here's to *you*—The Equalizer!"

The tequila goes down, and my spirits go up. And I set Sam Harrison in my sights.

A MOMENT OF SILENCE

As anxious as I am about acting on Christine Requa's information, I can do nothing about it but formulate a plan of attack for a future time. Rome wasn't built in a day, and neither will be my campaign to sabotage Garland Harper's plans for Sam's life. It's frustrating, because I want Sam back *right now*, but I know it isn't going to happen that way.

The main thing I need to do—according to my and Christine's compiled logic—is make sure the failed software never crosses my desk again so that in the event I convince Sam to leave Malia to her true love (alcohol), Harper's threat to ruin my business reputation is rendered barren. As upgrades for our products approach release, technical manuals and training videos need to be updated. This generates a lot of work—remember I told you I have more work than I can do?—and so I doubt anyone will be surprised or suspicious if I ask that Stella or Gretchen be put on the new project.

So two days after my meeting with Christine—which, by the way, ended up accruing a large taxi bill for me, as we sat there for three more hours discussing options and plans of action and just plain chatting. Over the course of the evening, I downed more than my fair share of a bottle of Cuervo Gold. I had to take a cab home, and then back the next day to get my car. Tequila and me…

Um…where was I? Ah, yes, two days after Christine… I go into Sam's office to talk to him about my workload. I've timed it carefully and wait to go in until Malaria is installed upon his leather sofa and they're going over the enormous workload of the office for tomorrow's progress meeting. She looks up with cold dislike as I hover in the doorway.

"Yes, Fran?" she asks in a chilly tone. Sam's head comes up and he pins me with a sharp glance.

"I just needed a quick word with Sam, if I can interrupt for a moment?" Malia's jaw clenches but she nods. She can hardly protest, since he's my immediate supervisor.

"What is it, Fran?" He lays his pencil down on the notepad on his desk. I wonder if she realizes that he's deliberately created a physical as well as a hierarchal separation between them. Funny, any time I've ever had to corroborate with him on a project, we've sat together at the desk or on the sofa, and that was even before we shared a bed.

"I was just wondering the ETA of the new inventory software. I know they're fixing the bugs, but—"

There's a flash of alarm in Sam's eyes and Malaria looks like a cat with cream. "In the next three or four weeks. Why?"

"Because I'm swamped, and by the time I get the updates done for the training videos and the instruction manuals for the current upgrades, I'm going to have a whole lot of patches and upgrades to other programs to deal with. I was hoping perhaps someone else could handle the new project. I can come on board when I'm freed up, if I'm needed."

Something changes in his expression, so subtly that I doubt Malia even notices. But I know him well, and suddenly he's moving very, very carefully. "If it eases your stress-level, Frannie—"

"Sam," Malia breaks in, practically purring. "You *do* remember that Art Driscoll in Concept Development asked specifically for Frannie."

Sam's mouth tightens to a thin line. "And when Art Driscoll is the head of this section, he can decide who bears the brunt of the workload. In the meantime, that responsibility falls solely on me. Do what you need to do, Frannie. If the software is ready before you are, I'll shuffle it to Stella."

Damn smart move. Gretchen is my best friend and perhaps as vulnerable to sabotage as me, and Morgan and I are pretty close as well. But Stella, while a good friend and a drinking buddy, is not in my immediate orbit. It appears as though Malia knows this, too, for her eyes narrow.

"Was there anything else, Fran?" she asks sharply.

"No, ma'am. Sorry for the interruption. Thanks, Sam." I duck out of his office and slip into my cubicle, feeling immensely satisfied that I was able to orchestrate even this seemingly small strategy. But if a twig can turn a river, my dawdling with my other projects and not testing this software can hopefully turn the tide of my potential ruination.

* * * * *

Two weeks later, Sam gets called away for an indefinite period because his mother is ill. God knows when he'll be back. Four weeks into his absence, we're all considering umbrellas in the office to protect ourselves from seagull droppings. And lookit that, here comes a seagull manager moment right now.

"Frannie, I can't get the data I need off these damn things without going through each record. Can you rerun them in date order instead of alphabetical?"

These damn things turn out to be two three-hundred-plus page reports, and Production is going to shit a brick if I run them again—as might Sam when he reviews the budget. But it's not on my head; she's the interim boss while he's absent, and while none of us save Malia are happy with *those* circumstances, we're stuck with them.

And *these damn things* turn out to be only the first of many idiotic time-wasters she comes up with over the next four weeks, and they all seem to fall on my head. But while she may be a crappy manager, I'm not a stupid employee, and I manage to make sure she puts in writing everything she wants me to do. No doubt, since she can't steal my ideas anymore (I take them directly to Sam), she's looking for some other way to make my existence even more miserable than she's already made it.

By the last Friday in May, I've had enough. The girls and I—including Christine—congregate at Tony's, and I make damn sure we sit in Enrique's section.

"She's making me nuts!" I fume, stirring the first of the two margaritas I'm going to allow myself. I must keep an eye on Enrique, who shows all signs of slipping countless icy concoctions in front of me, hoping to liven up this Friday's festivities.

"She's egging you on," Stella says, "hoping you'll either blow your buffer or go postal."

"Fat chance," I mutter darkly. I've been on my best behavior, not wanting to shoot myself in the foot.

Christine chuckles lazily. "Well, Fran, you aren't really surprised, are you? You *did* screw her husband senseless."

Gretchen chokes on her drink. "Jesus, Chris!"

"Oh, come off it, Snow White," says Stella with disgust. "Last time we tied one on, Frannie told all. Now it's your turn."

Gretchen settles herself in her chair primly, avoiding looking any of us in the eye. "I don't know what you're talking about."

"We're asking how many times Gus Haldemann has

snuck out the bedroom window when one of the kids gets up early," Morgan pipes up. Her belly is a round soccer ball under her shirt, and as I watch I see the baby shift. She signals Enrique for another club soda, eliciting a disapproving look from a woman at the table next to us.

"Club soda," Morgs says loudly. "And totally not your business."

Stella snorts. "*Seriously*. Anyway, Gretch, let's have it. What's up with the soon-to-be ex?"

"He's soon to be an ex," she says.

"And Gus…?" I ask idly. There's a beat of silence around the table, and I get the feeling there's already been speculation about the intricacies of social planning.

"We'll see how it goes. I'm not putting all my eggs in one basket."

"Are you dating other people?" Chris wonders, idly stirring her martini with the plastic-speared olive.

"Well, no," Gretchen says, blushing.

"Then I'd say all the eggs are in one basket," I remark. "But Gus is nice. Good-looking too."

Enrique stops with Morgan's club soda. "Anything else, Miss Morgan?"

"No, Enrique. That's all for now." Morgan smiles brightly at him, and he leaves beaming like a roman candle. "What?" she demands when she catches us all staring.

"Nothing," I murmur. "I've seen stranger things." Morgan and Enrique? And what might Stella say about that? I sneak a glance at her, but she seems cool with it.

Gretchen says, "I'm not going to exclusively date anyone. Besides, my divorce won't be final for several months, and that's *only* if James and I can agree on the settlement. The lousy bastard thinks it's all his."

I finish my margarita and signal Enrique for another. Gretchen gets a text message, and Stella and Morgan roll their eyes.

"Oh for chrissake, not you too!" Stella grumps. Gretch waves a dismissing hand at her, flicks a glance at me, quickly texts back, and puts her phone away.

"Just one," Gretchen assures her. "So Frannie, how many bullshit projects did you get put on this week?"

"I lost count by Wednesday," I reply. "It doesn't matter to me what she does. I make sure she puts everything in writing and I'm keeping a hard copy at home. She's slipped a cog, that's for sure."

"I heard she lost it in a meeting with the Board of Directors Thursday and shrieked like a banshee at them because they're thinking of scrapping the new program altogether and starting on something new," Christine confided.

She's still stirring her martini with her olive but only sipping it now and then. I wonder if she's just sitting back making a show of drinking but really is just gathering information. Such information, as I well know, is power. It makes me nervous that anything we say might possibly be used as ammunition or a bargaining chip, but at this point I don't think I have any other option but to trust her.

Stella chuckles. "The woman's a serious head case. I can't believe Sam—" She stops dead. "I'm sorry, Fran."

"It's all right, Stel. I'm a big girl." I spy Enrique winding his way through the crowded tables with my margarita, and not a moment too soon. He drops it off via Morgan's side of the table, which makes us all bust out laughing once he's gone. "Jesus, Morgs, you've tamed—Gretchen, what the *hell*?"

Because Gretchen's snatched up my margarita and is gulping it down at top-speed. With only a drink or two left in the bottom, she sets the glass down and holds a hand to her temple. "Owowowow!! Ice cream freeze!"

We're all howling, but I'm perplexed, too, because this is totally unlike my best friend, who can make a margarita last until the twelfth of never.

"Well shit, Gretch, what did you expect when you picked up *my* margarita and slammed it like a shooter?"

She holds up a hand to stop me, her other hand still pressing her temple. "I've always wanted to do that," she finally gasps.

"What the hell for?" Christine wonders acerbically.

"It's all good," I say, laughing at Gretchen. "You can pay for it. I don't need another one anyway. As a matter of fact, I have a date with Penguin, so I'm gonna go."

"Oh, come on, Fran!" Stella protests. "You big party pooper."

"Too much tequila puts Frannie in rehab," I quip, "and one rehabber in the office is enough."

It takes a while, but I manage to extricate myself from the crowd. I feel some inexplicable thing missing that makes it so I can't truly have a good time, and I know that thing is Sam. If I make it through all this without losing my mind, it's going to be a miracle.

When I get home I grab a blanket and a beer, put Penguin in his harness, and carry it all out to the boardwalk to watch the sun finish setting. The cat is in heaven, batting at the bugs that flutter past the spot where he reclines. After a while—and half the beer—I feel myself start to unwind, and that's when he comes, his footfalls soft on the weathered boards. I don't turn around; I already know it's him. Perhaps something in the way Gretchen gulped my drink after that mysterious text message prepared me for this. Conspirators, the lot of them.

He passes my chair and takes the one on my left, where he always sits. In meetings, at the table, walking down the street, in bed—he's always on my left. Penguin meows and jumps into his lap, where he curls up and purrs. After a moment, Sam's hand covers mine on the arm of my chair, and he twines our fingers together. We sit that way for a long time, silently, the cat purring in his lap and kneading his thigh, our hands clasped.

The sun finishes its descent below the horizon, and finally he speaks. "My mother died last week."

"I'm sorry, Sam."

And I am, because I know what this means to him: no chance ever again to build some sort of relationship with her. Raised by a paternal aunt, Sam had very little to do with his parents while growing up. Filled with wanderlust, no more than children themselves, they had next to no time to spare for the unexpected offspring of their union. He had a happy childhood; his aunt proved to be a better parent than the brother who pawned his child off on her, but still…they were his parents, and there was always a part of him that yearned for that normal *Leave It to Beaver* family.

And so we sit while the night deepens and the crickets sing, as the cat sleeps in his lap and my fingers cling to his. And I pretend not to see the silver tracks of tears down his cheeks because it's a private mourning even though he sits beside me.

The moon is high in the dark sky when he raises my hand to his lips and kisses the back of it softly. He puts Penguin down and as he passes my chair, his fingers brush my cheek, and then he's gone, as quietly as he came.

BLACK WIDOW

Late June brings warmer weather, and with my weight loss, I find I actually need the summer clothes I packed away two years ago when I outgrew them. Say what you want, but while Chunky Monkey, French dips, and Frappuccinos can't hold you and make love to you all night (although it *does* depend on what kind of French dips we're talking about), they sure can give comfort when you're feeling down. I put away my fair share of each after Sam married Malia, and eventually boxed up a whole wardrobe that I'm thrilled to now take out of my storage shed.

What I'm not delighted about is walking into the sticky, freeform webs of the black widow spiders populating the shed. Luckily I've prepared for it, and I'm wearing a long-sleeved over-shirt and gloves. The widow is relatively easy to control with just knocking down the web and crushing the egg sacks; the problem I have with this is it requires me getting within twenty feet of the damn spiders, and I have some serious issues with being that close.

But I do it and the rewards are worth the creepy crawlies I have the rest of the evening, because I have a goldmine of casual and business wear in those boxes. I run it all through the laundry and stow it in the closet and let me tell you, there's nothing like a whole new, skinnier wardrobe to make a woman feel like a million bucks.

I get lots of compliments on my appearance and Malia has called in sick (drunk) for the last week, so my Wednesday is actually going well except for the severe pain at the side of my left breast and the cramp between my shoulder blades. Damn pulled muscles from bucking boxes. Add to it the fact that I think I'm coming down with a cold or the 'flu, because I have a headache and feel a rolling queasiness in my stomach. Add to all that the fact that it's progress meeting day, and…oh fuck it, the day sucks and I want to go home and go to bed with a heating pad between my shoulders and a cold cloth on my feverish face.

"Fran?"

I made it through the meeting with my head propped on my hand, pretending to listen. I realize I've not done such a good job when I look up: the room is empty but for Sam and me.

"Oh, I'm sorry," I say feebly. "I was daydreaming."

His gaze is sharp on my face, disbelieving the lie. "You look like hell. Are you coming down with something?"

"To tell the truth, I don't feel very well. Maybe I should just go home."

"Are you all right to drive?"

"I'm fine, Sam." I smile reassuringly, grab my notepad, and take three steps toward the door. Well, my *mind* takes three steps toward the door; my body actually heads a little to the west and I bounce off the jamb rather painfully.

"Frannie, I can't let you drive home in this condition." I gain solid footing just as Sam grasps my elbow to steady me, and he guides me toward our department. "You're feverish. Why did you even come in this morning?"

"I didn't feel this bad when I got up."

He sighs. "I'll have Gretchen take you home."

"How am I going to get my car? I can't be stranded!"

"We'll figure something out. You shouldn't drive anyway. Sit." We've reached my cubicle by now, and he pushes me down into my chair while he gets Gretchen.

To tell you the truth, I don't remember a whole lot about the drive home except that I feel utterly miserable. Gretchen walks me in and deposits me in my bedroom, and I wake up a long time later and change into a comfortable tank-and-panty set and lie on top of the covers because I'm burning up. And it seems like no time has passed at all when the shadows lengthen and Sam shakes me awake.

"Gretchen was really worried about you, but she has to pick up her kids from the sitter by six. I told her I'd come by to check on you." He's wearing shorts and a tee-shirt and looks like he was on his way to the gym when she derailed him.

"Mmmm." I roll out of bed and stumble into the bathroom, vaguely aware of Sam chuckling behind me. And no wonder: my hair is sticking out in damp spikes and I look decidedly punk rock. I brush my teeth with some difficulty, because my fever is disorienting me and I'm damn near hallucinating.

I stumble back out and stop halfway back to the bed, overcome with a sudden rush of pure sexual desire. It's the fever, I'm sure, that makes me drape my arms around his neck and pull his head down to mine. He pulls away…but not until several seconds have passed.

"Frannie, you don't know what you're doing. You're burning up."

I giggle. Yes, giggle. My shame knows no bounds. "Touch me, turn me on, and burn me down," I murmur, falling against him. He staggers back, catching me under my arms. "That was a Marty Robbins song."

"Marty Stuart," he corrects me. He's trying to get me

back on my feet, but I just plain don't have any strength left and he's having a hell of a time.

"Oh," I say blankly. "Who the hell's Marty Robbins then?"

"You know, he did the song about El Paso."

"Why would anyone sing about El Paso? Bugs…lots of bugs. Sam, stay with me." I tug him toward the bed, and he resists.

"Not a good idea, Frannie."

I take a step back, trip over my shoes and tumble backward to the bed. As I go, I manage to snag his shirt, and down he comes with me. I laugh. The provocative tone stuns even me, but I can't seem to stop.

"Your lips say no, but…" He can't stop my hand soon enough. He sucks in a breath, trying to edge away. "Your lips are lying."

"Well, Fran," he says, and I have to hand it to him, there's a definite note of laughter in his voice in spite of his physical…ah…discomfort. "You have me at a disadvantage."

"Best just give in to me, then." I edge my fingers under the waistband of his shorts and he grabs my wrist.

"No can do. You have a fever, and a high one at that; you're not in your right mind. Where's your thermometer?"

I smile sweetly. "I don't have one." I drape my leg over his hip and mold myself against him, my lips pressing against his throat. "Sam…"

"Frannie, stop!" There's alarm in his voice, as well as a desperate desire, and I know I've won. Sam's neck is his weak spot, as I well know, and I exploit this knowledge shamelessly. He lets go of my wrist, his hand sliding across my stomach. His fingers find the hem of my tank as my lips find his, and his control explodes like a powder keg, consuming me so completely I'm unaware of anything but the wild passion of his kiss and the almost unbearable, combined heat of our bodies pressing tightly together.

His hand skates over my ribcage to cup my breast, and then comes a surreal landscape of pain like liquid fire, a clenching spasm in my chest, Sam's panic. I suddenly can't get enough air. He scrambles for the lamp, throwing light across the bed, and then he's raking up my shirt and turning me over, finding a little red ring with the pale center on the side of my breast that I hadn't known was there.

"Frannie, when did you get bitten? Did you see what bit you? Fran! *Frannie!*" His voice comes from a long way off and I let go of consciousness with relief, welcoming the cool, soothing darkness.

* * * * *

Whispered voices and soft singing beckon me toward full consciousness God knows how much time later.

"Found it in the bed, crushed. She'll freak when she finds out. She's damn near phobic."

There's laughter, and then a vaguely familiar male voice: "What is she singing?"

Sam: "Blue Oyster Cult. *Godzilla*, I think."

Other Guy: "Well, she has good taste in music, then."

Sam (ironically): "*You* can say that—you missed the theme from *Gilligan's Island.*"

Other Guy: "Just the first verse?"

Sam: "All four verses. Three times. And then she sang *Secret Agent Man*, only she said *Secret Asian Man.*"

Other Guy (laughing helplessly): "I'm sure *that* was entertaining."

Sam: "Well, it didn't even compare to *The Name Game Song.*"

Other Guy: "Oh yeah? Your name or hers?"

Sam: "Both. And Chuck's."

They break up laughing and I groan, the noise going

through my aching head like an ice pick. I feel a cool hand against my cheek.

"You awake, Frannie?"

"Go away, Sam," I mutter, wincing at the pain my own voice causes.

He chuckles. "Yep, you're awake. How do you feel?"

"Lemme rephrase. Go. The. *Hell.* Away."

"She's so pleasant when she wakes up," he remarks in a confiding tone, and I wonder just who the hell he's talking to. I crack an eyelid and glare blearily around, my gaze landing on Gus Haldemann sitting in a chair near the door. I close my eye again, resigned.

"I'm so humiliated."

The guys crack up, and Gus says, "I was just about to put in a request for a song, Fran."

"Kiss my ass."

"You've got your work cut out for you, Sam."

Sam sighs. "Don't I know it."

I hear the rustle of Gus getting out of his chair. "Well, it seems like you have things well in hand. I'm meeting Gretchen for dinner, so I'd better get going. Tell Fran she'll be by to see her later."

"Hel*lo!* I'm *right here!*" I snap waspishly. I hate it when people talk about me in front of me like I'm not there.

"What was that?" Gus asks, amusement in his voice.

"Dunno. Kinda screechy—must have been something by Yoko Ono."

Gus leaves, snickering, and Sam comes back to the side of my bed. "Wake up, princess. You're in the hospital. The doc will be by anytime to talk to you about your condition and when you can go home."

"I don't wanna go. But you can…any time."

He laughs. "You're so sunny when you wake up. C'mon, sit up."

I clap my hands over my ears. "My God, will you *please* shut up? My head is killing me."

Sam pries my hands away and pulls his chair closer to

the side of my bed. "C'mon, Fran, look at me." He waits until I open my eyes to continue. "You were bitten by a black widow spider, and you had a severe reaction. After you passed out on me, I called 9-1-1 and then I stripped your bed. I found the spider crushed on the sheet on your side of the bed."

I shudder. "Is that supposed to make me feel better?"

"Well, maybe this will," says a new voice, and I peel my eyelids open again to find a man in a white coat coming into the room. He takes my chart from a hook by the door and flips pages, reading as he stops beside Sam. "I'm Dr. Nelson. You're a sick puppy, Ms. Freeman."

Sam snorts, and I fix them both with a baleful glare.

"Are you allowed to say that?" I demand irritably.

"I like to speak in layman's terms," Doc says. "You had a nasty reaction to a black widow bite. Since the spider is generally shy and avoids people, I'd guess you invaded her territory. She managed to get into your clothes or your bed, and when you crowded her, she struck."

"Yeah, blame it all on me."

"She's a bit crabby," Sam explains. Doc chuckles.

"Can't blame her. While the spider bite caused the severe pain at the site of the bite—as well as the muscle cramps through her back and shoulders, the nausea, the chest pain and shortness of breath—the body aches, high fever, and headache are all 'flu-related. So you see, Ms. Freeman, you *are* a sick puppy."

"Fantastic," I mutter. "Now can you guys go the hell away, or perhaps you have some more forms of torture to inflict upon me?"

"You're right," says Doc, "she's crabby." Sam laughs.

I huff out an impatient breath. "Listen, I was right in the middle of a very…heated sexual interlude, so don't expect me to be happy about waking up in the hospital."

I pause. "I can't believe I said that out loud."

Doc turns to Sam. "And your...relation to Ms. Freeman?"

"She's my...um...*friend*," Sam says very deliberately, and if I could roll out of bed and fall into an abyss I would, because everyone knows—at least in the office world—that an "umfriend" is a person with whom you have a sexual relationship.

Doc snickers. "Well, then, my condolences on the...er...*coitus interruptus*, but the heat of the exchange was probably caused by the high fever. Hundred-and-four-point-three when she was admitted. It's gone down some since we administered the antivenin."

"Still here, guys!"

"Sorry, Ms. Freeman. I generally address the lucid party, and your...um...*friend* is the lucid party at present." And he goes back to talking to Sam as though I'm not here. "The widow toxin is injected into horses, who then produce the antivenin. There's always a risk of a reaction to the horse serum, but we skin-tested first, and got no reaction. I doubt she'll have any delayed problems. Curiously, exposure to the widow antivenin may make her sensitive to rattlesnake antivenin, so if at all possible, try not to let her be bitten by a rattler."

"I try many things, Doc," Sam says in a long-suffering tone, "but she still manages to get herself in trouble."

"One of those." Doc grins. "We'll keep her for observation tonight, and she can go home in the morning. And then, plenty of rest and fluids. Do you need a note for your employer, Ms. Freeman? I've taken the liberty of writing one for you."

I motion half-heartedly to Sam. "Give it to him, then. He's standing next to you."

Doc raises a brow but refrains from remarking as he hands Sam the note. "My work here is done. Goodnight, folks." A swish of the door and he's gone. I close my eyes, listening to the hushed, oddly soothing sounds of Sam moving about the room. A moment later the bed behind me dips with his weight.

"Move over, Fran."

"This is *my* bed," I grumble. "I seem to recall I had to grab you by the shirt and pull you down into the last one."

"I obviously wasn't thinking clearly," he replies with amusement. He doesn't wait for me, but shoves me over and fits his body against mine, his arms sliding around me.

We lay in silence for a while.

"Sam, are you going to have any awkward explanations when you go home?"

"She's back in rehab, Frannie. That's where I was Monday morning, putting her back in Betty Ford. No one's at the house to notice I'm gone." *The house*, he says, not *home*.

"Is it going to be like this—every time she's in rehab, we can have a relationship?"

Sam doesn't say anything for a long time. "That's not the way I want it," he says finally. "And I don't want to put you in that position, Fran. But things are…so very fucking complicated."

I pull his hand from its place on my hip to kiss his fingers, and only then notice he's not wearing his wedding ring. "Let me guess—you're working on it, right?" I understand now what he means when he says that. It's not that he's shining me on; it's just that he's navigating shark-infested waters.

I fall asleep, his hand clutched to my breast. When I wake in the morning he's gone. But he's left something behind, pressed into my hand: a little stack of magnetic words. I read them in order as I peel them apart: *goodbye was a lie love you.*

I stare at the words arranged across my palm—the words I'd left behind on my cabinet that were gone when

I came back—and suddenly I remember he'd said the spider was found on *my* side of the bed. I smile and close my fist, knowing I have something solid to hold on to.

FRIENDS IN LOW PLACES

Gretchen drives me home from the hospital and deposits me in bed. The girls all came over—all except Morgan, that is, who can't risk getting sick because of the baby—while I was gone and cleaned the apartment top to bottom to be sure there were no more widows or 'flu germs lurking anywhere.

I take a quick shower and swap my clothes for another shorts and tank set and slide into bed. I love the feel of a freshly made bed with clean bedding. There's something very soothing about it. I'm rather enjoying it when Gretchen, Stella, and Christine pile onto it with me, sandwiching me in the middle, and pop a chick flick into the DVD player. We spend the day and evening eating junk food and watching movies—some of which I sleep through. Morgan spent the day setting up a makeshift nursery in the corner of her bedroom with the help of Bud Mitchell, and she joins us via speakerphone for the last movie—no chancing her getting the 'flu while she's preggers. I'm glad I have friends—especially ones who don't hold it against me when I sleep during movies, drink too much tequila, face-plant in public, and fall in love with the boss.

When the Chunky Monkey, Doritos, brownies, and margaritas are gone, the girls clean up the kitchen and leave me to sleep. (Side note: I got none of the 'ritas because Gretch pumped me full of TheraFlu and said the two were not compatible. I rather think I got screwed in that deal, and not in the manner in which I was thoroughly enjoying before being stuffed into the hospital.)

I sleep the rest of the work-week away, and on the weekend Sam comes over to watch TV with me. He doesn't stay the night, and while I'm disappointed I understand the reason he gives. He doesn't want to appear to be taking advantage of Malia being in rehab. We have enough going against us without allowing reason for doubts between us.

I'm back at work by Tuesday and glad for it. It's unbelievable how the work piles up after a few days. We used to be staffed with four more employees who shared the workload, but those four positions were dissolved in one of those acid-rain showers coming down from the Adminisphere. We're pretty sure the reasoning for *that* decision was pulled out of a hat, too, because logic seems not to have been an element in the equation. Sam fought valiantly to keep the staff, and when he was shot down he showed us a rare display of his temper by slamming his door and throwing things around his office.

Thursday's Adminisphere meeting heralds bad news: the inventory software they were speaking of scrapping after my unsuccessful trial run is back in action. The code is rife with mistakes, which makes more people than me wonder if Malaria isn't the only one drinking on the job, but with several weeks of work it should all be corrected. I've heard this before and know that "several weeks" usually ends up meaning twenty or thirty, but this knowledge doesn't serve to calm me because Art Driscoll is adamant I test it, claiming (rightfully) that I'm the most thorough and if there's a bug I'll find it. Sam tries to beg me off the project, citing my workload is astronomical, but the Suits on a rung higher up the ladder merely advise him to shift my other duties to someone else.

I don't, of course, get any of this from Sam. We haven't discussed the reasons why he left me in March; he's only implied the reasons he gave me were crap. Christine overhears it in a conversation between Sam, Art Driscoll, and a senior executive, and she hauls me to Marty's Café for a tequila *cruda* and a chat.

Christine and I conclude that only a code monkey with expert skills can fix this software and keep Harper from having any leverage against me. And while I've worked with the programmers regularly, I'm not what you would call close to any of them—not close enough to plead my cause and beg help.

As you can well imagine, the stress is killing me, and I spend a lot of time this week in the restroom fighting off nausea. And before you ask, let me just assure you I'm not pregnant. The monthly blight comes without fail. Besides, I did a Clearblue Easy—the brand of choice around here—a couple weeks after Sam and I split just to be sure.

On Friday afternoon, I'm coming out of the coffee room when I hear what sounds like a major butt-chewing in the hallway. I pause, and finally I'm able to identify the section the employees belong to.

"I told you to make sure the AV equipment was set up correctly in the Executive Boardroom. I'm not happy I was called to go fix it. It's not my job. I write code, *that's* my job. Setting up the AV equipment, that's *your* job."

"They tripped over the cords while walking behind the equipment, where they shouldn't have been. How is that *my* fault?" The voice is familiar but I can't quite place it.

"Just deal with it, Stewart, they're waiting! And I'd better get good reports about you!" Hurried footsteps carry the programmer—a shifty-eyed guy who looks like a weasel—past the break room and down the steps to the lobby.

"Or what, ass-wipe?" the hapless Stewart grumbles to himself. "You're not my boss."

I step out of the break room and find my able laptop-saving Stewart from the training convention, pacing in the little alcove by the window at the end of the hallway. His face turns tomato-red when he sees me.

"Oh…hi, Ms. Freeman."

"Stewart," I say, rolling my eyes. "You don't have to call me Ms. Freeman. I'm not a Suit."

His hue deepens. "My parents raised me to believe it's just respectful."

I cock a brow at him. "Well, I appreciate it. What seems to be the problem with—ah—"

"Vince Parker? Some Suit stepped behind the AV equipment in the Exec Boardroom and pulled a bunch of plugs when he got tangled up. Didn't say anything, the meeting started, and the Suits flipped when nothing worked."

"How is that your problem?"

"I'm the AV guy. No matter what happens, shit rolls downhill and lands on me. I'm at the bottom of the pecking order."

I digest this silently. "Doesn't seem quite fair. Have you tried transferring sections?"

"Transfer freeze. No one's going anywhere." He rakes a hand through his red hair, making the waves stand up on end. "Look, Ms. Freeman, I really shouldn't talk about it here. If someone overhears me, I'll get in trouble."

"Seriously?"

"We have strict policies about griping and whining. It's considered creating a hostile work environment." Ah, I know *that* kind of policy well.

"But what—ah—Vince did isn't?"

Stewart shrugs. "Bottom of the food chain, Ms. Freeman," and he points at himself. "It doesn't matter that I can write code around those idiots. Look at the new software they're freaking out about. There're mistakes in that code that never should have been made, and it's because they have incompetents like my good buddy Vince working above his ability."

My breath has stopped in my throat. "You write code?" I ask, because I need to hear him say it again.

"Yeah. I graduated high school when I was fifteen, got a BA by the time I turned eighteen. That's just the tip of the iceberg. But they won't take me seriously. Jeremy Ingram—my section supervisor—seems to think I was given my degrees without having the skills to earn them. They have no idea how many times I've gone in after hours and fixed a major screw-up at the eleventh hour."

"And what's wrong with the new software?"

"Stupid coding errors, ones a programmer learns not to make his first semester in school. It's just carelessness, going too fast, not paying attention."

I swallow hard, and manage to keep my voice casual when I ask, "Could it have been done deliberately?"

If Stewart thinks this is an odd question, he hides it well. "Doubtful. A certain person makes these kinds of errors all the time—they're kind of like his trademark. I think it comes from trying to code on Monday after tying one on Saturday and Sunday."

"Let me guess—Vince?"

"Good guess," he says wryly, and checks his watch. "Ms. Freeman, I really need to get to the Executive Boardroom."

"My section's that way. I'll walk with you."

The red that had been fading from his face makes a startling reappearance. "Oh, that's all right."

"My pleasure, Stewart. Shall we?"

While we walk, we discuss mundane things, such as the fiery convention and the Sales department's subsequent bitching about landing the Business Solutions account. And then he makes an unexpected revelation.

"I used to go by your cubicle and play with the poetry magnets. I'm finishing up my degree so I can teach, and I'm taking a class on poetry. They helped me remember lines for tests."

I stop abruptly just outside Cubicle Row. "That was you?"

He blushes brightly again. "I'm sorry, Ms. Freeman. Did you think you had a stalker?"

"I wasn't sure, but it seemed rather sweet for a stalker."

"I'm glad it was your cubicle," he says, now flaming like a bonfire. "You deserve poetry, Ms. Freeman."

I'm not quite sure what to say, because I think that's the sweetest sentiment anyone's ever expressed in regard to me, so I take him by both shoulders and kiss him on each cheek.

"Thank you, Stewart," I say as Vince Parker whizzes by, his shocked expression comical and extraordinarily satisfying. "You've made my day in more ways than one."

Stewart scurries off, very nearly dying of fright when he sees Sam glowering at him with lowered brows. I stroll casually over to where Sam stands in his office door.

"A little young, isn't he, Frannie?" he whispers, a glint in his eye.

I grab his tie and pull him closer. "What of it, old man?" I smile wickedly, let go, and stride away. A last provocative glance over my shoulder assures me that I'll be seeing Sam tonight—perhaps more of Sam than I've seen in months, if we're both lucky.

In the parking lot after work I corner Christine at her car. "I found a code monkey."

Stunned, she drops her purse, and we spend the next five minutes trying to retrieve her favorite lipstick from beneath her car.

"Where did you find a programmer? Jesus, Frannie, you didn't tell anyone about any of this, did you?"

"No, but I'm going to have to if I'm asking for his help."

She sighs and holds her face to the breeze. "I know, I know. I just don't want anything to screw this up. If they have any inkling that you know anything, they'll find some other way, Frannie."

"I won't give them a reason," I assure her, and as I prepare my dinner that evening, as I watch television without really seeing it, as I read the same paragraph of a novel for half an hour before laying it aside and turning out the light, I pray Harper never catches on that I'm foiling his carefully laid plans.

Sometime after eleven-thirty, I wake from a doze to the heat of his body against mine. I know by scent it's Sam; he wears this aftershave with a clean, forest scent. His hands pay homage to every inch of my skin, sliding my tank over my head and my panties off my hips. And then there's motion and sensation, hushed whispers and quiet sighs, impassioned kisses and murmured endearments, and finally explosive release and shuddering reaction.

And when I wake in the morning, he's lying beside me, fully dressed with a cup of strong coffee in one hand, the other winding my hair around his fingers.

"Good morning, gorgeous."

I smile. "I thought we weren't going to do this, Sam."

"No way am I going to be aced out by a sixteen-year-old."

"Stewart's not sixteen." I swipe the coffee from him and take a swig. It doesn't taste as good as it will once I've brushed my teeth, but it's a start. "Sam—"

"Frannie, I have some things to talk to you about. I can't see any way out of this unless we work together. Some heavy shit—"

"—has gone down. Yeah, I know. But I think I have a solution—to some of it, at least."

"Oh? And how do you know what's going on if I haven't told you?"

I set the coffee aside, grab the front of his tee-shirt and pull him down to me. "I have friends in low places. Now shut up and make love to me."

God, I love obedient men!

AN OFFER YOU CAN'T REFUSE

"It's like walking a tight-rope with no net to catch us if we fuck up," Sam says a long time later.

The bed is made and I've showered, brushed my teeth and am working on my second good, strong cuppa joe. Sam's hair is endearingly mussed from my fingers; he looks like he's just been thoroughly made love to, which he has been.

"So let's not fuck up," I say.

"Easy for you to say. You don't know half of what's happened."

"So why don't you tell me, starting with the moment you left me in the lobby before going up to meet with Harper. That's when the world went insane."

He stares at me silently for a long time. Have I ever mentioned his eyes are like coffee grounds, framed with long black lashes? Or maybe like rich, fertile earth. Why are the naturally dark, thick lashes always wasted on men, anyway? Maybe it's like birds: the males have the more colorful, ostentatious plumage to attract the female. Or perhaps it's just men are graced with features we women covet because there's no other way we'd put up with them otherwise. Either way, Sam is handsome to heartbreak, and with his mussed hair and a day's growth darkening his jaw, he could ask me to parade naked at

Sunset and Vine and I wouldn't even hesitate, because remember: I'm a sucker for a man edging into unkemptness.

"I thought he wanted to talk to me about Malia's rehabilitation and transferring me elsewhere, given my relationship with you," he says at last. He leans back against the padded headboard, adjusting the pillow behind his back, and turns those rich brown eyes on the ceiling.

But it wasn't about Malia's rehab and return to the office—at least, not all of it. Harper sits Sam down and within ten minutes decimates his world with the one thing guaranteed to bring him into alliance: a plea for help.

"He asked me to stay with her while she's drying out, afraid that she'll never find her way out of the bottle if I leave her while she's in the clinic."

Sam hemmed and hawed and finally declined, explaining that their marriage has never been a real one in any sense of the word but the legal one. Feeling he owes his father-in-law complete honesty (although this is the first he'd known that Harper was his father-in-law), he unwittingly hands over the weapon Harper had only suspected existed—because we'd be fools to think the gossip about us hasn't reached his ears.

"I told him I was in love with you and wanted to divorce Malia so I could marry you. It all went to complete shit from there, Frannie."

The ultimatum comes down: stay with Malia until she's dry, or I'll be fired for deliberately tampering with the bug-ridden software, and Sam's business reputation will be slandered throughout the corporate world for diddling a subordinate. Whereas Sam doesn't give a damn about his own reputation—indeed he thinks given his reputation as a manager, no one will even think twice about an affair with me, especially if it leads to a long-term commitment.

But there's no arguing with Garland Harper where I'm concerned. Not only could I be fired for tampering with the program's code, I could be prosecuted for the destruction of property. Harper even intimates—circumspectly, of course—that it could even be made to look as though I've sold corporate secrets. Sam caves instantly.

He goes back to his office in the darkened wing we occupy, frantically trying to find his way out of the quicksand in which he's suddenly found himself neck-deep. And when he sees no way out, he flies apart, wrecks his office, and sits in the dark for hours. (Side note: I'm pretty sure he cries because he's losing me, only he's not about to admit it. But look at me: I'm gorgeous, sexy, smart, and damn good in bed. He'd better have cried for me—especially knowing I'm going to leak an ocean of tears because of how he ends us—or his ass is grass.) At one point, he dials my number but hangs up before it rings, because he can't tell me what's happened, he can't tell me Garland Harper has landed in the middle of our love affair like an atom bomb, for if he does he knows I will never accept us being over—and that means devastation for us both.

Sam leaves the office around four in the morning, passes the next few hours in a Wal-Mart parking lot, sitting in his car, numb. Once he's sure I've left for work, he goes to my apartment and sits on the boardwalk all day, steeling himself to do what he must. When it's quitting time at the office, he goes inside with the key I gave him and waits for me to come home, and you know the rest of *that* story.

He turns to sit on the bed facing me, cross-legged, his coffee mug secured in those long artist's fingers. He mostly stares into the dark liquid as he speaks, darting quick reconnaissance glances at me to gauge my reaction.

"It killed me to say those things to you, Frannie," he says hoarsely. His eyes glint suspiciously. "I hated myself for hurting you, but he didn't give me any time to try to find a way out of it. I had twenty-four hours to end it, and I couldn't tell you what happened. I had to make you go away and I knew you wouldn't for anything less than me saying that I didn't want you anymore."

"Well," I say quietly. "It wasn't fun, let me tell you."

"I'm sorry." He looks up, his eyes pleading for understanding. "But I had to make it convincing to buy some time."

"You took an awful chance, Sam. What if I'd written you off and wouldn't take you back?"

He smiles, blinding like the sun from behind a cloud. We both know that never would have been an issue, because—well, I don't even have to say it, do I? We're all aware of the things I'd do for Sam Harrison.

"All right. That's a non-issue," I admit, grumbling a bit.

"What did you do that night after I left?" he asks quietly.

I sit silently for a long time, and then finally get up to get more coffee, wondering if I should tell him. Does he deserve to know that I sat in a crumpled heap on my floor for two hours, paralyzed with shock and pain, clutching the phone and my crab-ass cat to my chest, not even able to cry? Does he deserve to see the blood my heart spilled and the tears my eyes shed, not because he was leaving me but because he was lying about not caring and was leaving anyway?

"Frannie," he says from behind me, and I jump, not realizing he followed me into the kitchen. I keep my back to him as I set my mug down and fill it from the pot.

"I called you a few names. Called my dad. And then I broke a few things." Namely our favorite Motown collection, but he doesn't need to know that just yet.

He draws in a breath. "I thought I was doing the right thing, the best thing to protect you, but I don't know anymore. One mistake after another," he says, more to himself than to me. "From Vegas to this…it's all my fault, Frannie, and you don't have to … if you don't want to…"

I glare up at him. "Are you a complete idiot?"

He grins, and I swear the world pauses for one of those breathless moments at the perfection of that boyish smile. I didn't get hit with Cupid's arrow when I fell for this man; I got vaporized by Cupid's nuclear missile. In his smile that reaches from his heart to his eyes, I suddenly understand that loving someone takes only one person, but being *in love with* someone means both of you have committed to it, both of you have decided to love each other every day you wake up. He's made that decision, despite the pitfalls of loving me—and there are more of those than just Malia and her interfering father.

He sees the moment I get it, and his smile slides from his face, leaving a serious, solemn look in its place. "We have to find a way to put this right. It's not going to escape Harper's notice that I'm seeing you again. He might take action against you, frame you up for sabotage or worse."

"Stewart," I say dumbly.

"Oh, the jailbait you were kissing yesterday."

"Oh, stop!" I smack him lightly on the arm. "Stewart is a programmer."

Sam looks confused. "I thought he was the AV guy."

"He is. But he's really a programmer. He writes code, though Jeremy Ingram won't give him the time of day. Stewart says he's gone in after hours and fixed major coding mistakes at the last minute."

He steps away from me. "What do you think we should do?"

I draw in a deep breath. "We're going to have to tell him what's going on, Sam. I need his help to fix anything they might break and try to blame on me."

Sam paces the apartment, considering, worrying, forecasting every possible scenario and weighing the benefits against the possible negative ramifications. Finally he stops and turns back to me. "Okay. I don't see any other choice. Do you have his phone number?"

"Yes, we exchanged them the other day right under your nose," I remark sarcastically. "No, I don't, silly. But I can probably corner him on Monday and ask him to meet us after work."

"Tony's?"

"No, too noisy. How about Marty's Café?"

He shakes his head. "No, this is too sensitive a subject for that place. Let's go to Hunter's Landing."

"All right. And we should have Christine meet us there, also."

"Why?"

"She's one of my friends in low places."

He stares at me. "Everything I told you today—you already knew, didn't you?"

I grin. "Yeah, but I wanted to hear it from your lips."

His smile makes a sudden reappearance. "You're amazing."

"Glad you realize it. Now we have some things to do today, such as take P-E-N-G-U-I-N to the V-E-T, stop by the dry cleaners—"

Sam laughs. "Did you just spell out the cat's name?"

"Yes, and once you've seen him turn into a Cuisinart with whiskers, you'll understand. Whaddaya say—you up for it, loverboy?"

"Well, I guess," he says, shrugging. "But if he understands his name in conjunction with the word V-E-T, I'll bet he can spell, too."

* * * * *

It proves no problem to waylay Stewart in the elevator with no one around and ask him to meet with

Sam, Christine and me at Hunter's Landing. He doesn't ask questions but sends me a speculative glance over his shoulder as he gets out on his floor. I hope I'm doing the right thing; at this point in time I don't see that we have any choice. We need help from someone with coding skills within the company, because they will understand our software. Stewart is the only person in Product Development whom I know, plus he's very dissatisfied with his job. The makings of a conspirator if I ever saw one.

"He'll meet us at seven," I murmur to Sam as I pass him going into the coffee room. I try not to glance at the deep scratches on his right forearm. He didn't believe me about Penguin until the cat turned into a demonic whirlwind when Sam tried to stuff him into the cat carrier. It was quite comical to see man and beast waging war—beast fighting from the top of man's head—but I don't think either of them appreciated the humor of the situation like I did from my vantage point as a bystander.

Stewart's about twenty minutes late arriving. Christine switches from brandy to tequila ten minutes after seven and is working on her third cruda when our boy finally skulks in. His eyes dart to all tables like a pinball as he weaves his way across the room and claims the empty chair next to Christine.

"We were beginning to think you weren't coming," I remark with relief.

"I wanted to be sure no unexpected parties were showing up," Stewart says, flushing. "You never know with this company who's laying a trap."

Sam, Christine, and I exchange a glance. Sam hails the server and points to my shot of Bacardi white rum.

"Oh, I'm not much of a drinker, Mr. Harrison," Stewart protests.

"Sam," Sam corrects, and says, "You may need it. If not, Frannie will drink it. We have something to ask you, Stewart, but first we have to make it clear this does not leave the table."

Our hapless programmer blanches, making his freckles seem like pox. "Am I in trouble?"

"No. We need your help, but only if you're willing. If this doesn't work, we could all end up worse than fired."

"Worse than fired," Stewart repeats, his eyes wide. "As in put-in-jail worse?"

"Could be," Sam confirms soberly. "We'd like to make you an offer you can't refuse. Maybe all of us can benefit from this."

Stewart's eyes bounce from Sam's granite expression to my worried one to Christine's tense, watchful look. He grabs my rum shot, downs it in one gulp, and gasps, tears standing out in his eyes. He's right; he's not much of a drinker, but I applaud his courage nonetheless.

"Okay," he rasps. "I won't breathe a word, even if I decide not to help you."

It's as though Christine's tension jumped from her to me; until now I'd been fairly relaxed, though a little jittery, and she's been wound like a spring. Suddenly I'm sitting rigidly in my seat, and she sits back with a sigh.

In a quick, concise manner, Sam explains the situation. It's a little embarrassing to have to talk about our affair, but Sam glosses over the intimate details, although I see Stewart's eyes slide over me and back to Sam, and he smiles a little. Christine and I let Sam do the talking, because—well, you feminists can get mad all you want, but women are emotional creatures, and we take the scenic route when giving explanations. Men tend to drive right the hell over the tundra, and we figured a minimum of bullshit will best serve us in this matter.

Stewart's shot of rum comes, and I take it since he slammed mine. He doesn't seem to notice. He's riveted on Sam right now, and I can't tell if he believes our story or not. He has very much a poker face, probably from having to work around assholes like Vince Parker and Jeremy Ingram for so long without blowing a gasket.

Finally Sam stops speaking, and it's all down to Stewart. He'd been leaning on his elbows on the table while Sam explained the situation, and now he sits back, frowning as he processes the information. We can do nothing but wait for him to decide, and hope his decision is in our favor. If not... I don't even dare think how screwed we are if Stewart won't help us.

"You're talking deliberate sabotage of the coding?" he asks Sam finally. Sam shrugs.

"It's messed up already, as you know," I put in. "When I tested it, I got stuck in a loop and couldn't get out. I had to shut it down through the Task Manager."

He mulls this over for a moment. "When was this, Ms. Freeman?"

"Frannie," I insist. "That was the day the sprinkler system went off accidentally."

Now he looks at me strangely. "Ms.—Frannie," he says carefully, "I'd been staying late every night for a month to fix things after everyone went home. That code was clean as of eleven-thirty the night before you got it."

"Perhaps someone went in after you and thought they were correcting something," Christine suggests.

"What, at three in the morning?"

Sam lifts a brow. "Does Ingram know you're correcting his programmers' work?"

Stewart flushes. "Doubtful. I just can't stand to see bad products hit the market. It's a compulsion to fix it; I can't seem to stop. Maybe someone did come in after I went home that night, but they would have to be a complete idiot to change what I'd done. But you know…Harper himself could set it up—he has access to everything, including logins and passwords, and God knows it would be child's play for him. He's an expert programmer."

My hand clenches on my glass of rum. "Will you help us, Stewart?" Before I can stop it, tears flood my eyes and spill down my cheeks. "I don't want to lose Sam," and as an afterthought: "And I don't want to lose my job or go to jail."

Christine snorts with laughter. "Notice how Sam comes first?" she says to Stewart, who grins.

"Before I say yes or no, can I ask a question?"

Sam's hand slides down my arm, his fingers twining with mine. I can feel the tension, coiled inside him as he replies, "Sure. We owe you that."

"Why are they doing this?"

Silence reigns at the table for a long moment while Sam considers how much else we should tell Stewart. I wait for him, because I don't want to overstep my bounds and tell anything he doesn't want known. Christine decides for us.

"If we want his help, Sam," she says quietly, "we need to tell him everything."

Sam sighs heavily. "My wife is Garland Harper's daughter from a...ah...relationship outside his marriage. She has a serious drinking problem, and when I refused his appeal for me to stay with her while she dries out, he resorted to...ah...more extreme measures."

"Well," says Stewart, slowly and thoughtfully. "You did vow for better or for worse. In sickness and in health," he adds, for good measure.

Sam flushes and fidgets in his chair. "I had no intention of marrying her to begin with, had no desire for her at all, but somehow I woke up in Vegas one morning married to her with no idea how it happened. Several months ago, I told Malia I intended to file for divorce because I'm in love with Frannie and I want to marry her."

Stewart puffs out his chest and fixes Sam with a fierce glare. "So you're intentions are honorable toward Ms. Freeman?"

Christine barks out a laugh, and I feel my face burst into flame. It's my dad, all over again. Sam struggles to suppress his grin.

"They always have been, Stewart, since the day I met her."

Stewart smiles at me, apparently not seeing my lobsterized face. "See, Ms. Freeman, I told you that you deserved poetry." I grin back in spite of my burning blush.

"So can you do a geek-tweak on this damn program and get us the hell out of this mess?"

"Will you give me a recommendation if I get fired?"

"Glowing."

"And what the hell is 'geek-tweak,' Mr. Harrison? Is that some kind of Adminisphere jargon?"

Christine and I burst into laughter as Sam's face takes on a shade close to mine. "I—ah—thought—"

Stewart holds up a hand. "Do me a favor—let *me* do the thinking now," he says, and behind his abused-AV-guy demeanor, I see a geek of steel. He glowers at Sam. "And no more techno-slang, all right? You sound like an idiot."

Christine orders another round of drinks and we all toast Stewart. Over my shot of Bacardi my eyes meet Sam's, and we allow ourselves a moment of hopeful relief. Everything's going to be all right now.

It has to be.

PUT THAT BACK—IT'S NOT DONE YET!

"I can't believe you're seeing him again."

Gretchen slices through a zucchini squash with a little more force than necessary, and half the veggie skids off the counter and onto the floor. There is no five-second rule in my house; if you can't catch it before it hits the floor, it's a goner because it will be covered in cat hair. Despite my efforts to keep the kitchen pristine even when the rest of the apartment goes to rack and ruin, the cat hair proves to be beyond my control.

"Gretch, you don't understand the situation." I throw the zuch in the garbage and look up in time to see her casting a look out the kitchen window to the back patio, where Sam and Gus are doing their best to burn our steaks into oblivion. Judging from the amount of smoke clouding the area, they are either trying to send signals to the Native Americans in South Dakota or are testing the fire department's response time.

"I understand the situation perfectly well, Frannie. While Malia's in treatment, you're sleeping with her husband."

I draw in a breath, trying to contain my temper. *Count to ten, Frannie*, I repeat over and over, but you know me—ten never proves to be enough. "No, Gretchen, I'm sleeping with *my* husband."

She slams the knife down and gapes at me, open-mouthed. "Frannie—you didn't!"

"Didn't what?" I ask, and belatedly realize what she's thinking. "Oh, seriously, Gretchen! I didn't turn him into a bigamist. I'm just saying that without her interference, Sam would be *my* husband."

"Says who?"

I smile wryly. "Says Sam, but thanks for the vote of confidence. Look, Gretch, I know you don't approve, but…"

Disapproval is a mild word for Gretchen's attitude toward Sam and me. When she and Gus showed up for an impromptu barbeque—unannounced, I might add—I didn't have time to reach Sam to warn him they would be here. When he arrived, Gretchen's mouth compressed into a thin line as Gus drew Sam out the back door to the grill, and she's been Pouty Princess ever since.

"I'm not going to rehash our disagreement about your relationship, Frannie. I just don't want to see you get hurt. I find it rather convenient that he only seems to be a presence in your life when his wife is in rehab."

Another deep breath. "So you're saying Sam is a jerk-wad who takes advantage of his wife's addiction to play around."

Gretchen frowns unhappily, her eyes searching through the billows around the grill to mark the location of her two oldest children, who are playing croquet in the yard. The two youngest are currently sleeping on my bed, Penguin firmly entrenched between their warm little bodies.

I can tell my question bothers her, because I know she likes Sam. "Jerk-wad" is not a term most people use to describe him.

"It just seems convenient," she answers finally.

"You don't believe he really loves me, do you?" I ask quietly.

Gretchen doesn't answer for a long time, and then

she says softly, "I guess I just don't understand it. I equate it to James and his floozy."

"But you can't do that, Gretch. This is totally different, and Sam is not James."

She lays down the knife again and looks me squarely in the eye. "Is there more to this than you're telling me, Frannie?"

"Why would you think that?"

"Just a feeling—and you keep saying *'this is totally different, Gretchen.'* I'd wager Christine Requa knows, though."

"It's not a reflection of my trust in you, Gretch. It's a matter of keeping you out of it, if possible, and of who has the information I need."

She starts cutting veggies again, the rhythmic snick of the knife somehow comforting. "All right. Do I need to worry?"

I smile. "I'm worried enough for both of us."

"Then it's bad."

"Bad enough."

Gretchen scoops the zucchini slices into a casserole dish, adds some pats of butter, and covers them with the feta cheese I just grated. "Did Sam drag you into this?"

"Inadvertently—when he told Malia he's divorcing her."

She shoves the casserole dish into the oven and bangs the door closed. "He asked her for a divorce?" I can tell she hadn't expected that.

"I don't think there was any asking involved." I glance out the window at Sam. "Gretch, is it just me or does there seem to be a lot more smoke?"

"Good thing we have side dishes," she says when she catches sight of the roiling mass of carbon particles obscuring both men and grill. "I can't see the kids; do you think they've succumbed to smoke inhalation?"

I squint, trying to peer through the smoke, just as the grill bursts into two-feet-high flames. The guys holler and slam the lid down to smother the fire, and a moment later we see Gus appear through the billowing white clouds, ushering the kids toward the apartment.

"Did we lose Sam?" I ask, trying to hide my grin.

"Beats me. I can't see a damn thing," Gus pants. Gretchen guides him to the sink, where he splashes water into his eyes.

Sam staggers in a minute later, choking and gasping. Gretch shoves him toward the sink, too, and a few minutes later he's able to see and breathe.

"I thought we were a man down," I remark.

Sam grins. "Had to scatter the coals or the damn thing would have kept burning. What do we do now?"

"We eat the side dishes, call for a sitter, and head to Tony's for some tequila," Gretchen says, which cheers the guys considerably.

And that's how we find ourselves at Tony's (seated, naturally, in Enrique's section). A phone call to Gus's niece secures a babysitter, and a phone call to Christine secures her, Stella's, and Morgan's company. Morgan resembles a little butterball, with her golden skin and round little tummy. Three more weeks and we'll have a baby—at least that's what the doctor says. That it will be three weeks, I mean, not that it will be a baby. That's a given.

Enrique positively dotes on her, pulling out her chair, hanging up her coat for her, bringing her club sodas with slices of lime. Stella finds this hysterically funny, and we spend a good twenty minutes teasing her about losing her Latino hottie to our pregnant, junior *femme fatale*.

Partway through his second scotch and soda, Sam gets a call on his cell phone. He screws a finger into one ear to block some of the bar's noise and practically presses the phone into the other. I don't pay much attention, for one of Enrique's clothes-removing margaritas has just landed in front of me, the glass rimmed with plenty of salt. The only thing I need is a tree full of squirrels and I'd be perfectly content.

"Sorry, folks, Gus and I have to go. Problem at the office and an emergency meeting has been called."

I set my margarita aside. "What happened? Do you need us to go in?"

Sam smiles, a little tense. "No, Fran, I want you as far away from that place in your off-hours as you can get. I don't know how long we're going to be—Morgan, can you get them all home all right? You're the only one who hasn't been drinking."

"Not a problem, Sam," she says. "Doc says I can drive for another two weeks, then no more."

As the men get to their feet, I don't miss the look Gus sends Gretchen or her answering smirk; I have a feeling she'll be having one of those late night visits from him that I'm used to from Sam. Not for the first time I wonder how she justifies the fact that she's still legally married—albeit hashing out her divorce through lawyers—and is seeing Gus, yet my relationship with Sam is somehow worse.

Sam leans down to whisper in my ear, his fingers twining with mine of the arm of my chair. "I'll see you later, Frannie. I love you." He kisses my ear and then he and Gus leave, winding their way through the tables to the door, turning heads as they go. I can't blame the women staring after them; two tall, dark, and handsome men with wonderful physiques...yeah, chick magnets. Sam stops at the door and turns, searching for me through the crowd, and gives me a long, slow smile before pushing through the door and out into the night.

"Ummm...wow," says Stella, fanning her face with her paper drink coaster, her gaze swinging between me and the spot where Sam had just been standing. "I feel like I just watched a porno, Fran-Fran."

Christine, in the midst of taking a healthy gulp of her martini, sprays gin and vermouth over the table and Stella, who squeaks and shoves away from the table as we break up laughing.

"Yeah, well, that's not nearly as interesting as the look Gus gave Miss Priss over there that *clearly* said 'I'll be seeing you later—*aaaaallll* of you!'" I tip my glass to drain the last of my 'rita over the last bit of salt on the rim and into my mouth. Damn, these things go down like Kool-Aid. But there's another one on the way, so I'm not worried.

Stella downs her Alabama Slamma and raps her glass on the table loudly, catching the attention of the table next to us. "Okay, Gretch, all this yapping about Fran and Sam, and you're setting the sheets on fire with the head of Human Resources."

Gretchen is blushing like a neon sign. "Oh, what*ever*," she mutters. "At least I'm not texting back and forth with him like a love-struck teenager," as her cell phone chimes with an incoming message. We all howl. "Okay, so I was wrong about Sam, Frannie. All right?"

"It's a start," I say, grinning. "You going to get that?"

"Eventually," she says coolly. She looks up as Enrique slips another margarita in front of her. "Thanks." Her hand stays studiously away from the Motorola on the table in front of her. Finally Stella can stand it no longer, and she dives for it. Gretchen gets there first, laughing, flips open her phone and presses a button to open the message. Her eyes widen and her blush becomes fluorescent.

"Well, Gretch?" Christine challenges. I notice there are four martini glasses in front of her; she's really drinking this time.

"In the words of Frannie Freeman, I'm not drunk enough for *that*," she remarks, making us howl again. Morgan stiffens in her seat.

"Oh my God…I think I just peed my pants." We're now laughing so hard we're falling against each other. Morgan blushes prettily. "It's getting harder to control."

"Especially with this group," I agree. "Do we need to

whip a jacket around your waist and usher you out, Morgs?"

"Oh, no," she assures me. "It was just a drop."

A long while later, I disengage from the banter between the others and notice Morgan's face has gone quite pale and sweaty, and she's gripping the arms of her chair with white-knuckled hands.

"Holy shit!" I exclaim, bringing heads around from other tables. "Morgan, are you in labor? Jesus! Gretchen, you've had babies—what do we do?"

Gretchen looks up blankly from her cell phone. "Uhhh…boil water?"

"She's shit-faced," Stella says disgustedly. "Great. The only one of us who's birthed a baby, and she's eighteen sheets to the wind."

"Good thing she has an overnight babysitter," I chuckle. "Can you imagine her trying to tiptoe into the house and change the baby's diaper before passing out?"

Christine smacks my arm. "Fran, you're babbling. What do we do?"

"One of the guys is going to have to come back," Stella says. "None of us can drive, and Morgan certainly can't if she's in labor."

Gretchen closes her cell phone and puts it in her purse. "No can do. They just went into the meeting— closed door and incommu…incommicado."

I peer into my 'rita glass suspiciously. "I think I understood that."

Morgan, meanwhile, is trembling in her chair, and she raises her eyes to mine, panicked. *"Frannie!"* she hisses. *"I think my water broke!"*

We all dive under the table, and sure enough, a thin stream of fluid is flowing from the seat of her chair.

"Holy *Christ!*" Stella barks out, shocked. She motions to Enrique, who moves sinuously around the tables in his path and leans down to hear her. *"She's in labor!"* Stella whispers. Well, she *thinks* she whispers. In truth she was as loud as Christine—at least I think she was. To tell you the truth, I've had one too many margaritas.

Have you figured out tequila is my downfall? Sam isn't the only man I've had troubles with. José and I have experienced turbulent moments in our relationship as well. In fact, once when I was in my early twenties, a friend had a birthday party for me, and we ended up in the kitchen matching shot for shot of straight Cuervo Gold—no salt, no lime—and man, was I completely annihilated. I don't remember much of that night, but—

"Frannie!" Stella shouts, exasperated. "Are you going to help or are you going to meditate about the outcome?" She stands up, teetering, and I'm thinking she's had one too many Slammas. What a great flock of mother hens our little Morgan has; we're all completely in our cups the night she goes into labor.

Enrique takes charge with an enviable efficiency. His hand dives into his pocket for his car keys, and a rapid glance around the table tells him who's sober enough to bring his car around. He slaps them into Christine's hand.

"Take Stella; she can show you what car is mine. I've got the Dodge tonight, Stella. Bring it around to the back entrance by the Dumpster." He shoves her off toward the door, motions to a nearby server, and hurriedly explains the situation as he disentangles himself from his apron.

Gretchen is holding Morgan's hand, trying to talk her through the contractions, but honestly no one can understand what the hell she's saying because she's piss drunk. Morgs frantically looks to me for sanity, and I wonder what kind of crazy-ass world we live in that she's looking to a tequila-soaked mother-of-none to help her.

"Do you have a jacket, Frannie?" Enrique asks.

"Umm, sure. A windbreaker. You think it might fit around her waist?" I look at Morgan's swollen belly doubtfully. I'm not even sure she *has* a waist anymore.

And I can't believe he thinks she's going to walk out of here under her own steam, let alone give a rat's ass about her wet pants.

He laughs. "No, silly. Childbirth is a shock to the body. She needs to stay warm. Put the jacket on her. Try not to jostle her too much; she won't appreciate it."

"Are you a freaking midwife?" I blurt out. "It wouldn't surprise me. Gorgeous, sexy…why not a midwife?"

Enrique rolls his eyes. "My sister is an OB nurse. And you'd be surprised how many women go into labor here. The jacket, Frannie," he reminds me.

"Oh, yeah!" I pop out of my chair and as carefully as I can wrap my windbreaker around Morgan. She's *not* very appreciative, and at one point I believe she tells me she's going to wrap it around my throat and choke me with it, but I backed away from her when she growled at me—yes, *growled*—so I'm not certain that's really what she said.

Enrique gets behind her chair and starts wheeling it toward the bar, motioning for us to follow. I wonder if bars have wheeled chairs just for this purpose. Not wheeling out pregnant women in labor, but drunks when they can't stand. We go through the kitchen and out the service entrance to the waiting minivan.

"A *minivan?*" I can't believe my eyes. Enrique, of the utterly hot Latin…hotness, drives a minivan?

"Hey, I have nieces and nephews," he defends himself. "Besides, this is my sister's car. She had date-night with her husband, so they took my truck. Good thing, too."

With a little maneuvering (and a lot of swearing and threats from Morgan), we get her into the van, pile in ourselves, and with the capable Enrique at the wheel, start the mad dash for the hospital. Let me just say that I didn't know it was possible to run an L.A. cab driver off the road, but Enrique did it…twice.

Modern childbirth is the oddest thing these days. Anybody can be in the "birthing room" with the mother-to-be; doesn't matter if they're family or aliens from Pluto as long as they stay out of the way during the pertinent times and don't cause any trouble. Gretchen passes out on the small sofa, obviously under the impression that a first birth is going to take most of the night. Stella, Christine and I mill around Morgan, making her comfortable and fetching for her.

A couple of hours after we arrive, it's obvious she's progressing through labor rather quickly. When the nurse asks her if she's doing natural childbirth, Morgan asks her if she's ever passed a watermelon out her vagina and how good did *that* feel? The woman scurries out to arrange for an epidural.

Enrique, our knight in shining minivan, returned to work with the promise of coming back when his shift was over. Morgan tells him he doesn't have to, but one look at the way his face lights up when he looks at our girl says he'll be back, no matter what.

And shortly after two in the morning, he saunters in, only to be ushered right back out by Christine because Morgs is in hard labor and has been given the go ahead to push. I'd like to join him in the hallway, but I'm held captive by Morgan—literally. She has my hand in a grip like a vise. Gretchen is still in the land of oblivion, and Morgan has shooed everyone away from her bed but me and the doctor. I'm petrified—what the hell do I know about having a baby? I've heard it's much like squeezing out a pumpkin and I'm definitely not qualified to help with *that*.

But it turns out I don't have to do a damn thing but maintain eye contact with Morgan, assure her that she's doing great even though I'm certain she's dying on me, and before I even realize how much time has passed, the nurse is passing a squirming, slimy red thing to the attending pediatrician to have his/her Apgar done. A swipe and a swaddle, and the baby is laid in Morgan's arms.

"Say hello to your son, Morgan." The nurse beams down at her, totally unsuspecting of the reaction about to come. "Is that Daddy in the hallway? I'll get him." She's gone to get Enrique before we can correct her.

"Holy hell!" Morgan exclaims, making everyone jump. She's staring at the baby with a look of revulsion, and she looks up at the obstetrician, holding the baby out to him. "Put it back—it's not done yet!"

After the first surprised moment, Doc laughs. "I'm afraid they all look that way, Morgan. Congratulations. What's his name?"

Morgan looks up at me, then at Enrique, who tiptoes in hesitantly, stopping in his tracks when he sees the baby in the crook of her arm. He stands transfixed at the sight of her tiny little son as though he's never seen such a thing before.

"Jacob Enrique Cassidy," she says, shocking us all. "For my Prince Charming to the rescue." She puts the baby in Enrique's arms, and as a beautiful smile spreads slowly across his face, I'm suddenly certain our little Morgan will be well taken care of.

By the time my turn to hold little Jacob rolls around, I'm exhausted and sobering up. I stuff myself into a corner of the sofa, cradling the baby, wondering at such a miracle—and damn me, I want one!

ROXANNE

Gus takes Gretchen and Stella home about half an hour before Sam retrieves me; Christine took a cab about an hour before that. Sam looks as exhausted as I feel. As he hugs me tightly, I catch the scent of smoke in his shirt and I wonder what the Suits thought of *that* in their impromptu meeting.

He seems a bit perplexed by Enrique's presence there, but he doesn't ask any questions as he washes his hands and takes the baby, one long finger stroking the tiny, petal-perfect cheek. Morgan is sleeping, so we don't stay very long. Sam gives the baby back to Enrique, who lays him in the bassinette beside Morgan's bed.

The drive home is made in relative silence, and as we get undressed to go to bed I pause, my heart stuttering in its beat as I turn to him.

"You'd better not be thinking of leaving me again."

Sam, preoccupied with whatever it is that's on his mind, looks up, startled. "*What?* Why would you even think that?"

I shrug, feeling utterly foolish now. "Just your whole demeanor."

"Oh, Frannie." He slides across the bed and pulls me down to him, kissing my cheek when I'm settled against him. "It was not a good meeting. I'll tell you all about it in the morning, but right now I'm beat."

"Are we in trouble?"

"Damned if I know. Oh, all right, I'll give you a little bit before we go to sleep." He scowls at me ferociously as I twist around to see his expression. "Vince Parker went into the office to work on that new software, supposedly because he couldn't sleep. He caught Stewart Drummond monkeying with the code. He immediately called Jeremy Ingram—their supervisor, you know him?—who called Garland Harper."

"Why did you have to go in? You're not in that section."

"Vince Parker saw you talking with Stewart Drummond that day—remember, you kissed the kid. Dirty old woman," he adds under his breath.

I chuckle. It's a high-pitched, humorless sound that sparks alarm in his eyes. He obviously thinks I'm going to become hysterical.

"Frannie, I don't know all the technical details—you know that. The long and short of it, as I understand it, is Parker told Ingram he thinks you and Stewart conspired to tweak the code and cause malfunctions. Stewart has been suspended without pay, pending an investigation. He almost certainly will be fired. Gus is holding Harper at bay regarding you, citing circumstantial evidence."

"He wanted to fire me," I say dully.

"More than that, he wanted to bring criminal charges against you. At least that's what he was ranting about. But don't worry; it won't happen. Gus is more than capable of protecting you while making it look like he's protecting them from an unlawful termination suit—probably because he really is."

I feel faint. "Harper knows we're together again. That's why he's doing this."

Sam nods. "Yes. He took full advantage of this snafu with Stewart to try to oust you. I must say, blood runs thicker than whiskey between Malia and her father. Much thicker than I'd imagined, given I hadn't even known he was her father and I've been married to the woman for two years."

"Why don't I just quit? I can find work somewhere else. I bet Richard White at Business Solutions would hire me in a second."

"No," Sam says sharply. "You can't quit now, not with what just happened. It would look like an admission of guilt. Stewart plans to lawyer up tomorrow, but the plain and simple fact is, he was working under Parker's login. He doesn't have his own, you see."

"Oh, that's bad!" I feel terrible for Stewart. I've gotten him into this mess and now his whole career is in jeopardy.

"From my understanding, as a security measure the keystrokes are recorded when anyone is working on the software. It should show that Stewart was fixing bugs rather than breaking code, but it doesn't look good that he had Parker's login information."

I snort. "He said Parker leaves it lying around on his desk," I reply scornfully. "So much for security. Maybe Ingram should be tightening up his employees' work practices."

"Be that as it may, Stewart doesn't have the authorization to be coding. He's the AV guy, remember? There is a whole complicated rigamarole the programmers have to go through to be authorized to work on the code, including very strict confidentiality agreements. He's in trouble no matter what—and Fran, he admitted to us that he's been fixing Vince's code for a long time."

"You didn't tell anyone that, did you?" I scowl.

"No, not even Gus knows. But we're not entirely at fault here; he knew he was violating company policy long before we came along and dragged him into our troubles. He could have been caught at any time without our involvement."

I digest this silently as I slide under the covers. Sam's body is warm against mine. "Do you think Stewart will be all right? He really should be promoted—Jeremy Ingram won't even consider him. And now, with this…it could ruin his whole life, Sam, his whole future career!"

"I know, Fran. I'll do what I can. Now shut up and go to sleep." He kisses me quickly but thoroughly and manages to give me his trademark heart-breaking smile in spite of his mental exhaustion. "Why was Enrique still at the hospital, by the way?"

"It's a long story, and I'm not sure I know all of it. Now shut up and go to sleep," I quip. He chuckles, snuggles in, and out he goes. Me—I lie awake for another long hour, wondering how this unexpected move changes the nature of our game.

* * * * *

Monday sees a flurry of excited clucking among the Suits. Men in power ties with rumpled hair and women in sedate business skirt-suits which they compulsively straighten scurry through the corridors, whispering frantically as they hurry off to their usual interminable meetings that offer no explanations or results. Their squawking reminds me of chickens (or seagulls), and in spite of my worry for Stewart, I find myself chuckling every time I see a group of Adminispherists wringing their hands and conversing with worried creases in their foreheads, strutting around with airs of importance that far exceed reality.

Sam has been in and out of the office all morning, looking more and more harassed each time he swoops in to try to accomplish something of value. Unfortunately, he usually ends up with less than fifteen minutes before someone else calls him in a panic. I don't know what they think Sam can do; his technological challenges are legendary at Harper & Lyttle, but he's a born soother, and I think they rely on him as a sedative when things get crazy.

Lunchtime heralds the arrival of the Board of Directors: eight men and one woman, none of whom those at my authority level have ever seen for more than a microsecond as they breeze through the lobby and into the express elevator that goes directly up to the Executive Suite. They, Sam, Jeremy Ingram, and Gus Haldemann are ushered behind closed doors.

This is when I realize just how serious this situation really is. Millions of dollars in potential profits ride on the spec and contract programs, and rumor has it (as relayed to me by Christine) that Garland Harper's mood has transcended angry and achieved the level of blind fury. The grapevine claims his rage in last night's meeting was likened to the nuclear detonation on Bikini Island.

I stop by Christine's station in the lobby for a brief moment after the Suits and the Board disband their two hour meeting.

"Mission accomplished?" I ask, meaning did they decide on a course of action. My stomach is tied in knots, wondering when I'll be called in to defend myself—or to receive walking papers—and Christine is bound to be one of the first to know.

Christine snickers and casts a glance around the lobby to make sure we can't be overheard. "They don't know whether to shit or go blind, Frannie. It'd be really funny if I knew for certain this wasn't going to land Stewart in jail."

"I know. I feel terrible, like asking him for help tempted fate just one too many times. It's killing me."

"Go for a walk. It might do you some good. But don't fall down this time." She sends a disgusted look at the Executive elevator as it chimes; the doors open and let out a wave of Power Suits, all chattering animatedly, sounding serious and knowledgeable as they throw out terms like "this could prove to be problematic" and "when we've consulted our experts, we'll reconvene" as though they're at a world summit.

As I head out the side door to go to the walking track, I hear Gus Haldemann murmur in an aside to Sam, "I bet they don't have these kinds of colossal fuck-ups at Microsoft," which cracks me up.

I cross the parking lot to the walking track, but I don't walk—no sense tempting fate anymore than I already have. I take a seat on a bench in the shade of a flowering almond tree and watch the traffic go by on the distant street. I try to gauge my level of worry but frankly, I'm so saturated with tension I'm numb.

"Do you mind if I sit with you? It's such a peaceful spot, and I'd like to share it with someone."

I look up to find an attractive sixtyish woman blotting out the sunlight. Her smart page-boy is mostly silver but her face is relatively unlined. Sharp green eyes, wide and friendly, remain steadily on mine as she waits for my permission to sit.

"Please do. It's nice to have company sometimes."

She slides gracefully onto the bench, settling her small handbag in her lap, and her relaxed posture belies an elegance that fairly shouts money. I wonder what she's doing just walking around L.A. in the middle of the day, sharing benches with strangers on private property.

"Do you work there?" she asks, motioning to the building behind us.

"At Harper & Lyttle? Yes."

"Do you like it?" Her voice is like the throaty chirp of a large, exotic bird, modulated low to invite the listener to lean closer to hear her, welcoming intimate conversation.

"Most days," I reply with a sigh. "I love the work I

do. I just don't care much for office politics, and that place if rife with it."

"Most offices are. What is the nature of your duties?"

I shrug. "Other than doing the impossible for the ungrateful? I'm a training specialist. I prepare training materials in the form of manuals, presentations, and videos for our clients, showing them how to best utilize our software."

She's silent for a moment, then smiles engagingly. "Is that recited off your resumé?"

After a stunned moment, I laugh. "Yeah. How'd you guess?"

"It's all in the tone and the body language. You straightened your shoulders and your voice became monotone." At my surprised look, she explains, "In my former life as a member of the business community, I held a degree not only in business management but in interpersonal communications as well. And you're an easy study, Miss—?"

"Freeman. But please call me Frannie."

"Is it your name?" Her brow arches as she pokes gentle fun at me.

"So they tell me, although truth be told, the name is associated with any number of humiliating events, so perhaps I should claim to be something more exotic, such as a Sabrina or perhaps a Chantal. I knew a girl in high school whose name was Tialene. Scandinavian, I guess."

"Or Roxanne," she suggests idly.

"Is that your name?"

She sends me a sidelong glance. "So they tell me," she quips, tongue firmly in cheek.

I grin. "So, Roxanne, do *you* work at Harper & Lyttle?" It's not really an odd question; there are some people I've never seen, never even heard of. The company is very large, and we're so busy in Training that sometimes we rarely see anyone outside our own division.

"No, ma'am. I...dabble in business here and there but I am, for the most part, retired and loving it." Roxanne turns in her seat to face me. "Tell me about your work."

I do, and she listens to every word as though I'm telling the most fascinating adventure story. And for some reason I find myself telling her about some of those embarrassing moments I mentioned in passing: my skirt stuffed into the back of my pantyhose; passing out after too many margaritas at Tony's and then subsequently giving my boss a hickey (I leave out the information that we'd already engaged in much more intimate acts); my neighbor videoing the humiliating end of my date with Eric Edwards and my airing of said video to all Eric's friends in a training meeting; being thrown up on; and, God love us, even the meeting during which Malia shoved the Clearblue Easy meant for me across the table to Morgan. All, of course, without naming names. I'm not a complete idiot, thanks.

Roxanne listens attentively, laughs unapologetically, and empathizes sincerely. At one point, when I tell her about taking down Sam in the hallway after the pancake breakfast, she laughs until she cries. Finally her hand falls on my shoulder—small, elegant, but strong and reassuring—and her smile fades.

"Tell me, Frannie, this mysterious man you keep mentioning—is he your lover?"

I blush so deeply my face burns and itches. "Well..."

"I don't mean to be indelicate, but is there a problem in your relationship with him?"

For some reason I can't look her in the eye. It isn't that I'm ashamed of my relationship with Sam, but I can't expect anyone to understand the circumstances unless they're in the thick of it. I mean, for God's sake, even my best friend doesn't understand it.

"Yes," I reply at last. "He's married. It's…the long and short of it is he was tricked into marrying her—she took advantage of the fact he was very intoxicated. He's told her he's divorcing her, but…he ran into some complications."

"Oh? Is she pregnant?"

I look up, shocked. But it seems an innocent question, not a knowing probe. "Good God, I hope not!" I exclaim. "I'll eviscerate him if she is! No, pregnancy isn't the problem. She's in and out of rehab—drinking, you see—and then…oh hell, there's been some interference from his father-in-law."

"Ah. Sometimes family can be intrusive."

"You're not shocked that I'm seeing a married man?" For some reason I can't identify, her coming away from our encounter with a good opinion of me is important.

Roxanne smiles brightly. "Darlin', I've seen it all. My own husband is a philanderer by nature. A leopard can't change his spots, and I knew he was a leopard when I married him. He, on the other hand, thinks his being discreet makes me blind, deaf, and dumb." She pauses, considering. "Men are idiots."

"Amen, sister."

"Does this man love you?"

"Yes."

"Then his father-in-law should have no hold over him."

"But he does. It's…rather complicated, Roxanne. Truth be told, he has us backed into a corner and I'm having a hard time seeing a way out."

Roxanne levels a serious look at me. "Are you talking blackmail?"

"I don't know if that's what I'd call it. More like…very severe ultimatums. I can understand," I babble on quickly, lest she think I'm being melodramatic. "He's very worried about his daughter, and he's afraid she'll spiral past the point of recovery if S—if her husband leaves her."

"Interesting," she murmurs. "A very interesting situation, Frannie."

I glance at her from the corner of my eye. She's in finely tailored business slacks and a rust-colored silk shirt. A strand of pearls circles her slim throat, and I'd bet my meager 401K they're real. Just who the hell *is* this woman?

"What's the catch?" she asks mildly.

I let out a long sigh. "Oh, being fired, framed for sabotage, careers utterly destroyed—you know, the usual."

That I'm telling this stranger such private information shocks even me. I'm not normally a chatty person with my personal troubles, so you aren't the only one who is stunned by my open revelations. There's something about Roxanne that just plain opened the floodgates. In fact, she reminds me very much of Sam.

She whistles. "Wow."

"I know it sounds fantastic, like some kind of corporate thriller on the New York Times Best Seller list, but I swear it's true. Now I'm sitting out here while the Suits are deciding whether or not to fire the guy I convinced to help me out of this, and all I can think about is whether I want to go to Arby's or Taco Bell for dinner."

Roxanne starts to laugh. Soon we're both whooping like loons, scaring the few brave sparrows in the flowering almond so they take noisy, offended flight.

"I'm rather fond of Taco Bell myself," she says, wiping tears of laughter from her cheeks. She takes a deep breath. "You're a very delightful young woman. I've enjoyed our talk very much, so I'm going to do something I rarely do: give unsolicited advice."

I slant her a wry look. "I'd say after I let all my dirty

laundry spill out of the hamper, I've solicited such advice."

"Perhaps," Roxanne remarks noncommittally. "People who hold power over you only do so with your permission. You can remove that authority at any time you wish."

"I don't see how," I disagree. "I'm in no position to lay down ultimatums. I'm a lowly training specialist. The ultimatums are being issued from the top."

She raises a brow and glances at the building behind us. "Oh? Harper? Or Lyttle?"

"Lyttle retired two years ago; had one too many heart attacks and wanted to enjoy what remains of his golden years. No, if Lyttle were at the top of the food chain, I wouldn't be in this predicament. Harper's my problem."

Roxanne smiles serenely. "Think things over very thoroughly, Frannie Freeman, and start thinking outside the box. I believe you'll find that this Harper is no problem after all."

I regard her solemnly. She's definitely more educated in the finer art of people, but I can't help but think that she's way off target in this situation.

"I'll give it a whirl," I promise her—and I will, because I always keep my promises.

Her smile blazes like a supernova and she stands abruptly, holding out her hand for me to shake. I take it; her skin is cool in spite of the heat, and she sandwiches my hand between both of hers in what I call a business woman's handshake.

"Frannie, it's been a very definite pleasure. I hope you enjoy the rest of your day."

"I will now. Thank you, Roxanne."

She pauses long enough to reach into the side pocket of her handbag, drawing out a glossy white business card with bold red writing on it. She cups it in her hand, hiding the writing while she cocks her head at me.

"If you find yourself in a bind and you truly are backed into a corner, give me a call. I may be able to help you find a way out." She presses the card into my hand. "Good day, Frannie."

With a last smile, she turns and starts across the parking lot. I watch her until she gets into the closest car: a shiny green Jaguar XKR. As the sun moves across the car the shade of green changes; custom paint job on top of a whole host of amenities, no doubt. *That* baby didn't come cheap.

Then she's gone, speeding away from Harper & Lyttle, and I look down at the card. My heart stutters and my breath stops in my throat at the unexpected words printed in red: *R. EVELYN HARPER, CHAIRPERSON, BOARD OF DIRECTORS, HARPER & LYTTLE, INC.*

Garland Harper's wife.

YOU WOULD HAVE DONE THE SAME

"I think I just messed up really badly," I whisper to Christine as I pass her desk.

She glances up from the copy she's keying into the computer. "What'd you do now?"

I motion her into a nearby alcove where she can still hear her phone if it rings but which affords us a small measure of privacy. A quick glance around the lobby assures me we're alone.

"I went and sat on a bench by the walking track, and this lady came and sat down beside me. We were talking about this and that, and for some reason I started telling her about all the stupid shit that's always happening to me. Next thing I know, I've told her about…"

Christine's expression is horrified. "Fran, you did *not* tell a stranger what's going on here, did you?"

"Well, not in specifics, but…well, enough." I have the grace to show my shame, which—as usual—knows no bounds.

She closes her eyes briefly and grits her teeth. "Who was she? Do you know?"

"Evelyn Harper," I whisper. Christine actually groans. "I didn't know who she was until she gave me her business card as she was leaving. Get this, Chris— she said to call her if I find myself backed into a corner."

"Women like Evelyn Harper don't help people like us, Frannie," she says in exasperation. "She's a Suit like any other Suit, only she's Gucci instead of Christopher Banks. Oh my God...sometimes I can't believe we let you walk around loose!"

"I'm sorry, Chris," I say meekly. "Do you think I'm screwed?"

She thinks it over for a long moment, and finally shrugs. "Damned if I know. But you better go back to your desk where you can cause the least amount of trouble."

"I think you're forgetting about the fire sprinkler incident," I remind her.

She grins. "Good point." She gives me a shove toward the stairs. The elevator bell dings, and I scurry up to my second floor section.

No one has even noticed I've been gone for more than an hour. Stella is conducting an on-site training for one of our new clients, and Gretchen is engrossed in her project, furiously clicking her mouse button and scribbling hurried notes with her other hand. She's left-handed and somehow she's developed the skill of mousing with her right hand so that she can take notes while she navigates the software menus. It's stupid, but I envy her this skill.

Gretchen grunts a response to my greeting, not even looking up. I take a deep breath, push aside the crushing worry that seems to be my constant companion, and dive into my own project.

Gradually, I realize the building is silent and the light filtering through the open blinds in Sam's office has gone soft and blue. The overhead fluorescents are programmed to go off automatically at seven p.m. I didn't notice when they blinked out; I always have my desk lamp on, as well as the under-cabinet light that came with my new cube, and when I get into my work nothing short of a bomb—or Sam—will get my attention.

"Going home tonight, Frannie?" he asks from behind me, leaning over the back of my chair to nuzzle my neck. His aftershave, that clean, woodsy scent that so drives me wild, catapults me out of the complicated video presentation I'm making.

"Thank God this video is by keystroke and mouse-click and not in real time," I murmur, letting my head drop back against his shoulder.

He chuckles. "Let's go home, Frannie. I've got greater plans for the evening than waiting for you to get done with this silly thing."

"This 'silly thing,' as you so eloquently put it, is my job, which I sadly neglected today."

His hand slips from my shoulder to cup my breast. I can feel the heat of his skin through my shirt and bra. His voice drops to an intimate whisper.

"I saw you loafing out on the bench talking to someone, but I couldn't see who it was." His fingers are now inching their way under the hem of my skirt.

Before I can tell him about my blunder with Evelyn Harper, we hear the snick of the emergency staircase door closing. No one uses the stairs at Harper & Lyttle, even though our building is supposedly secure and we have 24-hour security guards. We're still in L.A., and we have a healthy caution of secluded places.

Sam is obviously thinking along the same lines as me; the paranoia of our situation drives us to act. Being caught together in a compromising position could give Harper inarguable reason to get rid of either Sam or me—or both of us.

He puts his finger to my lips to caution me to silence and turns my chair so I can see him. His finger sliding across his throat cues me to cut the power to my lights and computer; I slip my foot under my desk and step on the power switch of my surge protector, the quickest solution.

Cautious footsteps are coming toward the cubicles. Sam lifts me out of my chair silently, and I slip off my pumps so that we can tiptoe silently out of my area and into the abandoned, dark cubes of our downsized comrades. He shoves me down to crouch on the floor behind him and leans around the partition, trying to peer through the darkness.

A light goes on nearby. A moment later comes the rustle of paper and the rhythmic whack of…the hole punch? Sam opens his cell phone to give us a glimmer of light, shielding it with his suit jacket, and mouths "What the fuck?" I shrug, unable to fathom why someone would sneak up here at nearly nine o'clock at night to use a hole punch.

The unmistakable pounding of one performing percussive maintenance on a faulty office gadget tells me the intruder is at Stella's desk; her hole punch is legendary for jamming. I bend my head to muffle my laughter against my arm.

It was bound to happen. It's been months since I've experienced abject humiliation, so I'm not really surprised when the back seam of my skirt gives way with a loud, stitch-popping rip. Sam puts his finger to his lips, exasperated, but he knows it's too late. The sound fairly echoes in the empty wing. He topples sideways off his knees and sits against the wall of the cube, body shaking with suppressed laughter, waiting for the intruder to ferret us out.

And not long after, the bouncing beam of a flashlight pins us in its glare. Sam holds his hand up over his eyes.

"Can you lower the light? I think you've burned my retinas."

"Mr. Harrison?" comes the incredulous reply. The beam is lowered and in the dim glow we can see the round, brown face of Harold, one of the night shift security guards. The light bounces to me. "And Miz Freeman? What are you guys doing hiding in here?"

"We were just getting ready to leave when—" I begin, but understanding has already dawned on Harold.

He holds up his hand to stop me, shaking his head. "I don't want to know," he says, and adds under his breath, "Damn office affairs."

"What are *you* doing here?" Sam asks. "Killing the hole punch?"

"Damn thing jammed. I was going to use Miz Freeman's, but her light wouldn't come on. Speaking of which…why don't we head over to the light? It's creeping me out standing here talking to you in the dark. What was that sound I heard, anyway?"

I can feel the color blooming in my face. "Ah—"

"Not sure," Sam interrupts, shrugs out of his suit jacket, and drapes it around my shoulders. He's a large man, tall and muscled, so the hem falls to my knees, covering my ripped skirt. He helps me to my feet and we follow Harold to Stella's desk. He's about halfway finished punching holes in a sheaf of paper.

"What's that, Harold?" I ask, trying to see the print.

"Ah…" he says, looking embarrassed. "It's a novel."

"You don't say!" Sam exclaims. "Mystery? Intrigue? Let me guess—spy game?"

Whoever says black men can't blush is lying big-time. "Ummm…er…no."

While he's dealing with Sam, Harold doesn't notice me reaching for the top-most sheet on the stack already punched. I turn it over and scan the text.

Her heaving bosoms showed every danger of spilling from her bodice, but in the heat of her anger, Charity did not notice. Marcus, however, could not keep his eyes from the rounded globes, rising like perfect, gleaming pearls from the silk of her gown, rose-petal tips a fraction of an inch from full exposure.

"WOOT!" I holler, startling the men. "You go, Marcus!"

Harold, mouth pressed into a grim, humiliated line, snatches the sheet from my hand and slaps it back into the stack.

"Awesome, Harold. Is it a historical romance? Would your wife mind if I read it?"

Oh, hell...I spoke out loud again, didn't I? I might as well admit it; denying it is like closing the barn door after the horse has escaped. I'm a sucker for romance stories, especially historical tales. Give me heaving bosoms and throbbing manhoods and orgasms couched in careful analogy. It's my secret passion, if you'll pardon the pun.

"It's...ah...not my wife's," says Harold. "Er...*I* wrote it." His hand hovers protectively over the manuscript and he glowers at me as though I've shown every indication of grabbing the sheaf of papers and running.

"C'mon, Harold. I love historical romances. I'll make a quick copy and give you back the original."

Sam covers his ears. "You are not really talking about taking a Xerox subsidy in front of your boss, are you, Frannie?"

"Oh, whatever. As if just last month you didn't photocopy all your tax returns since the dawn of time."

Harold wavers, and I fix him with a puppy-dog stare. He's apparently susceptible to such looks (unlike Sam, who usually just rolls his eyes and ignores me), for he hands me the stack of papers.

"Just be honest when you tell me what you think of it after you've read it."

Sam snorts. "Don't worry—she will. Look, Fran, I need to get home. I'm tired and my eyeballs feel like I just walked through the Sahara with no sunglasses. Can you get yourself out all right?"

"Don't worry, Mr. Harrison. I'll walk her to her car."

"All right, then. See you later, Fran." He smiles softly and sidles past me. I watch him until he's vanished around a corner, and catch Harold's smirk.

"Oh, just stop!" My own blush floods my face.

Harold chuckles. "All right. You don't breathe a

word about that manuscript to anyone, and I don't breathe a word about…that."

"It's a deal."

"Now, Miz Freeman, I have some rounds to complete. I'll meet you in the lobby downstairs in about fifteen minutes. That give you enough time to misuse company resources?"

I beam at him. "Plenty."

Still chuckling, he saunters off to complete his rounds, and I shove the manuscript into the copier and hit the GO button. It doesn't take long to copy; there are probably only 200 or so pages. In less than fifteen minutes, I tap my stack neatly, secure it with a binder clip (also belonging to Harper & Lyttle), and grab my things from my cube. My own hole punch is much easier to use than Stella's, so I finish Harold's interrupted hole-punching job—it's the least I can do—put everything away, and turn off Stella's light as I leave, heading for the stairs. Because I'm me, I hold onto the polished nickel railing all the way down, not wanting anyone to find me in a crumpled heap at the bottom when they come in tomorrow morning.

The lobby is just as dark as the Training section, which I find unusual. The security guards—there are three of them any given night—share the lobby receptionist's desk, and usually the brass desk lamps by each computer station burn all night.

I follow a shaft of sodium-arc light streaming in through the front windows and puddles at the bottom of the staircase and head for the seating area near the door, where I feel less enclosed by the darkness.

And as only I can do, the last three steps are taken with flailing of arms and loss of balance, with legs sprawling askew and my fall from grace (although it can be debated I have any) marked by the ding of the elevator bell. My cheek bounces off the granite floor and I see stars—literally: giant bursts of brilliant color that obscure my vision. I close my eyes, swearing a silent blue streak that is, no doubt, forming a giant swear bubble above my head that would put any of Stella's or Christine's to shame. When I open my eyes again, I see the pair of expensive black Marc Jacobs slip-ons directly before me. I curse aloud.

"Son-of-a-motherfucking bitch!"

"Agreed, Ms. Freeman."

I push myself upright and scoot backward to the step, hoisting myself up with a gingerness that is all too familiar, and heave a sigh that expresses all the things I have no words for—even curse words. Garland Harper hesitates a moment, then eases himself down beside me.

"Are you all right?"

"Oh, that? I'm used to it. Happens all the time." I wave a hand negligently at the floor where I'm sure I left a significant amount of my DNA; my cheek is raw and burning.

"So I hear."

"Who turned out the lights?"

"They stay off now unless security is escorting someone to their car," he replies. "Conserving energy."

"Oh. Well, that's good."

I can't believe I'm sitting here having a conversation about saving energy with the man who has become the bane of my existence. As though he's thinking about the incongruity as well, he lets silence fall between us, a silence so complete I can hear the faint sighing of the air conditioner and the rustle of paper somewhere as the cool air moves across it.

"You're seeing Sam again," he says at length. I don't reply. "I thought I'd made it clear what would happen if you did."

"You did."

"And yet here we are."

"Yes."

He frowns into the darkness, barely visible in the

gloom. "I admit I don't understand."

"I wouldn't expect you to, Mr. Harper."

We let the silence hang between us again. He knows he doesn't need to reiterate his threat; I know that pleading for mercy is futile.

At long last, he rises and starts toward the front door. Several steps away, he stops and half-turns.

"If you had a daughter, you would have done the same."

"There's where you're wrong."

He grunts and leaves without another word. Through the bank of windows, I watch him get in his Mercedes and drive out of the parking lot.

I probe my wounded cheek, wincing at the pain; it's already swollen, and I won't take any bets on whether or not I'll have a black eye tomorrow because I think it's a given. I wonder how I'm going to explain my disheveled appearance and bruised cheek to Harold; I guess I'll just have to try to keep my right side toward him.

But it proves no problem; Harold doesn't seem to notice anything's wrong as he takes his manuscript from me and walks me to my car. He wishes me a cheery goodnight and heads back into the building, whistling.

Sam's going to flip. I think about the business card in my purse and wonder if it's already time to use it.

2:07 ON A TUESDAY AFTERNOON

Remember I mentioned that universal shift to maintain balance every time something appears to be going well? It stands to reason it would work in the opposite order: For every time some schmuck is bent over the barrel, the universe equalizes by allowing something fantastically good to happen to said schmuck.

Not so. I offer 2:07 on a Tuesday afternoon as proof.

Sam did indeed flip when he saw my bruising eye, but only because it's one more injury on top of a long history of them. He doesn't say much about my conversation with Garland Harper, but he's distracted and thoughtful for most of the evening. By the time we go to bed, his demeanor has become that of a man who has made some difficult resolution, and I'm left with the uneasy feeling he's going to do something that screws all of us.

I don't explain my black eye to anyone but Christine, so for most of the afternoon I see Gretchen shooting suspicious glares Sam's way even though I've assured her he hasn't beaten me. She didn't even smile when I pointed out he doesn't even own wife-beater shirts. Mid-morning I hear her in a whispered conversation on the phone, and I surmise she's called Gus about my wound. Judging from the pinched look on her face when she hangs up, he's told her to mind her own business.

Stella doesn't even blink when she sees it; she just gives me a wicked smile and tells me not to brace myself against the headboard anymore. I let it ride; it's easier to let her think this happened in a rowdy bout of sex than it is to explain the convoluted mess that has become my life.

She has been abnormally quiet ever since; in fact, the whole section is unusually hushed, and there's a feeling of impending chaos that has us all on edge. I can hear the tick of the wall clock, and for some reason I keep checking the time and thinking *No, not yet. A little while longer until...* Until what, I don't know. Like I said, it's that feeling of impending chaos about to strike.

All morning and through the early afternoon, I debate the pros and cons of dialing the number on that business card. While I have every confidence, despite Christine's caution, that Evelyn Harper can and will help us for whatever personal motives she harbors (because her husband's a douche bag, perhaps?), for some reason I don't want to call on her unless there is absolutely no other choice. Call it stupid pride if you want—and hell, you're probably right—but her intervention on our behalf seems almost as bad as her husband's on behalf of his bastard daughter.

Also, I want to ask Sam first, and he's been in his office with some mysterious man who showed up with news that made him tense and angry. He ushered his visitor behind closed doors and drawn blinds. Sam came out for coffee once, and in the brief moment the door was open I saw the stranger pacing around the office as he spoke with someone on the phone, his hands raking nervously through his hair, his words unintelligible but his tone passionate. Then Sam went back in, and I haven't seen either of them since.

Tick...tick...tick...

I look up at precisely 2:07 p.m. and abruptly get up

from my chair. The tension is killing me, so I grab my coffee cup and head for the break room. Concerned, Gretchen and Stella tag along after me. I'm a little annoyed at the time, but in retrospect it's a good thing they follow.

The layout of Harper & Lyttle makes me think that some blind architect drew up the plans. You enter the main doors of the building into a lobby that occupies the front half of the main level (the back half is an on-site health center where employees work out). The reception desk is on the left, just in front of a wide staircase leading up to the second level—our floor. These stairs gently curve 90 degrees and end at a landing with a balcony overlooking the reception desk. The break room faces this landing.

A long hallway just past the break room runs past the restrooms on the right and leads to the Training section. Ordinarily, we exercise caution coming around the corner to the break room; you never know who's coming in the opposite direction carrying hot coffee—and for the life of me I'll never understand why, in a country where you drive on the right, people don't also *walk* on the right. As soon as they become pedestrians, it's a free-for-all. Seriously, I want to get a tee-shirt to wear when I go to the mall that says "Drive on the right? Walk on the right!" because there are some really rude assholes who will just mow you down in your tracks even though they're walking on the wrong side.

Anyway, we round this corner today without our customary caution, and I stop dead in my tracks, face-to-face with Malia Moreno Harrison, who is as drunk as a lord and wild-eyed with bad ideas. Gretch and Stella, not paying attention, ram into me from behind and cold coffee spills down the back of my shirt.

Malia wastes no time; she advances on me, swinging her fist, but apparently in her drunkenness she's forgotten she's right-handed. Her left-handed roundhouse misses me by a foot but sends her careening into me—off-balance in more ways than one—and down we go, taking Stella with us. Gretchen has the foresight and reflexes to jump out of the way at the last second. As Malia begins screeching obscenities like a banshee, trying for all she's worth to work her hands around my throat, Gretchen sheds her pumps and sprints for our section, hollering for Sam at the top of her lungs.

If not for the fact that it seems like Malaria has turned into an insane octopus with eight swinging fists hell-bent on causing mayhem and misery, I'd have to laugh at the entire scene: Gretchen trying to sprint in her slim-line business skirt, sans shoes, her shouts of "SAM! SAM COME QUICK! SHE'S KILLING FRANNIE!!" barely audible over Malaria's slurred shrieking: "YOU HOME-WRECKIN' WHORE I'M GONNA KICK YOUR FORNICATING ASS!"

As it stands, however, I have my hands full trying to keep her flailing fists from making contact with my face. I'm not a hundred-percent successful, either; as Sam's running footsteps approach, accompanied by Gretchen's implorations to intervene before Malia kills me, Malia's clenched right hand makes accidental contact with my already bruised left cheek.

"HA!" she cackles, and swings again.

I dodge—forgetting that Stella is at the bottom of this dog-pile, unsuccessfully trying to extricate herself. Malia's fist crashes into Stella's jaw, and it's like poking an angry bull in the ass with a pitchfork. Stella's arms shoot out, capturing me between her and Malia. Her hands grab fistfuls of Malia's hair, and we become a rolling mass of feminine fury. Stella is a liability to me; her insistence on shaking Malia by her hair bashes my and Malia's heads together no less than four times by the time Sam wades in.

Through nothing short of heroic effort, Sam

manages grab the back of Malia's shirt through the tangle of thrashing limbs, and with a strength borne of desperation, yanks her upright with one arm and sets her on her feet, holding on to her shirt when she tries to fling herself onto me again.

Gretchen helps me and Stella to our feet. We've gathered a crowd of employees who are watching the festivities with the undisguised glee which only a public cat-fight can inspire.

"YOU BITCH!" Malia screeches. "DID YOU THINK I DIDN'T KNOW WHERE HE WAS SPENDING HIS NIGHTS?"

"Malia, shut up," Sam warns her.

In her drunken state, she misses the steely tone of his voice. No hen-pecked, spineless twat here, thank you very much. This is a man—a *real* man—at the end of his patience and tolerance.

"What the hell are you doing out of the clinic? You have another thirty days of rehab."

"OH REHAB YOURSELF, YOU CHEATING BASHTARD! YOU AND YOUR LITTLE PIECE OF ASSS—"

By now I've had enough of being called a whore and other such pleasantries. "DON'T ACT LIKE YOU'RE ALL INNOCENT IN THIS, YOU CONNIVING BITCH!" She shuts up. "Have you forgotten how you roofied him and dressed like me to get him to marry you in the first place? Why don't you tell everyone what you did?"

"SHUT UP, WH—"

"YOU CALL ME A WHORE ONE MORE TIME AND I'LL KNOCK YOUR TEETH DOWN YOUR LYING THROAT, YOU FUCKING BITCH!" She falls into stunned silence. "Why'd you do it, Malia? You knew he didn't want you and you didn't really even want him, so *why*?"

She fixes me with a bleary glare, her unfocused eyes

unsuccessfully trying to stay locked on mine. There is such longing and disappointment and jealousy in her gaze that I flinch, feeling for a moment a flash of complete empathy. I'd felt exactly these things when Sam married her.

"Why should you have everything?"

I gape at her in shock. Everything? She thinks I have everything even as she stands there wearing a ring from the man I love, the man she's had for the last two and a half years? My empathy vanishes.

The elevator dings behind us and a collective gasp rises from our audience. I don't look away from Malia— one should never look away from a rampaging tigress. I'm vaguely aware of either Gretchen or Stella pulling me out of the way as Garland Harper steps between me and my quarry, an unmistakable, protective barrier.

"I'll thank you to unhand the lady," says Garland to Sam.

"That's no lady," Stella quips, *sotto voce*. "That's Sam's wife!" The crowd breaks up laughing; Harper is not amused.

Sam straightens his shoulders. "If by 'lady' you mean this drunkard screeching like the shrew she is, the answer is no. She's already assaulted two people."

Garland Harper equals Sam in height and build, and I think the years Sam has spent as his passive son-in-law—regardless of whether Sam knew that was their relationship—has given Harper the erroneous impression that he'll capitulate without question. So to say Sam's defiance comes as a surprise to Harper would be putting it mildly, although Harper is too shrewd to challenge him publicly. His fury at being defied shows in the set of his shoulders and his tightly controlled movements as he pries Malia's shirt out of Sam's grip.

"Let's go, Malia," he says gently to his daughter. He beams a laser glare around the crowd of employees gathered around us. "Everyone get back to your work.

This does not concern you." When no one moves, his scowl becomes positively frightening. "I have a very good memory. If you don't go now, I *will* remember whom I had to tell twice."

The crowd scatters like frightened chickens (squawking like them, too). Harper guides Malia to the head of the stairs and there he pauses, sending me a look over his shoulder. I don't need an interpreter to translate: I'm toast; completely blackened, utterly incinerated toast.

So there's really nothing to lose, is there—except Sam.

I step forward. Malia raises her chin in challenge, but before I can say anything, Sam clears his throat, his shoulders straightened resolutely.

"Harper."

Harper stops; his expression as he returns Sam's stare is dangerous. "This probably isn't the best time for this, Sam."

Sam doesn't back off. "I think it's the optimum time. Perhaps you'd like to explain why you burdened this company with a woman who has had four violent mental breakdowns since the age of sixteen, and who spent a year and a half in a mental facility in her early twenties after assaulting a coworker. And why, upon her release from that facility, you hired her here and promoted her to a position of authority despite this being an environment of tremendous stress."

Malia's face blanches white. Harper is furious.

"How the *hell*—"

"I just concluded a *very* interesting conversation with Bradley Moreno, Malia's first husband, who came to see me out of a sense of duty. Seems he thought there were a few things I should be made aware of—such as my wife's mental history."

From the corner of my eye, I see Christine—who is standing at the bottom of the stairs, unabashedly eavesdropping—give a violent start of shock. She swings around the railing and begins coming up the stairs slowly, hanging on every word for another mention of her former lover.

"Which brings my next question, sir. Why the hell did you put the rest of this company at risk? This woman has a history of assault due to mental illness! Did you even think about the safety of your employees?"

Hot color suffuses Harper's face, and he steps forward, his warning finger an inch from Sam's nose. Sam doesn't even flinch. "That's enough, Sam. None of this is the business of anyone outside my family."

"But you forget." Sam cuts across him, cold as a glacier. "I *am* family."

Malia sways on her feet, her hue on the grey side now. Harper flicks a glance at her, but I can't tell what kind of glance it is. He's a shrewd man and has the consummate businessman's ability to mask all thought.

"I hardly think—"

"I'd say that's a very accurate statement," replies Sam with some asperity. "You make your only child beg and crawl for your approval and acknowledgement—neither of which she'll ever have. Then you have the unmitigated gall to slap band-aids, such as meaningless promotions, over wounds that are bleeding like rivers and pretend everything is okay because she *looks* so successful. Never mind that she's really hanging on by her fingernails, because when it comes to the bottom line, you really don't care as long as she stays out of your hair and doesn't cause you too many problems."

A low moan comes from Malia, and she sinks to her knees. Harper's restraining hand hangs in mid-air as she collapses beyond his reach. She looks like she's going to throw up.

"You know nothing about this, Sam," he rasps, the color bleeding away from his face and leaving behind random blotches of red.

Sam ignores him, moving swiftly across the space to

his erstwhile wife. He kneels before her and takes her hands, drawing her to her feet. Tears stream from her eyes in a flood, but neither of them makes any move to blot them.

"I want a divorce. Not because you have emotional issues, not because you tricked me into marriage in the first place, and not because of Frannie, but because you and I both know this isn't right."

She stares at him, and for a moment I'm scared he'll be swayed by those dark, liquid eyes. But then her head bobs convulsively. "I think that's best."

Harper struts forward aggressively. "You've made your choice, Sam. It's a bad one, but—"

"Oh, I think it will stand him in good stead," remarks a pleasant voice behind him.

So intent have we all been that we failed to notice the pretty, petite woman coming up the stairs behind him, stepping delicately around Christine, who has stopped halfway up the steps. Elegantly attired and impeccably mannered, Roxanne Evelyn Harper insinuates herself between her husband and Sam, her fingers gently squeezing Sam's arm as she guides him out of the way.

"Evelyn," Harper says, a little worried.

"I think we've given enough fodder for the gossip mill, considering the crowd that is no doubt listening behind that door," and she waves a negligent hand at the closed door through which the second floor Harper & Lyttle employees had dispersed. "Let's go."

Without further ado, Evelyn takes his arm and draws him away from Malia, sending me a serene smile over her shoulder as she moves him toward the elevator. Harper sends Malia an eloquent look as he leaves, and her whole body seems to sag as she turns to make her own escape.

She hesitates at the top of the stairs, glancing without interest at Christine. A split second later her gaze flies back to her face. Christine wears an expression of intense smugness.

"You! What are *you*—" Her hand floats up to her hair, her fingers combing through the disheveled strands. "Your hair…I didn't recognize…"

"Yeah, new hair color, new job, new name, but I still couldn't shake you."

"Karma sucks," Malia says with only the faintest tremor in her voice.

"You're telling me," Chris replies. She flattens herself against the stair rail to give Malia as much passing room as possible.

Malia turns to give one last look at Sam, who stares back impassively for a long moment, and then nods once. She teeters on the step for a precarious moment— she's sobered up considerably since the cat-fight, or perhaps she's just more alert with the adrenaline surge, but she's still drunk. I reach out to steady her, but she's already tottering down to the lobby, slow and defeated.

"You all right, Fran?" Sam asks, tipping my face up to the fluorescent lights to examine my black eye, which by now should be the exact shade of black as the deepest, darkest pit of hell and is throbbing like crazy. My shirt is stiff with the drying coffee Stella or Gretchen poured down my back—and, I notice belatedly, is ripped in three strategic places—my head aches fiercely, and I have numerous other contusions and abrasions from the wild struggle on the carpet.

I feel fantastic.

"You bet I am."

"Then let's—"

"Sam, she's getting in her car!" Christine shouts in alarm. The whole front of the building is constructed of windows; ordinarily the view, especially at sunset, is spectacular if you can appreciate the beauty of an urban landscape. But the sight that meets our eyes is not beautiful in the slightest: a drunk, emotional woman getting behind the wheel of a *very* fast Porsche.

"*Shit!*" Sam yells and races down the stairs at top

speed, his "saving people" complex kicking into action. I hear his footfalls pound across the lobby tiles and the door slams open as he crashes through it. Then he's visible again, sprinting across the parking lot to the Porsche.

Malia finally figures out how to start the car—which tells you how drunk she still is—and she starts to back out just as Sam reaches her. He pounds on the back fender and jumps out of the way. She slams on the brakes, tires screeching, and gets out, red in the face and already screaming.

Sam shouts back, gesturing angrily with his arms. Malia covers her face briefly with her hands and then lowers them.

"Is she crying?" Christine snorts, completely unsympathetic.

Sam is still speaking vehemently, but Malia has stopped listening. She leans into the car and stands back up, leveling something at him that makes him shut up immediately. His hands held up in a placating manner, he begins to back away cautiously.

My heart stops. "Oh my God, she has a gun! Chris, call 9-1-1!"

I don't remember much about my headlong flight down the stairs, even though at the time it seemed to happen in slow motion. I fly across the lobby to the front doors, barely aware that Gus Haldemann is pacing me. We crash out the doors at the same time. Gus moves to the right to circle around Malia, unseen, but I'm barreling across the parking lot like a torpedo in plain view.

Thunder cracks the air, and I don't understand that it's gunfire until Sam stumbles backward and crimson blooms on the left-hand shoulder of his shirt. He yells in pain and falls to the blacktop, clutching his shoulder, blood spurting between his fingers.

"SAM!" I scream. *"OH MY GOD, SAM!"*

The gun swings my way. Someone yells my name and tackles me from the side as thunder booms again. The impact from the hard asphalt jars every aching bone in my body and I feel blood running in several places, but I'm not given time to assess my injuries. Gus hauls me to my feet and drags me back to the relative safety of the portico, where he takes cover behind a supporting pillar a second before a bullet punctures the window behind us.

I know Hollywood likes to show windows shattering from the impact of a bullet, but it doesn't really happen that way. Our windows are very thick and layered with polyvinyl butyral to withstand earthquakes. The bullet hits, leaving a neat hole and a small spider web of cracks.

I realize belatedly that… "She's shooting at me!"

"No fucking kidding!" Gus shouts back.

"Sam!" I start to lean around the pillar and Malia fires again, the bullet ricocheting off the side of our pillar.

Gus flinches as chips of stone shrapnel strike his cheek, leaving threads of blood, and he shakes me impatiently, pinning me against the pillar. "You can't help him if you're dead, Frannie!"

I can see Sam in the reflection of the front windows, his white shirt like a homing beacon for my eyes. He's dragged himself slowly to his feet and is staggering toward the unused guardhouse in the middle of the parking lot. His hand, cupped over the bullet wound in his shoulder, is streaked with scarlet. Malia hasn't noticed; she's intently watching for me to poke my head out so she can get a bead on me.

Breathing doesn't come easier until he's made it to the small structure and is out of her line of sight. He sinks down to the pavement, leaning against the structure and panting heavily.

Malia realizes too late her prey has escaped, and the distant sound of sirens coming toward Harper & Lyttle seems to penetrate her murderous fog. She jumps into the Porsche, fires the engine with a roar, and speeds out of the parking lot and onto the street, tires screeching, engine revving, car weaving dangerously. She cuts off two cars in the oncoming lanes, and they swerve and collide. Then she rounds a corner, bouncing up over the curb and nearly running down a pedestrian, and vanishes from sight.

I break away from Gus and race across the parking lot as fast as my skirt and pumps will allow, skidding to a stop beside Sam and adding fresh abrasions—and fresh holes in my pantyhose—as I drop to my knees beside him. A fine sheen of sweat coats his face, but the flow of blood from his shoulder has slowed.

"Oh God, Sam, she *shot* you! The bitch actually *shot* you!"

Sam chuckles weakly. "You think now that I took a bullet for you, Gretchen will finally believe I really love you?"

I start to laugh and cry at the same time. Sam reaches up with his good arm and pulls me down to him, trying to keep me away from the blood. But I don't care; he's alive and he'll be all right. I wrap my arms around him, blood and all, careful to avoid his bullet wound, and that's how the police and the paramedics find us.

FORGIVE

"So that's the whole story," I conclude, my throat raw and scratchy from my three hours of narrative. "May I have a glass of water?"

The cop interviewing me jumps as though I goosed him. His name is Palmer, and he's listened to my whole tale with very little interruption and undisguised, avid interest. And why not? It's full of sex, forbidden love, and corporate intrigue.

"There's a soda machine right outside. I'll get you one if you like."

"I don't drink soda," I reply, "but it's all right if you can't get me water. I'll do without."

He gets up with seeming reluctance and goes out the door, hollering for someone to get him a bottle of water. When he comes back, he plunks a cold plastic bottle in front of me, looks at the statement I had written earlier about the incident at Harper & Lyttle this afternoon, and looks back up at me.

"This should be a movie," he mutters. "Ms. Freeman, all I can offer by way of advice is next time make sure the man is not married."

I grin as I crack open the bottle. "There won't be a next time, Officer Palmer. The man is all I need."

He nods noncommittally. "We'll keep looking for Mrs. Harrison; a Porsche being driven like that won't be hard to find. Are you sure you don't want to press assault charges?"

"Look," I say patiently, wiping my mouth and capping the water bottle, the contents of which I half-drained in three gulps. "She's in a lot of trouble for shooting Sam. I don't really think I care about adding assault and battery. Besides, I gave back as much as I got. Call it square."

He sends me a stern look. "I think you're being dangerously lenient. I understand the lady has a drinking problem, but it doesn't excuse beating up and shooting people."

"And I'm not excusing her. She'll be in long enough for putting a bullet in Sam and shooting at me and Gus Haldemann. Listen, can I go now? It's been nearly four hours and Sam should be out of surgery. I'd like to get to the hospital."

I wasn't allowed in the ambulance. The cops at the scene tapped me to come down and give my statement right away once the paramedics were done patching up my knees and hands. I'm pretty sure I sprained my arm falling on it when Gus tackled me, too, but not surprisingly I have a sling at home I can use.

Gus Haldemann comes down as well, but since his statement only had to deal with the events of the day, he's sent on his way after forty-five minutes. Officer Palmer—I'm sure to his eternal regret—asks me the one question that opens the floodgates of this story: "What started all this, Ms. Freeman?"

And so I took him from beginning to end, and here we sit now, our backsides numb, my throat raw from talking, our eyes glazing over. Palmer sweeps my face with a practiced gaze and determines I've hit the wall.

"Sure, you can go. You need a ride?"

"Thank you, but no. Gus Haldemann's girlfriend brought my car down when she came to meet him."

He sighs. I don't know if he's glad to see me go

because it means the end of my chatter, or if he's sorry the whole sordid tale came to an end—he rather seemed to enjoy it. He holds out his hand as he stands, shaking mine as I rise with him.

"Thank you for coming down, Ms. Freeman. We'll let you know when we've caught up to Mrs. Harrison."

A blast of eighty-degree air hits me as I leave the air-conditioned confines of the police precinct and limp to my car. I fall into the driver's seat, my abraded knees and palms screaming with pain, my left arm and my head aching, and I head for Good Samaritan Hospital.

Sam is out of recovery and sleeping under sedation. Gus has beat me to the hospital, and he and Gretchen are sitting on the small sofa by the windows, holding hands. He stands immediately and offers me his seat—which tells me I must look as weary and wounded as I feel—but I shake my head and claim the armchair beside Sam's bed, turning it sideways so I can see them.

"Any news on Malia?" Gus asks.

"No. The police are looking for her. Looks like she'll be spending some jail time once they find her."

"Rich daddy, alcoholism…they'll probably send her to some country-club corrections center." Gretchen snorts her disgust. "Doctor says Sam will be fine; he'll have physical therapy for a while after his shoulder heals, and he may have limited mobility for the rest of his life."

"It's better than being dead," I remark.

"He would be," Gus interjects, "if she had been at a different angle when she shot him. The bullet ricocheted off his collarbone and went out the side of his arm. Had it gone the other direction, it would have hit his heart or his lung."

I glance at Sam, his face pale under his dark hair, IV line plugged into a vein on the back of his left hand, and I feel like doing some shooting myself. My dose of quinine will be swatting a malaria-bearing mosquito…

"Cops kept you a lot longer than they did me," Gus

ventures.

"They wanted to hear the whole story. I'm sure they regret it now—three hours later."

We all laugh quietly so we don't disturb Sam, but he mumbles sleepily anyway.

"What's that, big guy?" I ask, leaning over him to hear better.

"Wuzzufan," he clarifies, slurring his words every bit as much as his drunken, pistol-packing wife.

"That so?" I ask, grinning down at him. His eye closes and he trails off into silence.

I smooth his hair off his brow as he goes back to sleep, and I sit back down. "Anyone talked to Morgs today?"

Gretchen nods. "I called her while Sam was still in surgery. She says she'll bring the baby by your apartment once Sam's released. We'll drink and make bad jokes about Malaria."

"It's a date."

We make small talk for a while and when my eyes start to droop, Gus nudges Gretchen and they stand up.

"We're gonna go now, Fran. Tell Sam we'll be by to see him tomorrow." He surveys me critically. "You should get some sleep yourself."

"I'll doze on that sofa once you're gone," I promise, and I do.

There's something about the quiet hush of a hospital at night that lulls me right to sleep: the whisper of crepe-soled shoes on tiled floors, the quiet murmur of nurses conversing with patients and each other, the indistinct sounds of televisions in neighboring rooms.

I'm happily reliving one of my finer moments with Sam in my dreams when someone shakes me gently awake. I open my eyes. Jeremy Ingram, the head of Concept Development, is bent over me. He steps back as I sit up quickly.

"Ms. Freeman...may I call you Frannie?"

"Sure. Ah…Sam's still pretty drugged up, so you may have to wait to talk to him."

"That's all right. I'm actually here to talk to you. I was informed this would be the best place to check." His glance darts to Sam and then back again.

I rub my eyes, belatedly remembering I'm wearing mascara. Too late now; my knuckles are smeared with brown-black Clinique. I try to unobtrusively repair the damage while he tries to decide whether or not to mention I now resemble a raccoon. "What can I do for you, Mr. Ingram?"

"First off, you can call me Jeremy. Nice to meet you, Frannie."

He holds out his hand to shake, eyes my smeared knuckles, and draws back. The corner of his mouth twitches. He makes a motion under his eye, indicating where I've missed a noticeable smear. I take another swipe and arch a brow at him. He nods and smiles.

"What's up?"

"It's a long and complicated story," he begins, and then shakes his head. "So I'll give you the Reader's Digest version. I was Bradley Moreno's college roommate. When Brad—shall we say fell from grace?—he left SoCal, moved to Oregon, and started his own company. When he learned Amy was working here, he asked me to keep an eye on her, make sure she was all right."

"Amy?" I say, confused.

"Oh, I'm sorry. You'll know her as Christine. She changed her name after the whole…" He waved a hand to indicate the mess that had ended Christine and her lover.

I mull this over thoughtfully, wondering why Bradley couldn't be man enough to keep his own eye on his estranged lover. "And Bradley is…where? I know he was at Harper & Lyttle today talking to Sam. Why isn't he talking to Chris—er, Amy as well?"

He casts another glance at the bed and Sam's sleeping form. "You think we can take this down the hall to the waiting room? I don't want to disturb Sam."

I follow him to a nearby, softly lit waiting room, which thankfully is empty. There's a coffee pot and all the fixings, and I watch silently as he prepares a pot of steaming brew. I normally don't drink coffee this late—it must be nearing eleven p.m., but I'm groggy and ill-at-ease and wouldn't mind something to do with my hands.

Jeremy doesn't speak again until the coffee's made. He deposits a Styrofoam cup in my hands and takes his own to the chair opposite mine.

"So why doesn't he just come up and make sure she's all right?" I ask again. "I'm assuming he knows Malia works at H&L."

"He knows—I told him as soon as I learned Amy had been hired—which is why he was concerned." Something in my expression must speak volumes to him, for his lips twist into a wry smile. "Everyone makes mistakes, Frannie."

"Seems to me he let Christine pay for all of them."

"That's very unfair," he says with a note of censure. He scrubs a hand over his face and gives me a sheepish look, taking the sting from his reprimand. "Sorry. Barking orders and correcting behavior have become habits I'll be glad to lose."

"You're leaving Harper & Lyttle?"

He looks surprised. "It's long overdue. Truthfully, Fran, working with programmers the caliber of Vince Parker will be the death of me. I'm going to go work for Brad in Oregon. He needs an IT guy."

"You should have promoted Stewart," I reply sternly. "Age isn't always the determining factor in ability."

He ducks his head, looking like a small boy. A small, geeky boy.

"Jeremy, where does this leave Christine—er—Amy? Is Bradley…well, I suppose it's been a long time. With

Malia no doubt leaving the company, she should be safe enough."

Jeremy reaches into his back pocket for his wallet and takes out a business card, which he hands to me. "That's why I'm here. She can reach Bradley at any of those numbers. It's entirely up to her whether or not she calls, but he's never given up loving her. He can put her to work as well if she wants to come to Medford."

"Medford! Good God, who would *want* to go to Medford?" I blurt without thinking. He tips me a look, and I rush on, blushing, turning the card over in my hand thoughtfully. "I'll give it to her. Why didn't she recognize you?"

"She's never met me. The most she would ever have seen were college pictures Brad might have shown her, and quite frankly, I doubt she would recognize me from them, since we were drunk in most of them and my hair was long." He grins charmingly. "I only knew who she was because I screened her application for a position in my department; she listed her previous name. But anyway, please tell Amy that Brad really hopes she'll call."

I assure him I'll pass on the message. I can already hear her reaction now; no doubt there will be a large bubble of profanity hanging over her head that will rival the one over Stella's.

Jeremy stands, stuffing his hands into his jeans pockets, and offers me a crooked smile. "I must say, it was rather convenient that Brad was on the phone with Evelyn Harper when you and Malia started pulling each other's hair and scratching out each other's eyes."

I blush brightly. "Oh, stop. I wondered why she showed up just at that precise moment."

"Sam didn't tell you? Oh," he sails on without waiting for my response. "I suppose he hasn't been conscious enough. At any rate, I don't think you'll have any problems now. The problem software is being shuffled to a more skilled programmer, so poof." He clenches his hands into loose fists and then flings open his fingers in the universal *Poof! It's magic!* gesture. "Ammunition gone."

"You knew about all that? I thought we'd kept things pretty hush-hush."

He laughs heartily. "With a grapevine like ours...more like a vineyard," he mutters, shaking his head. "Actually, Stewart Drummond sang like a canary in a meeting with Evelyn Harper and me while Sam was in surgery."

"A canary, eh?" I laugh. "Well, I can't say I blame him."

"Take care of Sam, Frannie." He dips his head in farewell and scoots out the door.

I pour myself another cup of coffee and head back to Sam's room, where I sit for as long as I can keep my eyes open, pondering the tangled web caused by Garland Harper's inability to keep his pants zipped thirty years ago.

I sleep.

* * * * *

Sunlight is streaming through the open blinds when I'm shaken awake again, beams of brilliance stabbing my eyes. My head aches fiercely, probably from the impact with Malia's. I stare blearily up at Officer Palmer.

"I thought I'd find you here," he says quietly. "How is Mr. Harrison?"

"He'll be fine," I assure him, "mostly because Malia was too drunk to aim to kill."

"Good enough I can wake him?" Palmer asks seriously. He hasn't come with good news.

"No need," Sam speaks up. "I'm awake."

Palmer moves to the side of his bed and flashes his badge at Sam. "I'm sorry to trouble you, Mr. Harrison, but I'm afraid I have some bad news."

"You haven't found Malia yet," Sam guesses.

Palmer shoots an apprehensive glance at me. "No, sir—we *have* found her. She headed south and got on South Coast Highway. Witnesses say she was travelling at a high rate of speed and weaving all over the road. She lost control just south of Cardiff by the Sea, crossed into oncoming traffic, and struck a streetlight pole nearly head-on."

"Sweet Jesus!" I exclaim, standing up. "How badly is she hurt?"

Palmer shifts his gaze to me for a moment, and then back to Sam. "Concussion. They pumped her stomach at Scripps Memorial and kept her overnight for observation. She'll be transferred to a private mental facility sometime today."

Sam stares at him blankly. "Pumped her stomach?" he asks, completely bewildered. "Mental facility? For a concussion?"

"Oh, I apologize. I've left a few things out. Before the paramedics arrived, she managed to wash down half of a bottle of sedatives with some pretty good scotch. Because of the suicide attempt, she gets an automatic three-day vacation for mental evaluation."

"At least she'll be out of everyone's hair for a few days," I mutter.

"Longer than a while, I'll bet, given her history—both mental and criminal. I've obviously caught you at a bad time—I know I woke you both. We can have a more in-depth conversation later. I thought I should let you know the highlights as soon as possible."

"Yes," Sam says thoughtfully. "Thank you."

"Please let me know if you have any questions. You know how to reach me, Ms. Freeman."

I pry myself out of my shock long enough to thank him, and as the door swishes closed behind him, I turn to Sam.

"If you need some time alone, I can go. I'm getting hungry anyway."

"I'm her husband," he says, and my heart nearly stops. He smiles slyly. "That means I have more say in her care than, say, her father. I will be making sure she gets the help she needs, instead of more enabling. At least," he adds matter-of-factly, "until the divorce."

I breathe a deep sigh of relief.

We sit in silence for a long while, each lost in our own thoughts, and then Sam remarks offhandedly, "Do you think I'm to blame for driving her over the edge?"

"No, Sam, I don't," I reply firmly. "You said it yourself—she has a history of mental illness. I always knew she was nuttier than a retarded squirrel."

He grins. "And you know all about squirrels, don't you, Fran?" He catches my hand and tugs on it, bringing me closer. "Lie down here a while, Ms. Freeman. Let's shock the nursing staff."

I snort. "They've seen this before, I'm sure." I climb carefully onto the bed beside him, accepting his awkward kiss. The nasal prongs delivering oxygen to him scrape my nose.

"I love you, Frannie."

"I love you back."

He grins a pain-tinged but endearing grin. "I know that."

He punches the button on his morphine machine, and seconds later is slumbering peacefully. I lie beside him, watching him sleep, listening to the miracle of breath inside him. I think about Malia, chased through life and tormented by her own personal demons, and I feel my anger and hatred ebb and finally disappear. I'm usually a forgiving kind of person—hence my steadfastness with Sam regardless of the shit he's done over the last three years—and she deserves a large measure of that particular grace. I smile and settle into the pillow to doze, rolling onto the goose egg at the back

of my head where Malia pounded my head into Stella's.
   Fucking bitch.

BRAND OF CHOICE

Two years later

"She's here, Frannie," Stella informs me, careful to gesture at the new girl with her left hand, thereby throwing little rainbows across the room from her diamond engagement ring. We never thought it would happen, but our Stella's settling down and getting married, and check this—guess who finally caught her? Mario from Production. Things have changed a lot in that department, including Mario.

I shoot a glance across the room at Fresh Meat—er, Sarah-Jane Quinn, the newest member of the Training team. Over the last two years we've slowly built the staff back to its former level and Sarah brings us to full-staffing. She tested well in her skills assessment, but right now she looks petrified. I remember Morgan's first day, and I pray fervently that Sarah doesn't throw up on me.

Gretchen's showing Sarah her cubicle—my old one—and introducing her to the rest of the staff, who all pop up out of their chairs like prairie dogs from their burrows. In fact, Stella calls it "prairie dogging," one of her more attractive office terms (we had a temp for a while who "crop dusted," according to Stella, especially after lunching at Taco Bell).

Things have changed overall at Harper & Lyttle, the major difference being the "Harper" now refers to Evelyn. I don't know how she managed it, but she strong-armed Garland right into retirement and took over running the company. Lyttle has come out of retirement to chair the Board of Directors, and positive changes have rained down on us all the way to the bottom of the food chain. We still have the different layers of the Adminisphere, and I haven't stopped suspecting that the air at the top of the corporate ladder is thinner, therefore making logical thought damn near impossible, but all-in-all I'm pleased. The Senior Execs still manage several sections—called Divisions now—and the Division Supervisors still handle the individual departments, but now there's coherent rationale behind the grouping of divisions under a Senior Exec.

With the departure of Jeremy Ingram, the supervisory position in Concept Development came open. The man at the top in Production had been coveting said spot for a long time and was happy to move there, which left the top position in Production open. Since my relationship with Sam necessitated a separation at work, Sam moved into that open spot— hence the positive changes there. While he may have to wrangle with technology, his management skills afford him a high level of respect, and the attitudes in the Production Division have drastically metamorphosed.

Obviously, this left the Training Division without a captain. At Evelyn Harper's suggestion, our Senior Exec tapped me for that position, so you are now looking at Frannie, Training Division Supervisor. Yahoo, rah rah rah! Gretchen has filled Malia's position, renamed Office Manager and afforded a certain amount of authority. A new hierarchal level has made Stella a Senior Training Specialist IV. This position is considered part of the "inner circle" and thus our frequent trips to Tony's for margaritas are not a flagrant violation of fraternization policies.

And let's not forget Morgan. With the altering of a few company policies, Morgan has been allowed to telecommute from home. Harper & Lyttle even set up her home office at the company's expense. Another three years and she'll be back in the office—we can't wait!—but for now she gets to both keep her job *and* be home with Jacob. She married Enrique when the baby was four months old, which pleased his family to no end. I don't know if you've ever seen a Mexican-American family in action, but to say Morgan has been enveloped with loving relatives is an understatement. Enrique turned out to be quite a surprise; other than his brief fling with Stella, he's actually very conservative regarding sex and relationships. He's still tending bar while finishing up med school—yep, our little Morgs caught herself a doctor.

We lost Bud Mitchell, first to retirement (thank *Christ;* I don't have to watch my paperclip count or my Post-It usage anymore), and then to a motor-cross accident just five months ago. Yeah, you heard me correctly: motor-cross. The birth of Morgan's baby rejuvenated him and he turned into quite the daring-do. He left everything to Morgs and Jake, which was a considerable amount since he lived very frugally.

Gretchen stops before me, Sarah-Jane Quinn in tow. Sarah looks petrified, and she hugs her leather notebook to her chest as though it's a life preserver and she's lost at sea.

"Frannie, you remember Sarah-Jane. Will you please tell her to relax?"

I smile at Sarah reassuringly. "New jobs are scary, but we don't bite—not often, anyway."

"I don't know why I'm so nervous," Sarah says shakily.

"Nothing to this. We'll show you everything you need to know. Stella is an excellent trainer, and you'll be spending the day with her. The first thing she needs to show you is the coffee room and how best to hide a space heater under your desk."

This brings the expected laugh and she looks embarrassed, although she eases her stranglehold on the leather notebook.

"Gretch, why don't you turn her over to Stella and get some coffee in the girl before the staff meeting?"

"Sure thing, Fran." Gretchen salutes smartly and marches our newbie off into Cube Row.

Now Gretchen... I know you're looking for a happily-ever-after there, and certainly she's happy. I worry about her sometimes, because I think James broke something inside her when he left her, some intrinsic ability to trust. She and the girls live with Gus Haldemann, but although he's asked her no less than four times, Gretchen won't marry him. I know she cares for him, and I believe Gus truly cares about her, but she won't take that last step. She kept the house she and James had shared and rents it out, and she pesters me and Sam all the time about buying it.

Stewart's now a programmer, and I'm happy to say the quality of software coming up from Concept Development has risen dramatically. Even Vince Parker seems to have pulled his head out of his ass.

Christine—she kept her assume name—went to Medford for a visit shortly after Jeremy Ingram left. She came back angry four days later, followed by Bradley, who then went home to Medford three days later—also angry. About a month later, she went back up again and came home fuming. Bradley came down again and went home furious. It's been back and forth since, but I notice her stays in Oregon are getting longer. I think eventually she'll relent and just move up there; I can't fault her caution and her refusal to relinquish her pride. For a long time, pride was all she had. Poor Bradley...but honestly, I think the man is enjoying the chase, as exasperating as it must seem at times.

A month after Malia was admitted to a private psychiatric hospital—thankfully that bill is being footed by Garland Harper, most likely at Evelyn's insistence—Sam let his apartment go and moved in with me. We're comfortable and happy there with just us two and Penguin; we don't really need a house until we decide to have children. And speaking of Sam...

With one last glance at Gretchen and Sarah, I turn and head back into my office—Sam's former office. He's lounging comfortably on the leather sofa, reading the newspaper and patiently waiting for me.

"Got her all situated, Fran?" he asks without looking up.

"Sure do. But I have a staff meeting in about ten minutes, so you'd better put that paper down and kiss me like you mean it."

He obliges with that slow, burning grin that hooked me from the start. Then he leans his forehead against mine and smiles.

"Where were you this morning, Mrs. Harrison? I came up and you were nowhere to be found."

"So you thought you'd make yourself at home in here and mess up my newspaper?" I arch a brow at the scattered debris of the *Los Angeles Times* on the sofa.

"I didn't know how long you'd be. I had to amuse myself somehow."

I lean against him and kiss him again. "I was leaving a little surprise on your desk, Mr. Harrison."

"Is that right? A cinnamon-raisin bagel?" he asks hopefully.

Chuckling, I push him away. "Nope. Something much better. Now go back to work; I have to go to my meeting."

"You sure are bossy since you became a supervisor," he complains good-naturedly. "I'll see you for lunch?"

"Count on it," I promise. I'll see him sooner than

that, for what I left on his desk will bring him to me as surely as magnets attract steel.

As Sam heads back to his office, I grab my things and dash off to the conference room, passing George Stuckey—my boss—who's heading the other way with another Suit. He gives me a nod, and the Suit says *sotto voce*, "After his first wife shot him, I'm amazed Sam Harrison ever considered getting married again."

"Ah," replies George, "but he married Frannie Freeman. Can't go wrong with Frannie."

Damn straight.

Sam and I were married after what we considered a respectable time following his divorce from Malia—six weeks. We haven't looked back. Over the last year he's been pestering me again about having a baby—his latest tactic has been to remind me that I'm almost thirty—but I resist the lure of a family while I accustom myself to the rhythm of being in charge of a busy office.

Seven weeks ago, unbeknownst to Sam, I stopped taking my birth control pills.

This morning I left a card on his desk that says "Congratulations, Daddy!" along with the home pregnancy test I did when I arrived at work this morning—a test which shows positive.

My brand of choice?

Clearblue Easy.

About the Author

Sharon Gerlach was in training to be a ninja, but a dismaying lack of physical grace and balance—not to mention the inability to keep her big mouth shut—ended her ninja career before it had really begun. Now she writes. She doesn't write about ninjas because that's obviously a sore subject. But she writes about other really cool things and figures someone else will cover the ninjas. Life's really not all about ninjas, anyway.

Sharon lives on the dry side of the Pacific Northwest with her husband (who must really be fond of her as he hasn't left her yet despite her ninja failings); her three kids and numerous grandkids (none of whom possess ninja qualities either); and three cats. Yes, you guessed it—ninja cats!

Website:
sharongerlach.com

Twitter:
@SharonGerlach

Facebook Fan Page:
www.facebook.com /AuthorSharonGerlach

Facebook Beta Readers Group
(by approval only)
https://www.facebook.com/groups/SharonsWordWarriors/

PREVIEW

THE SECRET DREAMS OF SARAH-JANE QUINN
Harper & Lyttle Book 2

BET YOU A DIME

"Bet you a dime Stuckey says *umm* nine times while talking to Frannie."

I look up from my copy and in the direction my cubicle mate is pointing. Frannie Harrison, our supervisor, is standing just outside her office door, talking to *her* supervisor, George Stuckey. George appears to be an intelligent man, but when he's in the vicinity of Frannie he turns into a bumbling idiot, which always has some entertainment value.

"Sixteen," I counter, assessing the way Stuckey is leaning against the wall, his hands in his pockets. This could be a long conversation.

"Come on, Quinn—you been smokin' crack?" Coleridge Tate wheels his chair out of his cubicle and half into mine, and we cock our heads toward the Suits to see who will win.

"I just...umm...think we would...umm...be better served if we...umm...stationed a Training Specialist in Customer Relations...umm...permanently. It wouldn't...umm...you know, be a reduction of your staff, and the employee would still...umm...be doing some of the training materials, but they would mostly be...umm...assisting the customer service representatives. Then your staff wouldn't have to...umm...keep running downstairs to Customer Relations all the time."

"George, I'm not giving up any of my staff to Customer Relations. I will, however, consent to in-depth training for one customer service representative, who can then train his or her coworkers." A small frown creases Frannie's brow, and I can tell she's clamping a lid on her temper.

"How many times was that?" Collie whispers, leaning close enough to me that I can smell the tantalizing scent of his aftershave. "Seven or eight?"

"I thought it was six."

"No way. I was still closest. Pay up." He holds out his hand, and I rummage in my desk for a dime. Grinning like a pirate with mayhem on his mind, he escapes with his treasure, disappearing into his own cube.

Coleridge Tate would make a bet on how many times his own mother tripped going up her front steps. I don't know if he's a compulsive gambler or if he's just bored out of his freaking mind with his job, but ever since I started working here four months ago, he's been betting me a dime on almost anything, up to and including how many times our pregnant supervisor makes a trip to the bathroom on any given day.

I huck a paper clip over the cubicle wall between us, hoping to bounce it off his head. A couple minutes later it comes back over, holding a paper replica of a dime, which cracks me up. Not everyone appreciates Collie's sense of humor. Take Brooke Fields, for instance. She rolls her eyes at his jokes, makes muffled *mmphm* sounds when she finds him loafing, and is downright cross and impatient when, at the end of the week, she finds he's completed more work than she has in spite of his long periods of idleness.

This same chick, however, wastes no time cozying up to him at company functions or the rare times she joins us for Happy Hour at Tony's, a bar that seems to be a local tradition for the employees at Harper & Lyttle, Inc. For some reason, this job drives many to drink. (Speaking of… Frannie looks distinctly as though she'd like a big-ass margarita herself as she watches Stuckey shuffle away. When he's out of earshot, I clearly hear her mutter, "Moron!" Collie smothers a laugh.)

When I started working here four months ago, I was

paraded around and introduced to the rest of the Training Division staff like a prized cow. In fact, Collie calls it "the prized cow tour." I know why they do it—so that you can place in your mind where everyone sits—but still, it's a bit humiliating. *This is Sarah Jane Quinn, the latest addition to our herd. Make her feel udderly welcome.* Honestly.

Anyway, when I was taken around to Brooke's cube caddy-corner from mine, she flounced her perfect Baywatch-blonde hair and fixed me with haughty blue eyes. "Brooke Fields. I've heard all the jokes, so don't bother."

I didn't—and still don't—know what jokes she's referring to, but the chip on her shoulder is obvious. At the time, I dropped the *bitch on wheels* label on her, and I've yet to see any reason to lift it.

Needless to say, Brooke isn't often invited to our after-hours gatherings. Usually it's just me, Collie, Hannah, Lauren, and Allison, and we've drank more than our fair share of rum. The girls and I usually take it in the form of daiquiris, but Collie claims that's a frou-frou drink. He orders his straight up or in some vile concoction he calls an Acid Trip (rum, vodka, gin, Midori, and tequila. I call it a Get-Down-and-Crazy, and it's just begging for a What-Did-I-Do-Last-Night incident of epic proportions).

Collie kicks the divider between us. "Hey, Quinn, going to the Christmas party tonight?"

"Dunno."

"Come on. I don't wanna go if you're not gonna be there."

"I thought you had the munchkin tonight and couldn't make the party."

His voice lowers. "That's just what I told Brooke to get out of her trying to make this into a date. My parents are keeping Munchkin overnight." Munchkin is Collie's daughter. Her real name is Megan, but since he let her watch *The Wizard of Oz* and dress up as a munchkin for Halloween last year, she only answers to Munchkin.

Okay, I have a confession to make, and you damn well better keep it secret. There's something about a good-looking man in the daddy role that I find sexier than hell—not that I'd ever tell Collie that. It'd make things weird between us, and I don't want that.

I don't know much about the circumstances of his daughter's birth, but I do know that he's never been married and that he learned he had a child only when Child Protective Services contacted him after Munchkin's mother abandoned her at her daycare provider's. To get custody, he had to jump through a whole bunch of hoops, consent to two years of CPS monitoring, and get a better job, which is how he ended up at Harper & Lyttle, but he apparently did so willingly and with enthusiasm. His daughter is four now, and he's had her for just over two years. CPS lifted their monitoring about three months ago. He's a good daddy, another thing I find sexy as hell—with men in general, not Collie specifically. If you try to say any differently, I'll deny it to my grave.

"Bet you a dime you go tonight."

"Bet you a dime I don't. Why don't you just bring Munchkin over and we can watch classic Christmas movies all night?"

"Sarah," he says expressively. He only calls me Sarah when I've tried his patience beyond endurance. Otherwise I'm just Quinn—or, when he's trying to needle me, Prized Cow. "*Die Hard* is *not* a Christmas movie."

"The hell you say! I'm taking back your Christmas present. For what I spent I could buy the first two seasons of *Dexter* on DVD."

"Then you spent too much on me. You should have spent it on Munchkin."

"I spent more on Munchkin, so there."

"Told you not to."

"You're not the boss of me," I reply, grinning, knowing

he'll give up the argument now. And I'm right. He sighs expressively.

"Don't know what I'm gonna do with you, Quinn."

"You'll think of something."

He doesn't reply, but I can't shake the funny feeling that he's sitting over there on his side of the cube wall, grinning—and plotting—like a mischievous boy.

* * * * *

OTHER RUNNING INK PRESS BOOKS

MALAKH

Suzanne Harper had wielded supernatural abilities and super-athletic prowess while she was the lover of an angel. When a string of gruesome murders points to her former lover, Suzanne teams up with Icarus, an angel who hunts those of his kind who have fallen, because the choice of victims tells a terrifying tale: the next murder will be hers.

OFFICE POLITICS

Malaria is nothing a good dose of quinine can't handle, thinks Frannie Freeman when her vile office manager Malia—aka Malaria—marries their boss Sam, whom Frannie has loved for years. When Sam suddenly confides that he believes he was roofied the night of his surprise Las Vegas wedding, Frannie prepares for battle with a woman's three best weapons — a loyal heart, a willingness to fight dirty, and the strongest margarita money can buy.

THE WYCKHAM HOUSE

The Wyckham House has stood for centuries, its origin unknown, its history black and bloody. When Kimberly Owens' father disappears in Aaron Schaefer's town, all evidence points to the Wyckham House. Only one man has gone there and returned alive. But even if Aaron could remember what happened to him, he doesn't want to. For there are worse things than death.

CONDEMNED

Tools that relocate themselves. Shadows glimpsed from the corner of one's eye. The feeling of being watched when no one's there. Rachael Payne is delighted to be involved in renovating Bayview Manor for its new owner, Geoffrey Windsor. It doesn't bother her that the mansion's dark history is shrouded in rumor and legend, because she doesn't believe in ghosts. Geoffrey doesn't share her enthusiasm for his house. From its mysterious origins to the strange current events, he's certain something walks in Bayview Manor, unseen by the human eye. And he wonders if Rachael's faith in God protects her from the forces within the mansion…or blinds her to them.

BLINK OF AN EYE
One wrong blink sparked a global outbreak that mutated humans into brutal, conscienceless killers called Revenants. The Father of the Apocalypse, Ren Leonard is a legend whom Mackenzie believes is their only hope for survival. She appeals to Leonard to turn the tide against the Revenants. She is about to learn that everything can change in the blink of an eye and Revenants aren't the worst danger.

WHERE I BELONG
In the follow-up novel to *The Secret Dreams of Sarah-Jane Quinn*, the perfect storm descends upon Sarah and Gus Haldemann, bringing a quarreling sibling, estranged family, a mother-daughter feud, and old lovers together under one roof - theirs.

www.ingramcontent.com/pod-product-compliance
Lightning Source LLC
Chambersburg PA
CBHW020244180626
46810CB00006B/2349